NO SECOND CHANCES

WITHDRAWN

NO SECOND CHANCES

Don Bruns

severn
House

This first world edition published 2017
in Great Britain and the USA by
SEVERN HOUSE PUBLISHERS LTD of
Eardley House, 4 Uxbridge Street, London W8 7SY
Trade paperback edition first published
in Great Britain and the USA 2018 by
SEVERN HOUSE PUBLISHERS LTD

British Library Cataloguing in Publication Data
A CIP catalogue record for this title is available from the British Library.

ISBN-13: 978-0-7278-8756-6 (cased)
ISBN-13: 978-1-84751-872-9 (trade paper)
ISBN-13: 978-1-78010-934-3 (e-book)

All Severn House titles are printed on acid-free paper.

Severn House Publishers support the Forest Stewardship Council™ [FSC™],
the leading international forest certification organisation.
All our titles that are printed on FSC certified paper carry the FSC logo.

Typeset by Palimpsest Book Production Ltd.,
Falkirk, Stirlingshire, Scotland.
Printed and bound in Great Britain by
TJ International, Padstow, Cornwall.

AUTHOR'S NOTE

This is the third Quentin Archer New Orleans story. While the story rings true, once again I've taken liberties with the police procedures and the character information. Human trafficking mirrors the older slave trade that took place in the early 1800s. Trafficking happens today, and many locals and tourists receive the benefits of this illicit practice without being aware of it. Of course, some are aware. New Orleans remains a dichotomy. A playground for the tourists, a windfall for the restaurants and businesses that thrive on the reputation, and a hellhole for those who are working in the worst-case scenarios. I love the city, but remain conscious that everything is not as it appears.

ACKNOWLEDGMENTS

Thank you to the NOPD for being open with your information. Thank you to Linda Bruns, Nancy Merwin, Steve Stegall, Dave Bruns and all who have been first readers. Thank you to Jill Marr, my agent, and most of all to Kate at Severn House, who has always been a champion of my work. I appreciate my publishers, my agent and most of all my readers. Fifteen novels, fifteen stories. I am so surprised and so happy.

ONE

On the last day of his life, Nick Martin drove his Peterbilt 379 down Highway 90, the dark night made a little brighter with talk radio keeping him company. He liked driving at night, but he was constantly aware of the danger of making his living on the road. There were crazy people out there. Drunks and drug dealers. Drivers on the run from cops. And he'd seen high-speed chases with drivers who had little regard for anyone on the road. The talk radio host was bringing it all home, talking about a horrific accident on September 20th. A Chevy truck ran a red light in Santa Ana, hitting a church van with eighteen people inside, sending them flying into the street. Seven passengers died, including a woman who was eight months pregnant, her unborn child a victim, too. You never knew when your time was up.

The driver was still on the run. The announcer made the case that this guy was now a wanted killer who wouldn't hesitate to kill again. Damn. One minute you're coming back from a church camp, the next minute you're gone. All in the blink of an eye.

Martin's load, eight hundred cases of cigarettes, rode light in the trailer. Six thousand pounds of tobacco. Four hundred eighty thousand packs. Nine million six hundred thousand cancer sticks. Martin didn't smoke. He had no problem with those who did, but in his twenty-nine years he'd never even lit a match. For anything. Not even to light a candle. He certainly wasn't going to die of lung cancer. No way. Still, he had a solution for those who did smoke. Quit. How hard could that be?

But just like the American Cancer Society, the irony was, if everyone quit, Martin would be out of a job. The Cancer Society always said they wanted to be shut down, put out of business due to the eradication of cancer, but the thousands of full-time employees secretly hoped the society would last well into their retirement years. He smiled again. The world was full of ironies.

As he flipped the dial on the radio he caught the middle of a Wynonna Judd song, 'She Is His Only Need.' He thought about

Sandy and silently decided it was time to ask her the important question. In two weeks, he'd be thirty. His birthday gift would be her saying yes. She really was his only need. His mind drifted to the last time they'd been together, all wrapped up in nakedness, her firm breasts and hard nipples pushing into his chest.

The lights of the Peterbilt picked up a reflective sign just before an exit. *Detour Ahead.* He'd almost missed it. He braked and downshifted, slowing down and grabbing the handset on his CB radio.

'Breaker, breaker, this is Paw Paw Patch. Anyone know about a detour on I90?'

In a moment a voice answered.

'Paw Paw, this is Razor Back,' the drawl was thick. 'Drove the entire stretch today and never saw one.'

'Thanks, Razor Back. Must have just come up.'

'Ten-four, Paw Paw. They spring 'em on ya all the time.'

'I'll report back. Over and out.'

Spinning his wheel, he turned at the exit and drove half a mile to where the second sign was located. The arrow on this detour pointed onto a side road and he could vaguely see tall pine trees lining the two-lane road. He hoped he'd come out onto the highway in a matter of minutes, because he didn't like surprises. The long-haul driver had never been on this stretch of road before and the lofty trees blotted out the sky, blocking whatever light there was.

His birthday, the day he'd turn thirty, he already knew, would be a working day. He'd be on the road hauling tobacco, but the next week he'd ask Sandy to dinner to give her the ring. It was time. Thirty years old, September 30, 1992. Thirty was time to settle down. Make a commitment.

It was at that moment he saw the headlights, a vehicle coming right at him. Not in the other lane, but barreling directly toward him in his lane. It took him totally by surprise. It was big, huge, another semi. For a second his brain locked, the situation being so surreal. He stared at the oncoming truck, before finally realizing there was almost no room to escape. Two lanes, a sugar pine forest on either side. He could swerve into the left lane so he eased that way, praying no one was coming on that path. The oncoming truck swerved as well, still directly in front of him.

Taking a deep breath, Martin flashed his brights. At the same time, the truck in front flashed his, almost blinding him. Jesus. Somebody needed to give and the other driver didn't seem to move an inch.

His heart was racing as the vehicle bore down on him, never veering, never braking. So, Martin braked. He shoved his foot down hard, double clutching and downshifting, trying to slow the weight of his truck and load. It wasn't going to be enough.

A head-on collision was imminent. A standoff. There was a squealing and grating sound as his tires fought the pavement and at the last moment Martin spun the steering wheel. The oncoming trucker did the same, heading directly for him.

He felt the cab start to tilt.

'Dear God, don't let me flip.' His hands in a death grip on the wheel as he felt the right tires sink into the soft dirt on the berm.

God didn't get the prayer or else he chose to ignore it. The cab flipped, and the trailer went as well, as the truck plowed into the pine forest and down a slight incline. Forty thousand pounds slammed on its side, sliding into the trees. Forty thousand pounds of steel, rubber, tobacco and human flesh.

His seatbelt unfastened, Martin was tossed to the passenger side, thrown violently against the door. His neck snapped. Forever twenty-nine years old.

Three men scrambled from the trees, one with a rope and all three with red handkerchiefs covering the lower half of their faces.

'Tie him up, Joe. We'll start unloading the cargo.'

Joe scrambled down the incline, slipping in the pine needle straw, and opened the cab door to the semi that now lay on its side. The driver's head was at an odd angle, twisted, and blood poured from a gash on his face.

'Oh, shit.' Joe sounded shaken.

'What?'

'I think we just stepped in it, guys.'

'Tie him up and let's get on with this.'

'Motherfucker is dead, Jack.'

'No.'

'Yeah.' Joe spoke quietly. 'He's dead.' He wanted to quote Al Pacino in the famous drunken line from *Scarface*. 'I always tell the truth, even when I lie.' But it wasn't a lie. It was the truth. The man was dead. No question.

'Well, that's a first.'

The three men were silent, staring into the cab. Exhaust, steam from the engine and the smell of gasoline mixed with the musty odor of pine needles that carpeted the forest. They pulled their masks down, exposing two black faces and one white. The white man was even more pale than he had been.

'Guys, we're in new territory here.' Joe's voice was quivering. 'I mean, in the past, we've made out pretty well with the loads, and the drivers have all been pretty shook up, but we've never killed anyone before.' He shook his head. 'We stand to make eighty thou a piece on this heist, but was it worth killing some innocent kid?'

One of the men jogged up the road. The other two watched the body, hoping for some sign of life. A breath, an eye opening. There was none.

'What's done is done. We're not going to bring him back, Joe. Time's not going to stand still so let's start loading.' The man known as Jack pointed to their semi parked a little way up the two lane road. 'I ran up and pulled the detour sign so we should be alone for a while. The one out on the highway has already been picked up.'

The third man drove back in a front loader taken off their truck. 'Guys, there's nothing we can do. I'm not comfortable with it at all. I mean, it's a damned shame, but we've still got a job to do. Get these cases loaded. We've maybe got half an hour if we're lucky.'

'We killed someone,' Joe said. 'Andy, this is serious. We've just committed a murder.'

Andy was silent, thinking things through. He considered the loss of life, his family life, the money they were about to make, and the current situation. If he had it over again, he'd probably say no. No to the man who set this heist up. He didn't want to have a killing hanging over his head. How do you explain that to your wife? Your child? Then again, was this really his fault? Was this their fault?

'No, *he* had the accident. The driver made the decision to plow the truck into the woods.' Andy stepped off the loader. 'We're not going to let this interfere with our life. It's not like we shot him, strangled him, or beat him to death. We didn't. We weren't near him when this happened. And we didn't exactly set this up ourselves, so, let it go.'

'But, we caused the—'

'Shut up, Joe. Don't get so dramatic. You don't want to give up on this haul any more than we do. So, give it a rest,' Andy said.

'And, boys, never say anything to anyone about this,' Jack said. 'Ever. Do you understand? Don't go on a spending spree, use your heads. We've been here before. Never with a dead driver, but . . .'

Joe shut his mouth, wondering how he could live with himself for the rest of his life, knowing he'd been responsible for taking the life of another human being. Robbery, not a problem. Battery, some people needed to be taken down. But murder had never been a part of the plan. He had vowed to never even carry a gun in this line of work. If there was life on the line, Joe wanted nothing to do with it.

Now, there was a human life that had been taken. No, he hadn't pulled a trigger . . . never would. But he had helped set in motion someone's demise. He wasn't sure things were ever going to be the same again. He was shaking, his hands barely able to help with the loading and he tasted salty tears, which ran down his cheeks.

With crowbars and hammers they pried open the rear doors and started putting the cases on the front loader.

Forty minutes later the three hijackers stepped into their truck with the semi-trailer and drove back to the highway, leaving the wreck and Nick Martin's body for someone else to find and take care of. Two days later the lot of cigarettes was gone. The sale was always easy. They could save the retailer his taxes, half the wholesale cost and even more. Still, their profits were huge. The cigarettes hadn't cost them a penny. Not one cent. But this time there was another price that had been paid.

Joe thought about it. Was there any situation worth the cost of another man's life? Hell yes, the money was good, but he'd end up spending it on strippers, hookers, gambling and booze. He knew it. So a young man's life was expended so Joe could enjoy the pleasures of *his* life.

The killer bought a case of Four Roses Kentucky bourbon and spent the night of his payday getting blind drunk.

TWO

On the last day of Officer Johnny Leroy's life, he was on his computer, parked in front of Fontaine's drug store in a neighborhood known as Bayou St John. He'd answered a call about a disturbance, a fight that had broken out among three women; one with a knife, the caller had said. A big knife, maybe a butcher knife. It was strange because Bayou St John was usually a calm, peaceful neighborhood. There was a small-town feel to the district, with mom-and-pop businesses, quiet streets and even kayakers out on the bayou. He couldn't remember the last time he'd officially visited the area. But if there had been a fight, it was over by the time he arrived. There was no sign of any trouble in front of the Toulouse Street business and a quick interview with the store's employees simply proved no one had seen anything.

The assistant manager, Trace Benet, had been outside taking a cigarette break about the time the call had come in.

'There was no fight, no women,' he said. 'I'd be watchin' that battle, Officer. Believe me.'

Now, hunched over his computer and monitoring his radio, Leroy keyed in the information regarding the call. Time of arrival, interviews, survey of the area, enough to say, 'I showed up and nobody was home.'

The tapping on the car's window caused him to glance up. A sullen-looking young black man motioned to him to lower the window and he hesitated, resting his hand on the butt of his Glock. The kid may have seen the fight, it was just that Leroy really didn't want to pursue it, plus he was enjoying the air conditioning. He just wanted to drive away without an incident. He was looking forward to retirement and was cautiously avoiding any confrontation. But, he pushed the button and the window lowered, a blast of heat and humidity hitting him in the face.

'What can I do for you?'

'Got a question.' The young man wore a T-shirt and baggy shorts, a baseball cap turned backwards. He sported a tattoo that seemed to surround his neck. Thorns linked together. He'd buried his hands in his pockets and rocked back and forth on the balls of his feet.

'Fire away.'

The young man backed off, studying the officer. 'Funny you'd say that, "fire away".'

'Your question?' Leroy said.

'Do you recognize me?'

The officer studied him for a moment. 'No. Should I?'

'I'm André Brion's kid. You remember him, don't you? I'm Joseph Brion. Just thought you should know.'

Leroy blinked and that's when the kid shot him, right between the eyes, spraying blood, brain and bone inside of the cruiser.

'I knew the guy, Q. Stand-up cop. On the force maybe twenty-five years? Joined around 1992. Damn, this is so sad.'

'Not the case I wanted to draw, Levy.' Quentin Archer wiped the sweat from his forehead.

'Oh? In our line of work what case *do* you want to draw?'

The two homicide detectives watched in the sweltering heat as a photographer circled the blue-and-white cruiser, taking pictures from every conceivable angle. Archer stared at the blue crescent-and-star emblem on the car and thought about how someone could dedicate his service and eventually his life to protect others only to be unable to protect himself. He'd seen the TV stories about cops who were ambushed, but to be confronted with one of his fellow officers blown away in a squad car . . . It was a lot to handle.

'And no one saw anything?' Archer surveyed the area. Three employees from the drugstore stood on the sidewalk, a handful of tourists snapped photos with their cell phones and a couple of motorists slowed down to see what the commotion was all about. Other than that, it was an average afternoon. Except a cop was dead.

Officer Leroy remained slumped over the steering wheel, his chin resting on the plastic and his computer screen still glowing.

The radio blared as a dispatcher called for an officer in the French Quarter to respond to a drunken brawl. It wouldn't be Leroy.

'This time it's personal, Levy.'

'When she's done shooting pictures, Q, the ambulance is here.' He motioned over his shoulder. 'Personal or not, they're here.'

Archer turned and saw the white-uniformed attendants, a stretcher and body bag by their side. They had shown up, just like that, when his wife was killed in Detroit. Two attendants, a stretcher and a body bag. It was personal then, too. Death was serious enough. Death by murder was beyond serious. Someone wanted you dead. Someone felt that the world was a better place if you were gone. Or someone felt that murdering you righted a wrong. Maybe the act of murder avenged a crime. And of course, there was always revenge killing. All those thoughts played into the investigation. And then, this may have been just a random killing. Then again . . .

'No sunglasses, Q.'

'No body cam on the uniform. Probably wore it on his glasses.'

'The killer took them?'

'That would be my guess. Unless they're in the dash or on the floor.'

Levy nodded. 'Body cams aren't much good if they disappear. It's pretty clear the officer looked right at the killer when you look at the point of entry of the bullet. Leroy powered down the window. There would have been a clear picture on the cam.'

'When they go over the vehicle, I'll make it a priority. If it's in the car, we'll find the camera.'

'It won't be there. The killer took it, Quentin. Leroy was too good a cop not to have it with him. Especially on a call.'

Archer glanced at a uniformed officer standing watch over the scene, the bullet camera attached to the right temple of his sunglasses, following every move his head made. Leroy didn't have the glasses or the bullet cam on him.

'The department spent about 300,000 bucks on those cameras. I think we bought like 400 something. These little units are so sophisticated, when you witness something, you click on the camera and the camera, get this, Q, the camera records the fifteen seconds *before* you activate it. So it's always shooting but saves fifteen seconds before you turn it on. Amazing.'

'And when the criminal takes the camera away, all the technology in the world isn't worth squat.'

'That's what I said. They're only effective if we can view the content. So where do we start?' Levy asked.

Archer surveyed the growing number of onlookers, then glanced up.

'Apartments up there.' He pointed. 'Offices and shops across the street. Somebody saw something. Somebody always sees something. As always, let's start there.'

'Maybe something they didn't know they saw.'

'And then we ask why. When we figure out why the officer was killed, we're almost there. Was it a random shooting?' Archer squinted in the blinding sun. 'If it was random, that makes it really tough. We're taking shots in the dark, but if there was a reason . . .'

'Somebody Leroy arrested in the past?'

'So we go through twenty-five years of his arrests. It's a lot of paperwork but we may need to do it.'

'It's a place to start,' Levy said. 'I looked up the New Orleans *Officer Down* memorial page on-line. Since 2000, there have been six officers who died from gunshot wounds.'

'Now it's seven.'

'And one is too many.'

They were silent for a moment. Every day they wondered if they were going to be next.

Levy finally spoke. 'Let's canvass the area again. If we strike out, we go through his arrests. Find out who is still alive, who's on the street. Then we track them down.'

'Even someone in prison, they could connect with a friend, relative, and ask for help.'

Archer nodded to the paramedic team and they approached the car. Two paramedics, a body bag and a stretcher.

'It's going to be a tough case, Q.'

The detectives watched as the men carefully removed the corpse from the vehicle. They slipped him into the body bag and placed the bag on the stretcher.

'I've never been on a case where a cop was the victim,' Archer said, 'but my guess is that we've got the weight of the entire force behind us on this one. How many cops?'

'About 1,100 and some,' Levy responded. 'Should be more, but with our budget and the defections . . .' He let the sentence drift off. Everyone on the force was overworked.

'I heard there were defections,' Archer said. 'I'm not surprised but what were the reasons?'

'In 2014, 500 cops resigned or retired, Q. 500 cops. Feds came in, said they were restricting us from work on private security details during our off-hours because too many of us were abusing the system. Man, when you start out on the paltry pay we make, the officers needed that extra income. And it was like eight years since we'd had a raise. I don't have to tell you; this job is no picnic. They resigned. Retired. And the staff was short. Not just short but depleted. We were, we *are* in short supply. The Feds make unreasonable demands and force unfunded mandates on us and we are screwed. On a regular basis.'

'You're still here.'

Levy shrugged his shoulders as they walked across the street. 'Where would I go? I'm too young to retire and I actually know this job pretty well.'

'I think you do it pretty well, but you could make more money somewhere else,' Archer said.

'I could. But cops like Johnny Leroy, he didn't go anywhere else. I can stick it out if I feel like I'm making a difference. You know?'

Archer knew.

'This guy was respected, right?'

'Medal of merit, medal of commendation, Purple Heart, this guy was golden, Q. Helped out at the Boys and Girls Club for God's sake.' Levy pointed back to the hand-carried stretcher. 'The entire force is ready to do whatever needs to be done. You know that.'

'I got run out of Detroit for doing my job, Josh. I don't take anything for granted anymore.'

The paramedics slid the body into the vehicle and the EMS ambulance pulled away, leaving the scene quietly. No siren, no rush. The damage had already been done. The seven officers on the scene removed their hats, holding them over their hearts. A silent tribute to a decorated officer. One of their own.

THREE

'He was a cop's cop.' John Harris, superintendent of police spoke to the small assembly. Office workers and cops who were in the building. Archer and Levy stood in the back row, weary from the day and tired of the press and their insistent questions. There were no answers. Not yet. When Harris raised his hand and nodded, they slipped out. All the recognition, for good or bad, would come later. Right now, there was work to be done. A killer was on the loose and they needed some clues. Fast.

'We've got people running arrest records. Any idea what his average was?' Levy asked.

Archer glanced at Levy as they entered the elevator. 'These guys, they deal in a lot of stuff. Petty theft, shop lifting, rape, DUI, traffic violations, battery, drugs . . . maybe fifty arrests per year?'

'Higher.'

'Oh, so, this is a test. You've got the correct number, right? You've done your homework? I haven't and I have no idea. I'm not in the mood for a guessing game, Josh. You tell me.'

'One twenty.'

'Woah. One every three days,' Archer said. 'That's impressive. Twenty-six years on the force, that comes out to . . .'

'I figured it out,' Levy said as the elevator doors opened. 'That's 3,120 collars, give or take a few.'

'A lot of people who might have had it out for him.'

'But it's a list that we can work with, Quentin. There's nowhere else to start. Someone who had it out for Officer Leroy. That's probably who we're looking for.'

'Or, it just might be a random cop killing.' Archer opened the door and they walked into the blast furnace that was New Orleans in September. People in the north, east and west of the country were enjoying crisp cool fall weather. New Orleans, Louisiana was boiling. And with the killing of a cop, maybe even getting hotter.

'So,' Archer loosened his tie, unbuttoning his top shirt button, 'so far we've struck out on canvassing the area. I can't believe someone didn't see something or at least hear the gunshot.'

'Oh, we had one older gentleman, lives in an apartment across the street, second floor. He remembers hearing a pop about the same time as the shooting. Said he thought it was a car backfiring.'

'Must have been an old guy,' Archer said. 'I don't think cars backfire anymore.'

Levy smiled. 'With fuel injection and computer-controlled fuel mixtures, it doesn't happen often. Anyway, the old guy says he didn't check it out. Just another noise on the street.'

They quietly walked down the steps and out to the parking lot.

'It's becoming pretty serious all over the country these days, Q. Killing cops.'

'There's a lot of frustration out there, Josh. And I get that. Cops are shooting blacks *and* whites that are sometimes unarmed. It happened right here after Katrina.'

'I was here, Q. They used a drop to make it look like the guys were packing. Sometimes it's because cops are overreacting and killing suspects.'

Archer knew the story well. Cops shooting someone, then dropping a gun to make it appear that the men had been carrying weapons.

'Look, I know it happens, but we're on the line every day.' Levy stopped abruptly, staring at Archer. 'Good cops, bad cops, I'm not sure it matters. Killing someone takes it to a whole new level. Our lives are on the line. The perps, the bad guys, they're often a second away from killing us. If we overreact, it's usually an attempt to save our own lives. It's not pretty, but it's what happens.'

'I'm on the same page, Josh. It's just that some of the blues take the roll of bullies. You remember the case we worked on where the judge was murdered. Detective Adam Strand planted a gun to make the suspect look guilty. Tried to get him to confess to a crime he never committed.'

'Detective Strand was bad news from the start.'

'Yeah, well, we do have some bad news cops. My former friends on the DPD who ran the drug ring and probably murdered my wife are good examples. Listen, *I'd* kill them given the chance.

You know that, and there's no room for them on any force. Hey, I'm not saying that Leroy was—'

'Officer Leroy wasn't a bully, Q. He wasn't a bad news cop.' Levy headed to the left, Archer to the right. Over his shoulder, Levy shouted, 'I knew the man. He was a role-model cop and was about ready to retire. This is *not* a guy who threw his weight around. He was a responsible cop. Plain and simple.' He paused, then softly said, 'He stuck it out, Q. Didn't go when 500 officers resigned or retired. He wanted to retire on his terms. Obviously, that's not going to happen now.'

Archer nodded. He knew a thing or two about good people who died before their time. He walked the few blocks to the streetcar stop, the oppressive heat causing him to wipe the perspiration from his face every minute or so. Finally, he reached the stop on Canal as the streetcar pulled up. He stepped inside and sat behind the driver. Best seat in the house. A firsthand view of everyone who boarded. There was no point driving his car back to the Quarter since there were seldom any parking spaces, and the streetcar was cheaper than buying gas.

A grey-haired lady stared out the window, a ragged duffle bag between her legs. Next to her a young, attractive black lady flipped through the pages of a magazine with Denzel Washington on the cover. She didn't seem to focus on any of the articles as she continued to thumb the paper.

An eerie silence filled the space as people with their own problems, their own thoughts and solitude seemed to mull the concerns of their lives.

An older gentleman, pale and balding, lay on a seat, his head buried in his chest as he softly snored, his ribcage rising and falling.

Archer thought about Denise, and glanced around the streetcar, trying to find anyone who reminded him of her. Walking through the Quarter, he thought he saw her one hundred times a week. He'd hear the snippet of a song, maybe the Temps doing 'My Girl', and he'd see her in the distance. He would catch the whiff of Obsession and she'd be walking the other way across the street. Even the smell of food, a hot dog grilling on a food wagon, reminded him of Denise. They'd often connected at food wagons in Detroit when their schedules collided. He saw her every day.

Today, no one had any resemblance to the gorgeous, vibrant woman who had been his wife. She had been such a unique character. Warm, witty, caring . . .

Archer closed his eyes for a moment, silently praying for those whose lives had been taken, even though he wasn't at all sure there was a god or supreme being. Still, it couldn't hurt to ask for guidance, ask for salvation, ask for their eternal life. Just in case.

FOUR

She prayed for the marriage of her client to be successful. She lit a candle enhanced with patchouli oil, as a mint aroma filled the room. Then she sprinkled incense in the flame to encourage the gods of money to enrich another client. And she softly chanted a mantra to Loco, the god of health. The first two were for customers. One who was about to be wed, one who desperately needed money for an operation, and the third was for her own mother. Ma, who suffered with dementia, who was not in the present. Ma, who had been her mentor and best friend, who had taught her the ways of voodoo. She prayed every day, to a variety of deities, *Make my mother whole again.* But the prayers went unanswered. Prayers that may have fallen on deaf ears. Prayers that brought her to question her own faith. She wanted, needed, Ma back.

Stripping down to a plain white cotton T-shirt, Solange Cordray extinguished the candle and poured herself a glass of white wine. Her voodoo shop was closed but her small apartment in the rear was open for business. No tourists looking for a doll to cast a spell. No local who wanted to know if they were on the way to prosperity. No regular who checked in every week or month to see if the path was clear. Right now, it was just her communing with the spirits. Her time to find the portal to an answer, a solution to a problem. This late afternoon seemed to offer no solutions. She felt a void, an emptiness, and she decided to close down her session. Sometimes the gods were not cooperative. As if they got together and decided to shut her out. 'Not this time, young lady. We have nothing positive to offer.'

Solange never questioned them. Well, to be fair she did, but only in a confused state. Because, weighing in on the long haul, the gods responded to the majority of her requests. When she prayed for results for clients and friends, the deities often came through. It was Ma that she was worried about, and the dementia seemed to be more than the gods could handle. Here was a devout follower, Clotille Trouville, who had been a practitioner her entire adult life, and it was as if the gods she had prayed to on a daily basis had abandoned her. She would never understand the spirit world.

Sipping her Pinot Grigio, she turned the television on in her tiny bedroom, plumping her pillow and sitting back on the bed. *Breaking news*. She smiled. Every story every day was breaking news. A young lady with too much hair, makeup and cleavage faced the camera.

'Twenty-five-year veteran of the NOPD, Johnny Leroy was ambushed in his police car earlier today by what is believed to be a lone gunman. We now have a chance to talk to Detective Quentin Archer, homicide officer, who is in charge of the investigation.'

The camera zeroed in on Archer's face, somber and tight-lipped. Solange stared into his soulful brown eyes and could feel the hurt. Here was a man who dealt with violent death every day of his life, and the strain must be taking a toll. Now, a fellow officer had been killed.

'Detective Archer, what can you tell us about the shooting?'

Archer nodded. 'Officer Leroy was killed in his car by a single bullet. He was responding to a disturbance call in Bayou St John. At this time, we have no leads and we ask the citizens of Bayou St John, or anyone else in the vicinity, to please call us with any information. As you know, crimes are often solved with the help of our citizens giving us tips.'

'Officer Leroy was Caucasian, is that correct?' The officer's pale white face appeared on half the screen. Probably a department shot from early in his career.

'Yes.'

'Had he recently been involved in any altercations with black suspects in the community?'

Archer hesitated. 'We are currently reviewing Officer Leroy's past arrest records. He was on the force for twenty-five years so as you may imagine, that's going to take some time. We have no knowledge of the race or ethnicity of the shooter.'

'But has there been any outstanding case with minorities that—'

'Minorities?'

'There have been incidents around the country where blacks have felt the need to come out and confront an authority figure. I'm just wondering if the officer had any altercations with the black community that . . .'

'Ma'am, excuse me.' The camera honed in on his steely gaze. 'New Orleans is over sixty percent black. Sixty percent. That's hardly a minority.'

'Is there any indication that this may be a revenge killing, or—'

'I think your time is up. It's early in the investigation.' Solange noticed the irritation in his voice. She knew the reporter was trying to introduce the Black Lives Matter movement as a possible motive. Archer was doing an admirable job of stopping her.

'But, Detective, isn't it true that a number of years ago he did have an altercation with a black man?'

Archer was seething, gritting his teeth.

'Altercation? My understanding is that the man drew on Officer Leroy. A Smith and Wesson. Officer Leroy acted in self-defense and was exonerated.'

'Well, isn't there a possibility that—'

'As I said,' he held up his right hand cutting her off, 'we have no leads at this time. We are actively encouraging anyone with information to call the department and your privacy will be respected. Any leads no matter how small would be greatly appreciated.' Archer abruptly turned and walked away.

Solange pushed the power button on the remote and the room went silent. She took a deep cleansing breath, the incense-scented air filling her belly, and held it for five seconds. Then she slowly released it. She repeated the exercise, then stood up and walked into the shop.

She opened a cupboard door and removed a white candle in a glass vase. The reversible candle made by a wax master from New Orleans. Two black-and-white faces decorated both sides of the glass. She lit the two wicks and watched the tiny flames grow larger until they burned steady and bright. The wicks united under the wax. Two flames uniting as one. Duality. The measure of rich and poor, hot and cold, old and young and more importantly, good and evil. Good and evil. She felt it. As she stared into the flame, there was a moment of clarity. The gods had waited for this moment to connect. All other questions remained irrelevant, but this moment, the difference between good and evil, this was apparently important to them. It didn't matter which spirit, which god, spoke to her. She was in touch and that hadn't happened in days. Maybe there was hope for Ma.

She left the candle burning and walked back to her room, picking up her cell phone. She scanned through her contacts and pushed a button. The phone rang three times and then he answered.

'Archer.'

'Detective, this is Solange Cordray. I assume it's been a long day? A very long day.'

'You've apparently seen the news, Miss Cordray. It has been a long day. You can't imagine. And I can't imagine why you're calling. It's actually a nice break to hear from you after what's been going on here.'

'My call is related to your day. I lit a candle to try to get some vision, some idea of what you were up against.'

'OK. I appreciate that.'

'My communication with the spirits hasn't been that good recently. And then, suddenly one of them spoke to me.'

'No disrespect, but I'm always skeptical. You've helped me before and I thank you. But you know I question where you get your information. Of course, I question everything. It's my job.'

'Detective, can I see the body?'

'The body?'

'The officer's body. Officer Leroy? I assume he's at the morgue?'

Archer was silent for a moment. 'Have you seen a dead body before?'

'I've said prayers over dead bodies . . .'

'At the morgue? Where they have been subjected to an autopsy? Where, in this case, their heads have practically been blown off?'

It was her turn to be silent. Finally, she spoke.

'Detective,' she sounded very stern, 'I'm a big girl. I think I'm capable of handling that.'

'What do you possibly think you're going to gain?'

'Detective Archer, the last person to see the killer before Officer Leroy was killed was probably Officer Leroy. I would bet on it.'

'That's probably true, but—'

'The spirit leaves the body once it dies. I believe that. But the cavity is more than a vessel for the physical remains. The body retains an essence of its former occupant.'

'An essence?'

'Yes. An essence.'

'Solange, are you certain you want to see this? It's very raw. I was there today, I saw him in the squad car and—'

'The body, I know you think I'm a little bit crazy, but the body retains some memory of its last moments. And sometimes I'm able to pick up that retention. Isn't it worth a visit?'

'I don't know if this is such a good idea. I think you've—'

'I truly appreciate your trying to protect me from the gruesome realities of this murder. But, let's face the other reality. You haven't got one clue, Detective. You're sitting on the hottest case of the year, and you are rudderless. Let me at least try to give you some direction. I've helped solve other crimes, and I feel very strongly I can play a part in this one. And,' she hesitated, taking a deep breath, 'I worry about you. I know you carry certain things with you that are hard to let go. I'd like to help lighten your load.'

She heard him on the other end. She knew he was shaking his head, questioning his faith. She also knew that he would say yes. But there was a lot of tension between them.

'It's a strange request, but I know I can help.' She waited for his affirmation.

'No disrespect, but strange went out the window the day I met you. You know that.'

She smiled. He was coming around.

'Sure, I'll arrange it,' he said. 'How long will you need?'

'Ten, fifteen minutes.'

'Late afternoon tomorrow, I'll arrange for you to see the body. You know it won't be pleasant. I've seen people faint when they see the corpse wheeled out. What do you think you'll find?'

'I don't know,' she said. 'I'll tell you once I feel it.'

'I'll make it happen. I'm so glad you called.'

'I hope I can make a difference. It sounds like a tough case.'

'Can I ask you a personal question?'

Solange was silent. She thought she knew what was coming and wasn't quite sure how to answer. It wasn't the right time.

'Solange?'

He'd called her by her first name. Now she knew. 'Yes?'

'Would it, and I hesitate to ask, but would it be out of line for me to ask you to dinner? Just to talk.'

'About this case?'

'Sure, but just life in general.'

'And death.' She was immediately sorry she'd said that.

He was quiet for a short time. She wondered if he'd hang up. Then . . .

'In the short time we've known each other . . .'

'A year?'

'Sure . . . a year.'

'No. It would not be out of line. But, Detective—'

'If we're going to dinner in the future, it has got to be *Quentin*.'

'Quentin, let's deal with the cards on the table. First of all, I want to see him, Officer Leroy's remains, as early as possible. I want to know if I can shed some light on this horrific murder, OK?'

'Priority number one,' he said.

'I live here just like you, but unlike most of the residents in New Orleans, I think you'll agree, I've been able to do something about solving crimes. I didn't understand that at first, didn't realize that was part of what I should do, but you and I have had some moments, right? There's a certain chemistry. And please understand I want to help whenever possible.'

Archer paused for a second and she realized the word chemistry was probably not appropriate. A little chemistry of business, a little of something else. But now was not the time to define that. She made a mental note. *Don't talk about chemistry again.*

'You've definitely helped solve some crimes. You've given me some important information and I'm very grateful. I hope you know that.' He paused and she heard him take a deep breath. 'You also saved my life. What can I say about that?'

She'd walked into a crucial situation, and disarmed a criminal who had Archer in his sights. Yes, the detective would probably be dead if she hadn't shown up, but she didn't like to think about that. There were aspects of her profession that defied definition.

'I'm eternally grateful for that.'

Solange silently nodded her head. She had saved his life. It was important to know that occasionally she made a difference.

'Thank you, Detective.'

'It's Quentin,' he said.

She smiled, realizing she liked the new familiarity. It was comfortable.

'Quentin it is.'

'Tomorrow, Solange. I'll arrange for you to see the body. I need to solve this murder. It can't happen too soon.'

FIVE

The night produced no demonstrations in the streets. The chief of police had planned some precautionary measures and there were small riot squads positioned in select areas of the city, especially Bayou St John, but this was a white cop. And no one had any proof of the killer's race. Had the cop been black, the story probably would have been much different. As it was, the evening was relatively quiet and peaceful. At least by New Orleans standards. A shooting in Algiers, a knifing on the South Side, the beating of a homeless man in Central City and a purse snatching in the Quarter. No murders, no riots. A quiet and peaceful evening.

Archer simply called it as he saw it. There was more passion in the black community. White communities were a little more complacent. He was up at five thirty in the morning, drinking his hot chicory coffee on the small front porch of his former slave cottage, watching the sky show just a hint of light and hoping the sun backed off a little bit this day. He checked his phone to see if there had been any events overnight. He hoped there would be no dead bodies in the next twenty-four hours. His plate was full right now. Even though New Orleans led the country in shootings per capita, ten a week in 2016, Chicago was taking over as the murder capital of America and that was fine with him. It was his dream to be a homicide cop in Irvine, California, or Frisco, Texas where they seldom heard of violent crime. But then, those towns didn't really have any use for a homicide department.

Archer scrolled through messages on his phone. A note from Tom Lyons caught his eye. His cop friend in Detroit had seen the story about Johnny Leroy's death. Lyons always had his back.

Q. Saw the story about officer down and I'm sorry. Don't know if you knew him, but I looked him up. Impressive dude. Sorry for the loss. On the bright side, Chicago is finally taking some of the load off Detroit and Nawlins. (A little blue humor). Also, we got word that Bobby Mercer was somewhere down in South Florida. They're going to find him, my friend. And when they do we're going to bury him.

Bobby Mercer. The former Detroit cop who ran the drug ring, recruited Archer's two brothers and ran down Denise in a stolen car. *That* Bobby Mercer. Yeah, there *were* some bad cops out there. Cops who deserved to die. Archer would have loved to have Mercer in his gun site, but there were also the Josh Levys and Tom Lyonses. What had Levy called them? Role-model cops. Thank God there were more of them than the bad guys. He put the cup in the sink and took his morning stroll, past The Cat's Meow, the karaoke bar that kept him awake most nights, past Rita's Tequila Bar on Bourbon and ended up at his favorite breakfast restaurant.

He had his second cup of steaming-hot morning coffee at Café Envie on Decatur, where he poured over the *Times-Picayune*. Of course, the story was front-page above-the-fold on Leroy's murder. The headline. And of course, they reported that the police had no clue why this heinous crime had been committed. They ran several of his quotes, where he basically said they had no leads at this time. There was a slight tone in the story that insinuated the cops should know more than they did. Like they weren't doing their job. This, less than twenty-four hours since the killing. He read the story a second time, and Archer agreed. They should know more. A lot more. He needed to step up his game. Big time.

Officer Leroy's list of accomplishments was a huge part of the story. Two Medals of Merit for selfless acts of courage. Saving a baby from a burning car, and rescuing an elderly woman from drowning after she stumbled into a fountain. There were numerous other awards that had been presented to the man, most of them listed, including one for an investigation into a gang of armed thieves who hijacked trucks loaded with liquor, cigarettes and other valuables. Catching robbers, breaking up brawls, initiating community programs. The guy was a role-model cop.

Buried in the last part of the story was the shooting. A robbery suspect had drawn on Leroy, early in his career and he'd acted in self-defense. It was all aboveboard. Archer would look into it, but it happened a long time ago. There were more current cases to investigate.

Archer had never met Leroy, but silently toasted the officer as he took his final sip of the black bitter beverage. The wooden ceiling fans moved the air, but this early in the morning it was already hot and sticky, and the whirling fans only served to move hot moisture-laden air. He walked to Canal Street, his sport coat over his shoulder, hoping his shirt wasn't soaked by the time he got to the office.

On the streetcar, he called the lab to see when the morgue would be free for Solange to see Leroy's body. He texted, telling her any time after four would be fine and the address where she could see the deceased. He offered her a ride and she wrote back, declining. Archer wondered if it had been too soon to ask her out. For her, and definitely for him. He was still grieving. Every day, every hour, every minute. He was attracted to the voodoo lady in a strange, awkward kind of way, and they'd had several meetings over coffee and even a drink, but it had all been business. She was offering him advice. Strictly a professional relationship. And maybe she'd been put off by his offer. He hadn't asked a girl out in . . . He couldn't remember the last time. Still he had mixed emotions. How the hell did you deal with a dead spouse? How did you deal with the love of someone who didn't exist anymore? Love was never easy. And then it just got more and more difficult.

He exited the streetcar, walked down to the office and sat down at his desk at 8:30. He stared at the paperwork in front of him, at his computer screen, and knew that the first and only thing on his list needed to be Officer Johnny Leroy. Leroy's case was number one. And at the end of the day, the end of *this* day, he couldn't face his superiors, he couldn't face the news media, and say, 'Sorry, we learned nothing new today.' That wasn't going to fly. Work as long and as hard as possible and show some progress by the end of the day. Every second presented possibilities.

He had seventy-four paper messages, one hundred twenty phone messages and about twenty internal notes. One was from the Michael Landow, the mayor, telling him this murder had to be solved immediately. No shit. He'd never even met the mayor but he knew the pressure that man must be under. When a cop goes down, it's priority one.

The craziest thing was the fact that a voodoo lady thought she could help. Thought she could look at a body and help solve the murder. No, he was wrong. The *craziest* thing was that she *had* helped solve a couple of other murders too. Using methods only she understood. Archer was never sure how to deal with that. In Detroit it was cut and dried. Hard facts, concerned citizens, solid police work. No hokum. Here, in the voodoo capital of the United States, he'd found a woo-woo factor. And the times it was used it had worked. He was ill prepared to deal with that.

Archer reviewed a handful of messages. There were several hate-filled rants littered with tired phrases suggesting *5-0 deserved to die. More bacon gonna fry. When you kill a nigger, a nigger pulls a trigger.* Most of them were crackpot suggestions aimed at getting even with someone, identifying the killer as an ex-boyfriend, or an errant son who should have been in jail by now. One said it was a neighbor who always had it in for the cops, and another knew this one black cop who hated white cops. He was probably the shooter. Almost all the messages mentioned this supposed killer by name, and many gave contact information.

Ray Whitehead has been harassing me for years. I believe he broke into my home, stole some guns, some liquor, and in the last two weeks, stole my girl. I know he hates cops and I'm going to tell you exactly where to find him: 1219 2nd . . .

But some of the crazy leads, the ones the department was going to investigate, now they were going to take some serious manpower. Manpower they didn't have. And almost all those hours were wasted, but that was the nature of the business. You just needed one good lead. One of them might have the answer. Archer pushed them aside and closed his eyes, hands behind his head. A vacation would be nice right now.

'Q,' Josh Levy leaned on the desk. 'The old man, the one who heard the car backfire . . . he had a part-time caretaker with him yesterday.'

'And?'

'Caretaker, young black girl, she went to the second-floor window to see what the noise was all about. She saw a black male, five foot seven to five ten, walking down the street at a pretty-good clip. The girl says there was almost no foot traffic, so he stood out. And this caretaker said she wouldn't know what a car back-firing sounded like. But she could recognize the sound of a gunshot and she was pretty sure that's what it was. Somebody firing a weapon. She apparently lives in a neighborhood where she's heard gunfire before. We may have a witness, Detective.'

SIX

Joseph Brion sat on the steps over-looking Jackson Square. He stuffed the end of a shrimp po-boy sandwich into his mouth and started chewing, staring at the stately, glaringly white, St Louis Cathedral with its towers and dark spires framed against a cloudless clear-blue sky, and the statue of Andrew Jackson out front, his horse rearing up as the famous soldier, later president, held the reins with his left hand and waved his hat with his right. The words engraved on the stone base were quite clear. THE UNION MUST AND SHALL BE PRESERVED. A striking pose by a striking figure.

Brion had watched entertainment acts perform on these cold, concrete steps. His father had brought him as a child and they'd witnessed Dixieland jazz, acrobats who did handstands all the way up and down the concrete formation, magicians who could levitate people in the audience and the frizzy-haired banjo player, his favorite, who played something like five instruments at the same time. Drums, a kazoo, the banjo, an accordion and he couldn't remember what else. He could hear 'When The Saints Go Marching In', in his head.

Oh, I want to be in that number, when the saints go marching in.

At first, his father told him it was about the pro football team, the New Orleans Saints, and the song referred to *number* eight, Archie Manning, quarterback for the Saints for ten years. Manning had nine losing seasons and was sacked three hundred forty times. Not a stellar career, but his father had been a huge fan. It turned out, the song was written long before Manning and his sons Peyton and Eli played the game. Joseph Brion remembered his pop as quite the kidder.

He felt a chill run through his spine. This place, the concrete steps were mesmerizing. So many of his childhood memories had happened here. He and his pop. They'd had quite a time.

'Hey, mister,' a young boy about six years old stood one step down, pointing at him.

He stared at the kid, then glanced up and saw the mother, a heavy-set black lady, who was wrapped in a too-tight red dress.

'Lady, is he yours?'

'I'm so sorry,' she said.

'What's that around your neck?' the child pointed again.

'Sammy, stop. The man has a tattoo. Now leave him alone.'

'No, it's OK.'

'It's like a necklace,' the boy said. 'Is that what it is?'

'It is a necklace,' he said. 'It's called unity. People, events that stay together, that are connected. When someone leaves the unity, it falls apart.'

'It goes all the way around your neck,' the child said. 'It didn't fall apart, did it?'

'No, it didn't,' he nodded, 'but it's printed on my skin. Things change and I can't undo the printing and there are some people and events that have gone away. Connections have been broken. The necklace is a memory of when everything was perfect.'

The young boy looked to his mother, not at all sure what the strange man had said.

'Have a good day,' she smiled at him, hugging her son tightly and quickly walking away.

He usually savored a po-boy sandwich; deep-fried shrimp, with a rich, mayonnaise-mustard rémoulade sauce, but today his heart wasn't in it. Nor were his taste buds. Today he was probably the most wanted, hunted man in New Orleans, and for the first time in his life, he'd killed someone. He'd planned it. He'd executed the act with precision. Still, it was hard to deal with the emotions. Oh, he'd had some skirmishes with the law before. Shoplifting, some petty crimes, but obviously, nothing like this. There had been an assault charge when someone who worked for him collected a drug debt but decided not to pay him his share. It was a small debt, but he felt the man needed a lesson. Breaking the man's face and dislocating his shoulder got Brion thirty days in the city jail. Worst place he'd ever been. The New Orleans jail was a rough sentence.

He smelled the sour odor of hot sweaty horses even before he saw the two carriages pulling up in front of him, letting off their tourist passengers. The sad-looking animals, their heads lowered in shame, were toweled off by the carriage drivers, and those same drivers surveyed the area for the next couple or family to put the horses through their torture again.

Brion studied his options, sipping a watered-down cola from a cheap plastic cup. If no one had seen him shoot the officer, the possibilities were endless. If no cameras had captured the act, he could leave town, or stay. He could watch the cops chase their tails, laugh at the media reports, because there were no leads. He could move on to the next phase of his business. Three more events. He'd scoped out the area in Bayou St John. Three days he'd walked up and down that street. He saw no evidence of any surveillance camera in the area, but technology being what it was, cameras were everywhere. Private residents, city sites, businesses and every street corner in the world. Hopefully there were none that captured his crime. He was fairly certain. The only camera he was certain of was in his possession. Officer Leroy's body cam. He'd stripped the sunglasses and the camera from the cop and that camera was never going to be evidence in the shooting. He was pretty sure that his somber face and the barrel of his gun would be front and center on the video. So no one was ever going to view that picture. He'd made sure of that.

A clown-costumed character hand-pulled a small cart front and center to the sparsely populated stairs. The man had dressed himself to look like Weary Willie, the Depression-era character made famous by Ringling Circus clown Emmett Kelly decades ago. Brion's father had shown him pictures, videos, of the world-famous clown and now, this imposter was setting up shop. Pulling out a broom and a bucket for 'contributions', the impersonator started sweeping the street. Brion remembered an Internet video of Kelly, sweeping the spotlight, chasing it off center ring in a Ringling Brothers Circus production. This guy was no Emmet Kelly. The shows he'd seen with Pop, the atmosphere, it wasn't the same today. The entertainment just wasn't like it was when he was a kid. He desperately missed his pop. Missed his childhood. And Pop had promised to take him to the Ringling Brothers Circus. It was something they were so looking forward to. Ringling had recently shut the circus down. No more elephants, prancing horses, no more high-wire acts or clowns. The circus wasn't coming to town again. Ever.

Stuffing the sandwich into a paper bag, he gave the terrain one last look, remembering his loving father, remembering the city that his pop had referred to as the Big Easy, as one big circus with endless possibilities. That all ended twenty years ago, and nothing he could do was going to bring it back. But that didn't stop his mission. He'd mapped out his agenda, the locations, the timing, and the victims. After all these years, he needed revenge.

Brion caught bus 88 on St Claude at the fringe of the Quarter and rode the line to the Lower Ninth ward. Stepping off, he walked by empty lots, overgrown with tall grass and weeds. Vines crawled up cement steps with no porch or house at the top. A rusted-out Ford truck rested on blocks, it's tires long since removed. The nice thing about living in the Lower Ninth, you didn't have a lot of neighbors. And the crime rate wasn't that high. Basically because no one lived there. There was nothing to steal, no one to assault. The neighborhood still struggled to come back from the devastation known as Katrina. A long, slow climb.

A mangy dog snarled at him, a rumbling growl deep in its throat. Its brown fur was matted and the animal's teeth bared. Pets had been abandoned during the storm and today they continued to reproduce, mangy feral relatives of their ancestors.

Bald tires covered the next lot and sodden old couches and chairs were scattered like colorful sea sponges. The Ninth was a dumping ground for animals, tires and furniture, and there was an odor of rot in the air. He shook his head in disgust as a black snake slithered by on the broken sidewalk; a raccoon warily watched him, mostly hidden in the tall weeds. The press had announced that slowly the neighborhood was coming back. Very slowly. It had a long way to go.

He walked up the steps to his small shotgun house and opened the door. The gray cat, called Cat, brushed against his leg in a friendly manner, he thought because she was still thankful for the rescue six years ago when a Rottweiler was threatening to eat her. In reality, this time her bowl was empty, and she was sending a signal. She was hungry. He took five steps to the tiny kitchen and picked up the bag of cat food.

'I was about to do that,' the voice startled him. She seldom came out of her small bedroom.

'No problem, Mom.'

She pushed her unkempt gray hair back from her worn face and adjusted the threadbare blanket over her lap. Nodding at him, she spun the wheelchair around and pushed it the few feet back to her room. He heard the door slam. She was in a mood. A mood she'd been in for years.

'Mom,' he watched her go and yelled out, 'will you want some dinner? I've got half a shrimp po-boy.' She didn't answer and he put the sandwich in the refrigerator. Twenty years ago, her endless possibilities had ended as well. She decided she had nothing else to live for and waited every day for the good Lord to take her. And the days dragged on. And on. And on.

He eased himself down in the worn leather easy chair that his father had relaxed in, nights on end. It was always his father's chair and he never forgot that. Flipping on the remote, he settled on the local news channel. Of course, the stories were all sidebars on the shooting. Speculation, stories about Officer Leroy's legendary awards and commendations. Nothing about the Leroy that Joseph Brion knew. Nothing even close. They should have interviewed *him*. He poured himself a tumbler of Hennessy and changed the channel. The news didn't change. He should have been energized. Should have been elated. Should have been high-fiving his friends. Instead, he felt an emptiness. A dull ache. He'd eliminated a problem, not exposed one. There was still work to be done, and it all fell on him. There were others involved, but he had taken the mantle of responsibility. He would shoulder the work. His posse had his back. He paid for that service. They would be there if he needed them, but he'd made the decision. He'd suffered the greater loss and therefore he was going to give more than anyone else. There was work to be done. He took another sip of the cognac and closed his eyes. In the darkness, he felt his father, grasping his hand, keeping him close as they walked into the big top. Cotton candy in one hand, his father's hand in the other. The possibilities were endless. Until they weren't.

SEVEN

'You saw this man from the window here?' Archer sipped a cup of green tea as the young woman nodded. The window provided a broad, almost aquarium view of the street.

'I heard the noise.' She motioned to the older gentleman, sitting in a recliner, his head bobbing on his chest. 'Raymond said it was a car backfiring. I don't know what that means. Apparently, cars with faulty engines or bad gasoline used to make a banging noise?'

'Before your time,' Archer said.

'Anyway, I walked to the window and looked down on the street. Same view that you can see.'

It was a spectacular view from Archer's perspective. You could see up and down the whole street from only two stories up.

'The police car was parked in front of the drugstore,' she continued. 'I assumed an officer either needed some medicine or there had been a problem. Maybe a robbery. I've been coming here for several months and there isn't a lot of excitement in Bayou St John. It's pretty quiet in this area of the city. But I thought the sound was a lot like a gunshot. In my neighborhood, we have some gangs and in the evening, we often hear weapons being fired. There's a certain popping sound. You get used to it. It happens a lot. I'm pretty sure the sound was a gunshot.'

'Can you tell me about the man who you saw?' Archer wanted any identification. Whatever she could describe was better than what they had now. Anything.

'I only saw his back. He had a T-shirt on and cargo shorts. By his arms and legs I knew he was black. Slightly muscular, maybe five ten, although it was hard to tell. He was walking but walking fast and I was trying to put together everything I heard and saw. The gunshot, the police car and the man walking down the sidewalk. It wasn't that important, you know what I mean? This is New Orleans, Detective. A lot of things happen. But I was trying to figure it all out.'

'Did you observe the officer in the car?'

'The windows were reflecting the sun, Detective. I recall that, but I don't remember seeing anything in the car. You say that the driver's window was open but maybe it was the sun blinding me. I didn't pay a lot of attention. I was just aware the car was there. I thought maybe a policeman had fired the shot.'

Archer wanted a positive ID, but he would take what he could get.

'Tell me everything you can about the man walking away.'

'T-shirt, baggy shorts, a cap, and he kept shaking his head like he was talking to himself. Probably was.'

'Any sign of a weapon? Something in his hand?'

'Both hands in his pockets, Detective. I remember that. He was hustling down that sidewalk, shaking his head and his hands in his pockets. I remember thinking, *This man is having a conversation. Maybe with the devil.* Then I realized that *he* might have shot someone. I had no reason to believe it was the police officer in the car. I didn't know there was an officer in the car. But, you know how sometimes you just have a feeling?'

Archer had a brief moment where he thought he should hook her up with Solange Cordray. Apparently, several people had epiphanies.

'If you have any other thoughts, recollections, please call.' He handed her his card, then walked back to the full plate-glass window and stared out on the sidewalk two stories down. A young couple walked by, the girl pushing a baby stroller. He could easily see the child, almost bald and wearing only a diaper. The heat was oppressive and . . .

'You've got a great view from up here.'

'Raymond has a great view. I agree.'

'You saw this man walking down the sidewalk. And all you can tell me is that he was black and wore baggy shorts. Think a little harder.'

'Think a little harder?'

'Close your eyes. I want you to recreate the moment. You saw this man walking away from you. Concentrate. What did his hair look like? Was his head shaved, how did it look from the back?'

She closed her eyes. He waited. Witnesses always saw more than they remembered. They just didn't realize what they had seen. He was actually a fan of hypnotism. The professionals could often bring new information to light. Something the witness would have never remembered on their own.

'He's walking away from you. Look at his head. His shoulders, his torso his . . .'

'I see him, Detective. A cyclist almost ran him over, but the man never stopped or slowed down for a second. Hurrying down the street as if he needed to be somewhere else.'

'Good, good,' Archer encouraged her. 'Look at him again. How about the hair?'

'He wore a ball cap. Backwards. I'm sorry, I saw it; I think I mentioned that to you. But it's very clear right now.'

'What was printed on that cap?' He kept a calm, almost monotone voice. 'Keep your eyes closed.'

'The cap was backwards,' she said. 'I think it might have been maroon. Maybe there was a logo, a mascot, an animal like a cat or tiger.'

'You're doing great,' Archer said. 'And your view was behind this man, correct?'

'Yes, I was watching him from behind as he hot-footed up the street.'

She was silent, obviously concentrating. Finally, 'Saints.'

'On his hat?'

'No, I told you. That was an animal.' She kept her eyes scrunched tight as if concentrating. Archer hoped she was.

'The T-shirt. I don't know why I didn't mention that. The back of his shirt said Saints.'

'Good, good,' Archer encouraged her. 'Colors?'

'Black and gold.'

'You're doing well,' Archer told her again. 'Let's again concentrate on the physical, the body. Do you remember what kind of tattoos he wore?' Sounded like a ganger and all gangers wore tattoos.

Her eyes still closed, she answered. 'I assume he did, but he was in shorts and a shirt, Detective.'

'Look at his arms,' Archer coaxed her.

Nothing.

'His shorts, they came down below his knees? Baggy cargo shorts? Keep your eyes closed and see what was out the window.'

'Yes.'

'Yes, cargo shorts?'

Her eyes squinted tight, she shook her head.

'Tattoos around the ankles? On the calf. Any color? Ink?'

'No.'

'How about his face?' Mike Tyson had a tattoo on his face. Maybe he'd done something . . .

'I can't see his face. He's walking away. Oh,' she gasped. He heard amazement in her voice.

'What do you see?'

'He has a tattoo. He does have a tattoo. How did I forget that?' An upward tilt to her voice as she sounded surprised.

Archer nodded. 'Keep your eyes closed. Now, tell me where it is. Look at him closely. You can see his legs, his arms . . .'

'No, no, I don't even remember thinking this,' she said. 'But there was a tattoo on his neck. Yes, I see it.'

Bingo. Archer kept the smile to himself.

'His neck.'

She opened her eyes, a half-smile on her face.

'So, you saw a . . .'

'Wreath.'

'This tattoo, what kind of a wreath was it?'

'I remember it now. Like a crown of thorns. The one Jesus wore before he was crucified. It covered his neck. I don't know why I didn't remember that. But it was very evident.'

'It covered his neck?'

'I only saw him from the rear, Detective. But it appeared to go all the way around his neck. Thorns, stems, that's all I could make out. It was a dark tattoo, and sort of blended in with his skin, but it was definitely there. I can't believe I didn't remember before.'

'Sometimes you can wake up in the middle of the night,' Archer said, 'and remember something that you'd been worrying about for months. Sometimes that memory will solve a host of problems. We store a lot of information that we don't know is there.'

'Yes!'

It was a start.

EIGHT

On the last day of his life, Old Joe Washington was cleaning out the cash register from a convenience store in Algiers in the East end of New Orleans. He wasn't that old, really, just forty-five, but they called him 'Old Joe' because of his gravelly voice, his gray hair and his stooped posture. God knows he felt old. A life of petty thefts, grand-theft robbery and hijackings left him feeling ancient. But it was the only life he knew.

The cringing Korean owner huddled down in a corner behind the counter, begging for his life. This crying man was truly old. Probably in his seventies. The oiled wood floor of the small store spoke to the age of the establishment. It must be a mom-and-pop operation, and the take was going to be a lousy three or four hundred bucks. Still, a man had to live. And this was the way Old Joe made his living. And not much of a living at that.

His right hand was in the pocket of his hoody and with his left hand he pulled bills from the register, shoving them into his other pocket. Damn. He needed to hit some high-end targets, but with cameras, security alarms and a stepped-up presence of police and private security forces it was getting harder and harder to make a hit.

'Shut up, old man, or I swear I will shoot you right now.' He turned to the man and moved his hand inside his pocket. He mimicked the accent of Jimmy Cagney from old-school cinema. He liked to pretend he was an old-school criminal.

The man whimpered, but stopped his begging.

Old Joe reached under the tray and pulled out an extra hundred and two fifties. Enough to get by for several days.

'Ah, a little extra here,' he said. 'You didn't tell me about this, little man. I swear if you are holding out on me, I will bring down a wrath of vengeance on you.' Channeling Samuel Jackson from *Pulp Fiction*.

He shoved his left hand into his pocket, feeling the money, and quickly walked to the door, eyeing the supply of wine displayed on shelving down the right side of the store. He could use a bottle or two right about now. Or a bottle of Four Roses. That would be perfect, but the Korean didn't carry the hard stuff. The next time he'll pick a place that carried the hard stuff.

'Don't you get up, you kink; don't you go to the phone or push any alarm for ten minutes. Do you understand me? Your life isn't worth the paltry sum of money I'm taking. For your own health, stay there until I'm long gone. Do you understand me?'

'I understand,' the man mumbled.

Pushing open the squeaking door, Joe stepped into the glaring sun.

Glancing left he started walking. He'd go one block then jog down the alley that he'd scouted out before. Right behind the pawnshop and dollar store. There was no sign of any security camera. Stupid shop owners. A couple of blocks and he'd be home free.

'Stop. Police.'

He'd heard that before. Kept walking, a steady stream of traffic muffling the order.

'Hands out of your pockets. Now.'

He kept walking. Guy wasn't going to shoot him in the back. Not that stupid. A Harley roared by, monopolizing the sound on the street, but the voice was still behind him. He glanced to his right, wondering if he could cut through the cars and make it safely to the other side. It wasn't possible. Too much traffic and it would be a sad ending to a career to be mowed down by somebody's Kia or Prius.

'Sir, I'm warning you.' A high-pitched voice, some young buck. 'Pay attention. Hands out of your pockets. Stop now. Do you hear me?'

Joe heard the steps behind him, upping the pace. The officer was running, shoes slapping the sidewalk, and Old Joe started running too, breathing hard and heavy. Too many cigarettes, too many boilermakers. He *was* definitely old before his time.

'Sir, stop. I'm armed,' the cop was shouting, his voice high and hoarse. 'Take your hands from your pockets. I'm not going to warn you again.'

Panting, Joe stopped abruptly. He wasn't going to outrun this cop. He simply wondered how this guy knew the store had been robbed. This should have been one of the easiest heists he'd ever made, and it just pissed him off how little he'd actually scored. Had someone ratted him out? Who? He'd only mentioned it to two people. He spun around, confronting his accuser.

'What the hell do you . . .'

'I'm asking you again. Hands out of your pockets. And they'd better both be empty. No weapon, sir. Do you understand?'

The fresh-faced kid couldn't be more than twenty-five years old. He had both hands wrapped around his Glock 22. He was squinting into the sun, and Joe could sense the young man was scared. Not the look of a seasoned pro. This might be the first time the youngster had ever confronted someone with his pistol. Old Joe thought about the money in his pocket, he thought about the number of times he'd skated on thefts much bigger than this. The time a truck driver had died, just so Joe could take a big payday. He'd even skated on that job. No problem. It just didn't seem fair.

'Slowly.' The cop was shaking, the gun in his hand slightly moving up and down. 'Take your hands out where I can see them. Slowly . . . slowly, and no weapon, sir.'

Joe watched his eyes. That's where you saw what this white kid's intentions were. The officer was still squinting, but there was dread in those eyes. He didn't know if Joe was packing or not. Probably had a wife or girlfriend at home and scared he might not see her again. And Joe briefly considered his own girlfriend, his three illegitimate kids from two other women, and realized he really wasn't that great a provider. No one was going to miss him that much if this guy pulled the trigger. It was a little sad to think he probably didn't have much of a support base in his life.

'I don't see those hands,' the cop shouted. The boy was terrified. It was obvious.

Old Joe slowly pulled out his left hand with the bills and let them fall to the sidewalk, a light breeze blowing them into the street.

The white cop's eyes briefly strayed, watching the money.

'Sir, now the right hand.'

Old Joe smiled and quickly pulled his hand from his right pocket and that's when the young cop pulled the trigger, an explosion that ricocheted off the surrounding buildings. The bullet hit the robber in the stomach and exited out his back. He grabbed his abdomen, surprised at the pain and realizing he couldn't stand up. It felt like his spine had been cut in half. Looking down he saw his hands and shirt covered in rich, red blood as he dropped to the ground, closing his eyes. He felt that same blood filling his mouth and as he choked and gagged, the last thought he had was that the kid was going to be surprised when he found out that there was no gun. Joe never carried a gun, never owned a gun. There was just a hand in his pocket. That was all. Just his hand.

NINE

'**S**hit. Shit. Shit. We all know where this is headed.' Sergeant Chip Beeman pounded his fist on Archer's desk. 'We've got an alligator by the tale, Q. Shit is going to hit the street.'

Archer pushed aside the pile of papers he'd been addressing and looked up at Beeman.

'I agree, Sergeant.'

'Internal affairs is already on the scene, and we've moved Officer Montgomery to a safe house. There's a team of investigators talking to him. Of course, there will be an immediate in-depth investigation, but I'm afraid we may be looking at a murder charge.'

'And that involves me?' Archer realized he had no idea how this played out. If this was a homicide case then . . .

'No, of course not. At least not at this time. I'm not sure how this plays out. All I know is, the vic was unarmed. We've got the officer's body cam. Montgomery yells for the vic to pull his hand from his pocket, numerous times, and when he does, Jethro Montgomery fires his weapon at close range. As I said, they're interviewing him right now and you and I both know it's not going to be pleasant. The kid is going to go through hell, Archer. An unarmed black man. We'll be front page news this time tomorrow.'

Archer pushed back his chair, looking up at Beeman. 'The store owner says that this Joseph Washington had a gun when he robbed the convenience store, right?'

'That's what he said, but responding officers found no weapon. They've had this guy, this Korean shop owner, in interrogation for a couple of hours. He's apparently still shaken. Thought he was going to meet his maker.'

'He could have ditched the weapon.'

'He could have pretended he had a weapon. The owner seemed a little confused.'

'But you said that Montgomery was positive the perp had a weapon.' Archer shook his head.

'When officers arrived on the scene, the first thing Officer Montgomery said was, "When I got the call, they said the perp was armed." I imagine Montgomery is still shaken too.'

'So, the dispatcher called, said there was an armed robbery in progress and Montgomery responded. How did we know he had a weapon?'

'Cold call. Somebody phoned 911 and said a robbery was in progress and the perpetrator had a gun,' Beeman said. 'Apparently, the caller was adamant that there was a gun. As you know, we have to follow up as if there is a weapon. We sent out the message. Montgomery was under the impression. Puts a lot of pressure on a man, doesn't it?'

'No trace on the call?'

'Not at this time. It was probably a burner or someone found a pay phone. That said,' he smiled, 'I'd be surprised if there is somewhere you can find a pay phone.'

'Could it have been a setup?'

'Hell, anything's possible, Q. You know that. Obviously it's much too early to know, but I can't wait to hear the recording.'

'Somebody insisting a gun is in play, then there's no gun? And how about Officer Johnny Leroy? We got a call saying there was a knife fight in Bayou St John. Leroy shows up and there's no fight. At least no one saw any evidence of a fight. We're pretty sure that was a setup as well. I hope they pursue that line in the case of Officer Montgomery,' Archer said. 'Sounds like a strong possibility to me.'

'I'll tell you, Archer, look over your shoulder. There's going to be a riot in the streets and none of us is safe.'

Archer gave him a grim smile. He'd been looking over his shoulder for over a year. There were Detroit cops who wanted him dead. His brothers, one in jail, one on the loose, wanted him dead. Officer Bobby Mercer, head of the notorious DPD drug ring and now on the run, probably wanted him dead. Archer had turned on his own department, trying to stop this drug ring and they'd killed his wife and run him out of town. Look over his shoulder? Hell, nothing new. He couldn't imagine a life where he wasn't looking over his shoulder.

Joseph Brion got the call on his cell phone from one of his drug runners. The second movement had been performed flawlessly. He couldn't have planned it any better. Old Joe was toast. There'd been a backup plan if the responding cop hadn't killed him. Joe was going down anyway, but this was perfect. A white cop shooting an unarmed petty burglar. One more step toward retribution. One more step to judgment. Old Joe Washington. His nemesis. Joe finally got his comeuppance. Brion had called 911, warned them of the armed robbery, and so far the plan had been flawless. Tonight would be his party. Tomorrow night, his grand finale. Justice would be served. Hellfire and damnation, it had been a long time coming, but this would be a celebration his father would have enjoyed. All but the end. But still, this was going to be one of the greatest circuses ever to hit New Orleans. There was a surprise ending even he wasn't sure of.

He knocked on his mother's bedroom door.

'Mom, there's food in the fridge. Cat's been fed. I told Marjorie, if she doesn't hear from me, she needs to look in on you. Do you hear me?' He'd talk to her always but she never responded.

As he turned, the door opened. He heard it and spun around.

'Are you coming back?' The shriveled black woman in a wheelchair stared up at him.

'I live here,' he smiled and reached down, taking her hand.

'Are you coming back?'

'Mom . . .'

'Your father never came back. You're not coming back either, are you? Tell me.'

'Yes, Mom. I'm coming back. You'll be fine.'

'You've got a backpack, a sleeping bag. You're leaving and not telling me where you're going.'

'I'll be gone for a couple of nights. Don't worry. Pop needs some help and I'm simply going to step in, OK? You'll be fine.'

'Pop is dead. What help can you give him?'

The old lady lightly squeezed his hand, gazing into his eyes, connecting for the first time in weeks.

'Mom, again, you'll be fine.'

'I'll be fine, Joseph. But will you?'

He squeezed her hand back and walked out the door. He couldn't answer that question, but he needed to be a part of the final round. He owed it to his father. And if something happened to him, so be it. The church was a tight-knit community into itself and they would rally 'round Mom. Her quality of life was almost non-existent as it was. They'd give her shelter and food and make sure she was comfortable. And maybe he'd come out of this just fine. Go back home to Mom and care for her like he always did. Like Pop would have wanted him to. Maybe he would watch the circus from a bleacher-seat in the big top, finally feeling like his father had been vindicated. Worst-case scenario, or best, he might see his father again. In another world. And maybe there would be a square with a bright, shining cathedral and steps with endless entertainment. Maybe a banjo player who was a one-man band. He blinked back tears. Slim chance, but he could dream.

Joseph walked to the bus stop, past the overgrown, rat-infested yards, past the smoky piles of burned trash, past the putrid smell of rotting garbage and discarded tires. He wouldn't miss his neighborhood. Absolutely not.

'Solange, as I'm sure you know, things have changed in the last several hours.'

'I've been following the story, Detective. As I would guess everyone in New Orleans has.'

'Listen, I want to solve this murder of Officer Leroy. But it may not be a safe time for you to be on the street by yourself. I'll either give you a ride and stay with you while you . . .' he hesitated, not sure exactly what she was going to do, 'while you examine the body, or we can set this meeting for another time.' Another time would be much better.

'Quentin, this problem . . .'

'You'll have to be more specific. I've got like . . . a number of problems going on at the same time.'

'I understand. Two of the incidents you are referencing, they are related. I know this.'

'I'm worried that you might get caught up in some protests. I don't want that to happen. I'm not sure where they may spring up. We're going to be warning people to stay off the streets.'

'If there are protests—'

'Actually, a *protest* would be mild.'

'If there are protests regarding the killing of the black man in Algiers,' she said, 'they could relate to the killing of Officer Leroy. The two shootings are connected. I feel certain of that.'

'You think Montgomery and Leroy are linked?'

'I do.'

Archer took a deep breath. 'I appreciate your input, seriously. You've been right before. However, I don't think we should meet today. It's going to be a tough afternoon.'

'Detective Archer,' there was no more familiarity, 'if you want to solve this murder, I need to see Officer Leroy's body. I'll deal with the protests. Please, let me visit at four p.m.'

Joseph Brion took the bus to the foot of Canal Street, then caught the Canal Street ferry on a short ride to Algiers. The ride was only two bucks, probably less than a buck when he was a kid. He and his father had taken the ferry, several times, just for the fun of crossing the river. The first time, he'd clutched the man's hand, tight. He'd never been on the water before and he wasn't about to let go. Pop was his rock, and he held onto that rock. The second time, he remembered, he'd felt like a grown-up. When his father had grabbed his small hand, he'd pulled away. He could handle it this time. And they watched the Quarter and the city slip away across the river as they traveled, what seemed to Joseph, a million miles. New Orleans getting a little smaller. Ten minutes later they were in Algiers.

The plaque at boarding announced that the ferry had operated continuously since 1827. Parts of Algiers were involved in the Battle of New Orleans, 1814, where the British tried to separate Louisiana from the United States. Andrew Jackson, whose statue stood proudly in Jackson Square, faced the British with forty-five hundred troops to England's seventy-five hundred soldiers. Two thousand of the British died. Eight of Jackson's troops were killed. Only eight. Brion remembered the pride that his father had shown when he told him the story about the Kentucky and Tennessee sharpshooters who put away the well-mustered uniformed troops from across the ocean. And he was reminded of the funny song Pop had sung about fighting the British with a cannonball, gunpowder and using a gator as the cannon. Pop could be a funny guy.

He hadn't been to Algiers in years. It wasn't a tourist spot and if he remembered, there wasn't much to do. Grab some gumbo, watch New Orleans and the Quarter from this side of the river, and go home. Except tonight. Tonight should be very active. There would be a lot going on, no question. The slight breeze over the Mississippi was a welcome respite from the oppressive New Orleans heat.

There was going to be some more heat tonight. In the streets. Almost 90 percent of Algiers was African American. They were not happy that an unarmed black man was gunned down by a white cop. Tonight, Brion was fairly certain, there would be hell to pay. Time for a little payback to the NOPD. And after that, if he still was functioning, his final act. His final tribute to Pop. He closed his eyes and held his breath. He was not, as a rule, a vengeful person. But this was for Pop. He had to buck up and get the job done.

TEN

'They've scanned in over one thousand of his arrests, Q.' Levy sat on the edge of Archer's desk. He glanced at a clipboard he held. 'They've discarded speeding charges and domestic disputes, except for violent confrontations. He's got an arrest on someone passing counterfeit bills. Obviously the guy got federal time, not local, so that got tossed. Drugs, most of those charges they've ignored. Assault charges have been reviewed but only severe instances. If a guy slapped his wife and she swore out a complaint, they didn't include it. If a guy took a pool cue to a bar full of patrons, then it made the list. Probably should, don't you think?'

'He arrested a guy who used a pool cue on a bar full of drunks? That's a true story?'

'The guy put something like fifteen in the hospital.'

'A pool cue. Unique weapon.'

'Anyway,' Levy said, 'there's a method. If we don't get a hit off the ones we're flagging, we'll go second tier. The guy who slapped his wife and got arrested for battery? We'll call him in.' Levy put his hands on the desk. 'Now, what you got?'

'There's the girl who saw the guy with the tattooed necklace. It's not much, but we've got a bulletin out, looking for a five-ten guy with a crown of thorns necklace. We're contacting every tattoo parlor within twenty miles. So far, no feedback.'

Levy smiled. 'My final bit of good news, Q. Before I came in I got a message. There's a pawnshop across the street from the drugstore. Lady who works the counter there says she didn't see the shooting, didn't hear anything.'

'And how is this good news?'

'Two days before the shooting, two days before Leroy was gunned down, this young black guy walks into the store. He's looking at guitars. She was showing him the inventory but she said he was a little shifty. Kept looking at the ceiling, gazing around the store. She wasn't sure why, but she paid attention to him and thought about that incident when she saw our bulletin.'

'And that was because?' Archer stared up at him.

'He had a tattooed necklace. She remembered that.'

'Now that's a start.'

'We get the populace involved, we've got a chance of solving this,' Levy said.

'Well, we've got a whole lot more than we did yesterday. However, nothing we can cash in. Let's get out to that store, interview this lady, canvass the area and see if anyone else was visited by the necklace killer.'

'Agreed. The guy was scoping out the neighborhood. Probably looking for cameras,' Levy said.

'And we haven't found any. In that narrow block, no one seems to have video,' Archer shook his head. 'I'd think somebody, some business or residence would have video. You can't walk across a street in this town without a camera picking up your actions. And we definitely don't have the officer's body cam. Damn. So what? We have another thousand arrests records to go?'

Levy nodded an affirmative. 'Everything points to Officer Leroy being a straight-up dude,' he said. 'A guy who followed the rules, came up with answers and was a damned good cop. Married, a couple of kids, one who's a lawyer, one who is a public defender. I can't possibly imagine why someone needed to put him away.'

'And it could be,' Archer took a deep breath, 'as simple as someone just wanted to kill a cop.'

'Could be,' Levy nodded, 'but I don't think so. It seems this was staged. Too perfect.'

'Funny you would say that. Solange Cordray said—'

'The voodoo lady? You're still in touch?'

Archer nodded.

'Q, anything going on between you two?'

'No.' He didn't think so. Well, nothing physical. Nothing that either one of them was willing to admit. She had mentioned chemistry in their last conversation, but . . .

'So, what did she say?'

'She told me that she felt the death of Washington and Leroy were connected. And I think that Officer Montgomery got set up. Someone made sure he thought there was a gun involved in that robbery. I think there's a good chance that's why our guy Officer Montgomery pulled the trigger.'

'I truly believe it was staged. It really seems that someone orchestrated it.' Levy nodded his head. 'Too convenient that we were on top of that call. How did someone know the perp was going to hold up the carry-out?'

'Staged,' Archer said. 'I agree.'

They both paused, logically putting the sequence together.

'A call, either from a pay phone or a burner, told us that there was a robbery with a weapon. No trace of the call. The caller refused to give any contact information. Our Officer Montgomery responds and believes the dispatcher. He has no other choice. This is an armed robbery. He—'

'He's pretty much a rookie, Q. He got spooked and wanted to

go home alive. When the perp pulled his hand out, the hand that was supposed to hold a gun, he defended himself. And of course, there was nothing there. I feel so sorry for that kid.'

'Yeah. I get it. And somebody, or somebodies will decide whether that was the right move, but regardless, he shot an unarmed man. That is going to be a huge problem.'

Levy stood up. 'Anyway, addressing the case you're on, I am hoping that later today or by the latest tomorrow the rest of Leroy's arrest records and incidents will be listed. Then you can go over them and start interviewing the suspects. Tedious.'

'It's going to be a rough night, Josh.'

'Probably.'

'You know, we had riots in Detroit. I'm not unfamiliar with what's about to happen.'

'I've read about some of your infamous riots.'

'Reminds me of a T-shirt I saw before I came down here. *Detroit vs. Everybody Else.*'

Levy chuckled.

'I came to one conclusion back then, Josh. I am certain we can avoid this. It's all very simple.'

Levy nodded. 'Oh, I see. So you've got the answer?' Sarcasm dripped from his words. 'Why haven't you called the chief, the mayor? I'm certain they'd like to hear of this great idea.'

'I'm convinced that they wouldn't listen.' Archer gave him half a smile. 'It's really an easy solution.'

'You're going to stop any chance of a riot tonight? You've got this all figured out.'

'No. But I could stop it. And yes, I've got it all figured out. It's not a brilliant idea, but it's an idea that would save a lot of problems.'

'Pretty cocky, Detective Archer. All right, tell me what we should do? How do we stop a riot.'

'Don't show up.'

Levy paused. 'Don't show up?'

'We don't show up.'

'You're crazy.'

'Josh, the rioters need an audience. Sane people stay off the street on nights like this so if we don't show up, if the media doesn't show up, the protestors have no one to interact with except themselves. There might be some minor looting, a little damage, but the riot doesn't really start until we get there and the cameras are rolling.'

'So, your feeling is we just make it worse. You said, "Sane people stay off the streets." These are not sane people, Q.'

'I've always thought . . . you line the streets with uniforms and swat team riot shields, you bring in the vehicles, which they love to torch, you bring in the tear gas, and the riot begins. Now they've got something to react to. You back it off, say two or three blocks from the scene. You quietly monitor the situation just in case, but no confrontation. It's over almost before it starts.'

'You may be right, Quentin, but the governor has already asked for help from the National Guard. The Highway Patrol is sending in troopers and, of course, our police department and some of the sheriff's deputies will be there in full regalia. There will be riot shields and there will be vehicles.'

'Then we will most certainly have a riot in Algiers.'

'And I'm not going anywhere near the place,' Levy said. 'I wish them all the luck in the world.'

'You won't have to be there,' Archer shook his head. 'Every network and every cable company in the country will have full coverage. There will be satellite trucks all over that neighborhood. News anchors will broadcast from here this evening. They're showing up already. New Orleans will be the biggest story of the night.' Archer paused. 'You won't have to be there, Josh. You can watch it on every channel on your television.'

'Biggest story of the week, the next two weeks,' Levy said.

'I swear,' Archer shook his head, 'all they've got to do is ratchet it way down. If those people have no one to play to, they'll go home. The game is over and we win.'

'Interesting concept, Q.'

'Too bad no one will put it to the test,' he responded.

'Let's just hope that no one loses a life tonight.'

'Let's definitely hope it's not one of the good guys.' Archer was tired of the good guys losing. He fervently hoped that wasn't going to happen this time.

He silently prayed. No loss of life. There had already been too many killings in this case.

ELEVEN

She rode her motorbike to the morgue and Archer met her in the lobby.

'Are you sure you're up for this?' She looked great. He had tried to prepare himself for the meeting, on a purely business level, and she was dressed appropriately, but the black leggings, the black blouse top and the short boots took his breath away. Solange Cordray was hauntingly beautiful.

'Detective, I told you. I've dealt with dead people before.'

'And that's my job, dealing with dead people. However, it doesn't make it any easier when I see them. I just wanted to be sure you were comfortable.'

He ushered her into the inner sanctum.

'They've brought the body out, covered in a sheet, and Officer Johnny Leroy is through that door. Would you like me to walk in with you? Do you need me to stay . . .'?

'No.' She glanced at the doors. 'Don't take any offense, Detective, but I work better alone.'

'OK. I'll be right here when you're done.'

Solange nodded, and pushed through the double doors.

It was a matter of seven steps and she looked around the corner. The antiseptic smell of alcohol assaulted her olfactory senses. On a stainless-steel cart, a sheet strategically placed over the body from neck down, lay the naked remains of Officer Johnny Leroy. Two days dead. In two more days, the man would be under the ground, but today, there was essence of the body. She sensed it. He could tell her something. Anything at this point would be helpful.

And yes, the sight of his head was not for the faint of heart. A large hole in his head, the back of his skull blown out. For a brief moment, she shuddered, the shattered face a brief distraction. Then she concentrated on the aura. She was in the same room as the maimed man. She closed her eyes and the odor dissipated. There was no reason to view him, only be aware of his presence. Sometimes it worked, sometimes it didn't.

'Fill me with your presence, Nanchons of Loa, spirits of the afterlife. What words, what thoughts are in the cavity? The shell of Johnny Leroy? Why was he killed?'

And the thoughts came pouring out. Solange was overwhelmed with strong feelings.

Nothing concrete. She had expected that. But she experienced a broad view of the man. And foremost was that he wanted to escape. That was her immediate revelation. He wanted to be free of the past. Her initial reaction was that his wish had been granted. Because she felt, very strongly, that he'd had a violent past. A history that he possibly regretted. It shook her. A man she didn't know, only aware of him through media reports. Reported to be an upstanding member of society. Honored, decorated, yet . . . he wanted to escape his past. And he had. At least in this life. In the next life, she was certain that everyone would be confronted with their past, and forced to atone. His soul may have departed, but his spirit remained. His chi was powerful; it was asking for a higher acceptance, a ruling that would forgive him for his past transgressions.

There was money involved. Quite a bit of money. And she was somewhat overwhelmed when she considered the source of the money. He'd been a cop, and by all appearances lived on a cop's salary. But this was far more money than a police officer could make. And it seemed as if the money was still to be found. She closed her eyes, concentrating, but the source and the final destination of the wealth eluded her.

Maybe a mattress, although she thought there was more money than a mattress might hold. Possibly he'd buried it or maybe deposited the ill-gotten gains in an offshore bank account? She did feel the money angle was important, but she really wanted to offer Detective Archer, Quentin, something more tangible. Things seldom worked out like that.

She turned and stared at the mirror-shiny stainless-steel drawers that housed the cadavers. Leroy's temporary home. Solange was jarringly aware of her own reflection. She stared back at the young woman dressed in black. A dark priestess, almost a perfect likeness.

She raised her hand to brush back her hair and watched her mirror image do the same thing. She gasped. Something, a cloud, a vague image skirted across her mind. And she knew this was important. She closed her eyes and concentrated.

There was a reflection in his past, she was convinced of it. The officer lived two lives. A mirror image of himself, one side good, one side bad. She'd known it when she first lit the reversible candle. Two flames uniting as one. Duality. The yin and the yang.

And how did you explain to someone like Quentin Archer these mystical, vague interpretations. How was he supposed to act, what possible investigation could he mount based on her observations? He wanted facts, solid leads, concrete information, and she was unable to conjure up those leads. Gazing again at the reflective surfaces, the stainless-steel containers, she let out a breath she didn't know she was holding.

Leroy's transgressions, she had a strong sense, were severe. As she stood there, her hands clenched tight, the body called to her. The corpse spoke directly, asking her to intercede, begging for some peace, forgiveness. For what, she wasn't sure. But this cavity, this former breathing, feeling human being was reaching out. He wanted to possibly confess, maybe find a way to make up for past sins. And that was ridiculous. The past was the past. There was no way to make up for your sins. Oh, society had imprisonment, fines and the death penalty. Religions offered forgiveness; some of them promised absolution for a price, but none of them quite made up for the transgressions of a person's past. Your sins were imprinted in time.

A mugger put fear in his victims that followed them their whole lives. A rapist destroyed the confidence and trust of his prey. Killers who were put to death never brought back those they had killed. There was no atonement. Whatever evil a person had been responsible for . . . it was irreversible. The damage had been done. You could ask for forgiveness, do good works, even ask a higher deity to absolve your sin, but what happened in the past was cast in stone. When you were born, there should be a warning sign.

Whatever you do, whatever you are responsible for, will last through eternity. Get it right the first time, for there are no second chances.

*   *   *

Solange shivered. Her body shook, a cold spell chilling her spine. The empty carcass was again talking to her. She prayed daily that she could be delivered of these signs, these intense feelings. But she knew in the next moment that Johnny Leroy had been responsible for a death. Directly, indirectly, he'd helped kill someone. An innocent. The revelation was a shock. This was an officer of the law and she certainly never expected to accuse him of a crime, a crime as hideous as murder. Yet there it was.

And that could be what he desperately longed to escape. But that escape would never happen. If you killed someone, there was no escape. You just prayed that you never met up with that person in hell.

Walking out into the lobby of the building, she nodded to Archer, not sure what to tell him, not sure how to interpret her impressions. All she was sure of was that the forgiveness, the money and the reflection were subjects that had to be addressed. To accuse the dead officer of murder . . . she'd ponder that for a while.

'So,' he asked. 'Any revelations?'

'Yes.'

'What? What did you learn?' He was genuinely enthused. The detective seemed to be taking her visit somewhat seriously.

'Your officer Johnny Leroy, he is asking for forgiveness. That is the first impression I had. It's obvious, at least to me, that he's been involved in some bad situations. He wants someone, a person, a deity, maybe the police department to give him absolution.'

'But you have no idea what he did.'

'It involved a lot of money. I am assuming, only assuming, that it was ill gotten. I don't know that for a fact.' And yes, she did know what he'd done, what he'd been involved in. But no, she wasn't going to mention it to Archer. Not yet.

'So far, there's nothing I can use. You understand that.'

'No, I personally think you can use all of my information. Figure it out. But there's one more thing you need to know. Officer Leroy was involved in a reflection.'

'A what?'

'Before you ask me questions, can I please explain? I seldom am able to give you solid information. You know that. I can't point to his killer. I can say the reason he was killed may have been money, possibly ill-gotten gains. And a factor in his death may have been a reflection. You have the ability and resources to delve into his past. If you find his need for forgiveness, a trail of money or anything to do with reflection, then I feel strongly that will lead to the reason he was killed. And as I've heard you say, when you can answer the question *why*, then you are close to solving the crime.'

'We've been looking into his records, checking on people he arrested. We're trying to narrow that search down, but twenty-five years on the street—'

'And that may very well be where these three observations are hiding, in the arrests he made, but are you running any background checks on the officer himself?' she asked.

'No. He was on the force for twenty-five years. His record was exemplary.'

She studied him for a moment. 'Detective, Quentin, I'm certain you were given a rigorous background check when you joined the force.'

'I was.'

'A company went to the Internet,' she said, 'checked your profile. They found out that you had uncovered a drug ring in Detroit, they knew that your wife had been run down by a motorist, they understood your father was in law enforcement and they also saw that you had turned on your two brothers who were part of the drug cartel. Am I right? They found that one of your brothers was in jail and one was on the run.'

'I assume so. What's your point?'

She reached into a small clutch purse for her cell phone. Holding it up to him, she smiled.

'Detective, twenty-five years ago, about the time they hired Officer Leroy, phones didn't take pictures. Google wasn't even a dream. Facebook's Mark Zuckerberg was probably in the first or second grade. Now today you are very aware that with this device, the phone I carry in my hand, I can run a check on anyone in the country in three or four minutes. Just give me any name. Am I right?'

Archer smiled and nodded. 'Good point. Background checks twenty-five years ago—'

'They were not what they are today. Not by a long shot.

I wonder what we could find? You have hundreds of employees on staff who may never have had an updated background check.'

'I'm not sure that we don't update,' he paused, 'but damn. That's a good point. A current check might pick up something they missed when Johnny Leroy joined the force.'

'I think it's worth looking into.' She put the phone back into her black beaded purse. 'There may be something you missed.'

'Anything else?' Archer seemed somewhat chagrined. It was obvious he hadn't considered the check on Officer Leroy. Solange knew that the policeman's tenure with the NOPD seemed to show a spotless record and for some reason Archer hadn't considered that anything might be uncovered with a new check. Chances were that a new check would turn up nothing radical, but she felt he couldn't leave any stone unturned.

Besides, she was certain Leroy had been involved in the death of someone. Of course she'd seen Archer on TV talking about a shooting in the line of duty. That wasn't the killing she was worried about. She was convinced there was another killing and the secret of it was buried. In any case, she had no proof and felt she had no right to mention the accusation at this time. She wondered how she might suggest Leroy had been involved in another killing, maybe one that happened while he was investigating a crime?

'I didn't pick up any other thoughts, but you know I'll call you if something comes to mind. Just out of curiosity . . .' she hesitated, 'was Officer Leroy ever involved in a shooting, other than the one you mentioned on the TV interview?'

'One of the first things we looked at,' Archer said. 'The answer is no. A robbery suspect drew his weapon, and the officer shot him. The incident was well vetted and it was clearly an act of self-defense. Other than that, nothing.'

'The suspect was killed, right?'

Archer nodded.

She looked back to the room where the body lay. 'I think I saw that,' she said. But she would have sworn the victim was innocent. Not an armed robber threatening a cop. 'Again, I'll call you if anything else comes to mind.'

'I look forward to it,' he said.

'It was good to see you again,' she smiled.

'Solange, before you go, do you have any other feelings about the suspect who was shot in Bayou St John? Joseph Washington?'

She closed her eyes and took a cleansing breath. 'I'm sorry, I don't. I told you that I feel Officer Leroy and the Bayou St John shooting are related. I obviously don't have reasons for all my thoughts. That's all. I pray that no violence or bloodshed happens because of his death.'

'I do too,' Archer said, 'but that's one prayer that I don't believe will be answered. I told you, we expect protests. I just don't know at what level.'

'Quentin.' Her voice was almost a whisper.

'Something else?'

'He didn't carry a gun.'

'Joseph Washington? We didn't find one,' he said. 'The officer who shot him was certain he had a weapon. If he carried a handgun, it wasn't on the scene when our team arrived.'

She was starting to fall into a trance. An uncomfortable mental cloud. The trance was acceptable in the privacy of her quarters, behind the door and curtain. In a public situation, in front of a client, especially this client, it was not the time or place. She closed her eyes.

Solange shook her head, trying to dislodge the feeling and instead appearing to have a small seizure. She wished the uncontrollable sensation away. *Please, not at this time. Not at this place.* Her hands were clenched, her eyes squeezed shut as she shook.

'He didn't want to kill again,' she whispered in a guttural, throaty sound. 'Do you understand that?'

The tension suddenly evaporated. Her limbs were loose, her eyes opened and she saw Archer's face, his eyes filled with concern, his mouth open.

'Jesus, Solange, are you OK?'

'I'm fine, Detective. It was a moment of . . .'

He stared at her and she had no answer.

'A glass of water? Should I call an ambulance?'

'No, please. I'll be fine. It happens sometimes.'

'You're sure?' He reached out and touched her shoulder and she shuddered.

'I am. Please, it's time that I leave. Possibly seeing the body . . .'

'You mentioned a second death. This Joseph Washington killed someone before?'

'Joseph Washington?'

'You said he didn't want to kill again.'

'I don't remember saying that.'

'Solange? What's going on? Please, if you know something . . .'

'Nothing. I told you, I have no other feeling about the man who was killed. Somehow, his death and death of Officer Johnny Leroy are connected. Other than that, I can't help.'

She turned and walked out the door. The blast of heat didn't faze her. She wanted to go home. There were times when whatever gift had been given her didn't feel like a gift at all. It was a curse, and there were moments when she gladly would give it up.

'Baron Samedi, welcome this Johnny Leroy into the realm of the dead,' she whispered. The skull-faced god of debauchery with his dark glasses and a penchant for rum and cigars was a spirit she seldom if ever communicated with. But he could welcome Officer Leroy into death and possibly give him the escape he begged for. As for the other shooting victim, this Joseph Washington, he hadn't called out to her, and she simply wished him the best in whatever after-life he found himself.

She said a silent prayer that Detective Archer would find her discoveries helpful. That he would act on what she had offered. She felt certain that if he explored the three elements he would be much closer to solving the murder of Officer Johnny Leroy.

Escape, money and reflection.

Maybe the detective needed to reflect on how Leroy had accumulated his money. Maybe the officer had wanted to escape from his own reflection. She would think on it, discuss it with Ma, to no avail, but in the meantime her brain was tired. Her head ached. She was emotionally exhausted and felt that her spirit, her inner core, needed a long, slow timeout.

The voodoo lady fastened the chinstrap on her black helmet and straddled her red-and-black Honda Forza. The ride, the wind, it might refresh her. But a glass of white wine sounded even better at the end of her trip.

TWELVE

New Orleans's Fifteenth Ward contained Algiers, on the west bank of the Mississippi. Slaughterhouse Point, named so for the slaughterhouse that used to be a large industry there, and now named Algiers Point, sat directly across the river from the French Quarter.

Joseph sat on a bench by the river, staring at the city. Pop had taught him a lot about the history of New Orleans, and he knew the community. He'd studied it, he'd been here.

Algiers understood violence, playing a large part in the Battle of New Orleans, in which Andrew Jackson decisively beat the British. That in itself should have given the name Slaughterhouse to the piece of land on the Mississippi. In April of 1862, in the middle of the Civil War, the Confederate army burned a shipyard so the Union couldn't use the facility to launch boats. They set cotton bales on fire, broke into private warehouses and stole rice, bacon, sugar molasses and corn. What they couldn't carry away, they dumped into the muddy river. Anything they could do to stop the Union army.

A mob of Confederate supporters broke into powder and gun factories on the spit of land and carried away rifles and ammunition. Algiers was well aware of mobs, protests and violence. For almost two centuries the community had played key roles in resistance, helping shape the history of Louisiana and the country as a whole.

To this day, violence erupted regularly, and crime ran rampant. Now, Algiers's population consisted of 90 percent African Americans and a portion of the area had the lowest income in America. New Orleans cops, Fourth District police officers of all races, dreaded calls in Algiers. Armed robberies, shootings, battery, they were a daily occurrence. While there were some upper-scale neighborhoods in the community, most of the area consisted of downtrodden unemployed blacks. Mixed neighborhoods were not rare in New Orleans, but Algiers was an entity unto itself.

Pop had told him several stories about how Algiers got its name. The one he liked the best was that it was named by a soldier who came back from the capital of Algeria and saw similarities to that ruling city, this poverty-stricken community that was once again about to be besieged. An unarmed black man had been gunned down by a white cop. Close range. No sign of any weapon on or about the thief. The burning of warehouses, the stealing of staples like bacon, cotton, rice, corn and molasses, the robbery of guns and ammunition may have been more chaotic, damaging and violent, but the chance of violence tonight was serious enough. There were no records of the populace that was killed during those past riots, those violent protests. Tonight would be well documented. An entirely different story.

Joseph needed mass confusion, a crazy sense of unreality. Then he could have his final act of vengeance.

Twenty-four-hour news channels would monitor the situation. Satellite trucks and media vans had been pulling up all morning long. Major networks would have a field day with this story. News outlets lived for tragedy. Child-kidnapping stories, rape stories, serial killers and race riots. They licked their chops, salivating, knowing that ratings would soar through the roof if the populace took to the street in protest. And Joseph had studied these protests. He knew what kept them alive.

The angry, incensed, politically motivated moved in. Some drove, some walked. Some took public transportation . . . not much public transportation in Algiers. However, the protestors from the other side of the river could ride the ferry for two bucks. They would show up.

Curiosity, anger, social networking, they all worked to build this unrest. Then there was the second tier. The unemployed, the paid protesters, the ones who simply wanted to loot and steal: liquor, appliances, jewelry and paper towels. Whatever they could carry out of a store. Handkerchiefs over the bottom half of their faces when the riots started, they'd wait. Then, when the media and the cops got there, they'd break some windows, force some doors, then grab and run. Beer, computers, cigarettes, liquor, whatever was available. Few of them ever got caught, and even with a little tear gas it was worth the effort. These were the ones Joseph was counting on. He knew they'd be there.

And it built. Groups who didn't know each other roamed the streets around Whitney and Newton. The numbers grew by the dozens every half hour, then by the hundreds. Wary of each other, wondering what motives the others might have.

There were sign makers frantically scribbling on cardboard and poster board the words *Black Lives Matter*. They huddled with Sharpies on curbs, writing phrases like *Am I Next?* and *A Badge Is Not a License to Kill*. And as if they were an organized militia, the protestors lined up to accept and carry the slogans, often fastened to a stick and held high.

We Will Not Be Silent. Police the Police. The slogans kept on coming. *I'm the Future – Don't Shoot. #WhitePrivilege.* And of course, the signs were not the problem. Peaceful protests were common to a situation like this. The problem was the bottles of gasoline with a rag stuffed into the opening. A Molotov cocktail. The thugs carried these in the open, like they would a hurricane on Bourbon Street. The problem was the pistols shoved into their pockets, their waistbands. The problem was the crowbars, the buckets of rocks and bricks used to destroy cop cars and break merchants's windows. The problem was there were thugs in every race. People who seemed to live for the violence, who relished in destroying whatever semblance of peace there appeared to be.

Algiers was tinder. A highly flammable material that could catch a spark and burst into flame, then become a roaring fire.

Yet all the signs, all the slogans, all the posturing meant nothing if the world at large never saw them. When slogans fell on deaf ears, when homemade bombs only caused fire rather than world-wide rage or applause, then what was the reason? The purpose? A case of liquor, a TV, a six-pack of beer? There were those who reveled in that, of course; but the movement, the outrage needed to be shared to be fueled. For those who wanted to shake up the world, they thanked God that the NOPD didn't see it that way, didn't see that the coverage was necessary to the purpose. The Louisiana National Guard showed up and the State Troopers and Sheriff's Department were along for the ride. And camera crews by the dozens, maybe fifty or more, they picked up on every nuance. Every sign that had been made was photographed and broadcast around the world.

An industry had arisen, people made a living on setting up the protesters. Bodies were shipped in from surrounding communities, given directions and told how to behave. They would get thirty bucks plus a box lunch and transportation. Better than sitting in their over-mortgaged shack or trailer, worrying about payments and hoping they weren't going to be foreclosed. It was never mentioned during this recruiting stage that they might be gassed. They might be roughed up. They might be shot. They might die. Protests elevated. Riots ensued. It was a dicey proposition, but the participants didn't have much to lose. Not much except their lives.

Algiers was on the edge. Ripe for a takedown. Ready for disaster.

THIRTEEN

'Used to take two and half months to complete the background check,' Levy said. 'Now, they've shaved off about twenty days.'

'Still almost two months to vet a new hire.'

'I don't know what you think you're going to find, Q. The guy was pretty much an open book during the time he was on the force. And even with a full court press our investigators only move so fast.'

Archer nodded. He knew full well how bureaucracy moved at a snail's pace. Television shows found DNA, records and finger-prints at a record pace. They had only one hour to find the culprit. Real cases took much longer. And he didn't have that luxury of time.

'We can dig into this ourselves.'

'We?'

'Josh, I could use some help.'

They both knew the problem. Recommended staffing for the department was thirty-two homicide detectives for the department. At the moment, there were eighteen on the force. With one hundred thirty-six murders so far in the year, each detective was handling almost eight cases for the year against a suggested six. The number kept going up. This was truly a staff that was overworked and underpaid.

'I've got a pretty full load, Quentin. But I want to catch this guy too. Where do we start?'

'I want to get the killer before we lose another cop.'

'Agreed.'

'OK, let's consider his first background check, twenty-five years ago. Let's see if there's information someone overlooked. It could mean we put in some late hours, but I feel Solange is on to something.'

'Escape, money and reflection. I hope you're right, Q, because it sounds pretty strange to me.'

'Hey, she's helped us in the past and I see no reason not to follow her instincts now.'

The officer's arrest records had been fairly easy to find and categorize. The background information on Officer Leroy was not so easy to accumulate. Twenty-five years ago, very little information was digitized and due to a tremendous shortage of manpower, there was little time or desire to transfer NOPD paper files to digital files now. No one cared what had happened almost three decades ago.

'We're going to have to pick and choose, much like his arrest warrants, Q. We'll never get anywhere if we look at every file. It will take forever.'

And there was a pile of files. Not everything, but enough to consume serious amounts of time.

'Damn.' Archer stared at the folders bursting with papers. 'Let's start with before he was a cop. Education, employment, friends, associates . . .'

The folders were clearly marked, stuffed with yellowing sheets of paper. Archer sorted them then handed EDUCATION to Levy. He grabbed one that said EMPLOYMENT.

'Anything that jumps out, feel free to chime in.'

Sitting at a long conference table the two detectives silently read and flipped through pages.

'Not a stellar student,' Levy said. 'Cs and Ds in high school. It would seem our officer didn't exactly apply himself.'

'Back then you had to have some college to be a cop, right? Even to apply.' Archer looked up from his file. 'So, he must have done well enough to get into a school.'

'They've backed off that requirement recently,' Levy nodded. 'Tends to shrink the employment pool quite a bit.' He read further. 'Yeah, he has a year at a community college,' Levy said. 'Delgado Community College in Slidell. Didn't really have a major, just some basic courses.'

'His employment is a little spotty.' Archer studied the page he was reading. 'Part-time job for a pool company, a roofing firm, stocking a grocery and at twenty-one he got a job with a security company, night watchman at a manufacturing company. Pretty elementary stuff.'

'Education runs out after that year at Delgado Community. Stuff from high school like a year on the track team, Spanish Club, I don't see much sense in delving into that.'

'No, let's pick him up here at twenty-one. Night watchman. Gets his first taste of law enforcement. Probably carried a gun.' He pushed the file to Levy and started taking notes. 'How long did that last?'

Levy riffed through the papers. 'I guess a year, year and a half. He was actually working as a private contractor, as a security guard at a manufacturing company in Algiers.' He paused. 'Ah, here it is. Worked for the security company, Security First, for a little over a year. He left that job right after he turned twenty-three.'

'Quit college after a year, quit his job after a year . . .'

'Hey, kid's trying to find himself, Q. Did you know what you wanted to do at twenty-one?'

'Actually, I did.' Archer glanced up from his notes. 'I wanted to be a cop like my father. It's never changed, Josh. Never changed.'

'Even though it pretty much broke up your family and killed your wife? You still think it was the right decision? Becoming a cop? You must have had some second thoughts.'

'I admit it hasn't been easy. I've been defined by this job, but we're getting the bad guys off the street. We're making a difference, aren't we? That's something of a noble profession, don't you think?'

'I told you. There's nothing I'd rather be doing. But at twenty-one, twenty-three, I'm not sure I was thinking that. I was still going to be an NFL quarterback or the next Eminem.'

'A Detroit rapper?'

'Oh, you pick up on the rapper but you don't find the football reference questionable?' He laughed.

'I'm glad you're a cop,' Archer chuckled. 'It suits you, Josh. I actually met Eminem in Detroit and you are no Eminem. Thank God.'

'So am I, Q. I'm glad I'm a cop.'

'Let's get this guy, Josh. What's next in Officer Johnny Leroy's employment background?'

Levy continued to read. 'Here's an interesting tidbit. You ever work security, some event or for a private company?'

'Off duty? Sure.'

'Anything ever happen on your watch?'

'Bounced a couple of drunk guys at a fundraiser once. I remember it got a little physical. And as I mentioned, I worked security for an Eminem concert one night. Had to push some people away. That was about it.'

'I don't think I ever got into something like that,' Levy said. 'Just walked around and tried to look tough and important. But Leroy, he's got a different story. Read this.' He handed a copied newspaper story to Archer.'

NOPD reports that Saturday night, private security officer John Leroy with Security First LA apprehended two intruders at the Fox Glass company in Algiers. Owner Matt Fox says the company had recently taken delivery of three pounds of gold leaf for a major home building project in the Garden District and it was apparent the two intruders were intent on taking that gold.

According to Fox, Leroy detained them during the attempted robbery, contained the two men by wrapping them with packing tape, and waited for law enforcement agents to arrive. Names of the suspects were being withheld pending further investigation.

'Wow, catching gold thieves.' Archer laughed. 'Our Officer Leroy was a perfect fit for NOPD.'

'Read on,' Levy said. 'There are three other instances where he interacted with trespassers. No other arrests.'

'He made up for it on the force.' Archer scanned the report. 'His arrest record is impressive.'

'So, by all accounts in the check, Leroy performed admirably.'

'It would appear so,' Archer said.

'What was gold worth back in 1992?'

Archer pulled out his cell and keyed in the question.

'Three hundred eighty-six dollars an ounce.'

'So, with a pretty good head for math, that means the gold leaf was worth around $18,000. That would be pretty good for a night's haul, even by today's standards.'

'I think first-degree grand theft charges start at $10,000.'

'Back then,' Levy said, 'it was probably less. Either way, these guys probably did some hard time.'

'So far,' Archer said, 'we know he was a mediocre student, probably flunked out of community college, and had a stellar career, albeit short, as a security officer. Not a lot to go on from that.'

'No.' Levy shook his head.

'Escape, money and reflection.'

Levy stood and stretched. 'I think we'll find the killer in the arrest records, Q. I'm not saying your voodoo lady isn't seeing clearly, but I believe that Leroy was a clean cop. Nothing so far has colored that.'

'And those arrest records . . . how are they coming along?'

'They should have another batch cleared by this evening.'

'And we're looking for the guy with a thorn necklace tattooed on his neck. The word is out. The tattoo parlors are being canvassed, and if any patrolman sees the man, we've got a prime suspect. Everyone on the force is looking for him. Someone said that an officer in Central City actually stopped a guy who had a real thorn necklace.'

'*That* is good police work, Quentin. That is how we proceed. How we catch the bad guys. By the book.'

'Look, I know you don't think that Solange has the believability to bring a meaningful solution to a case, but . . .'

'I don't want to get into it, friend. She may have hit on some things a couple of times. I owe her that. She actually showed up at a crucial time several months ago to save our bacon, but you're not going to convince a lot of blue that her ideas have any serious validity.'

Archer was quiet for a moment.

'I've got the same problem, Levy.' He drummed his fingers on the table. 'I don't want to believe that just because she visited the corpse of a deceased police officer she has answers. My wife worked with dying people every night in downtown Detroit. She was a nurse and she experienced death on a regular basis. Yet she never came home with images of their past or what they went through. If they were stabbed to death, they were stabbed to death. End of story. She was never aware of some eerie spirit. These dead bodies didn't talk to her from the grave. If they were killed in a gang fight, or a domestic dispute, so be it. No ghostly feelings about the things that haunted them, or how it happened. I'm having a tough time dealing with this lady's supernatural findings too, but at least two times now she's—'

'Quentin, I'm probably way out of line here, but I think it's obvious that there's something more to this relationship you have with her than just business.' Levy pushed his chair back and closed his eyes, rubbing his finger and thumb over his eyelids.

'And just what else is there?'

'Come on, don't make me spell it out. I think you are attracted to Solange Cordray. Emotionally, physically, and hey, I get that. I don't know how she feels about you, but I would hate to think you are letting your feelings interfere with good police work. You know this is a top-line case and we can't let personal feeling interfere.'

Archer simply nodded.

'Fine, we can work with the three things she suggested. I don't mind reworking the background check on Leroy. After twenty-six years, it couldn't hurt. But don't let this girl get in the middle of you solving the case. If I'm wrong, I apologize up front, but you seem to be conflicted and that's not a good thing when you're working a murder.'

Archer was quiet. He wasn't exactly broadcasting his feelings, but wasn't exactly keeping it a secret. He decided that he needed to scrub the dinner invitation. Keep the relationship strictly business. He believed in transparency, aboveboard transactions. He'd bow out of any personal relationship.

'That won't happen, Josh.'

'Johnny Leroy was a good cop and I don't want to think that our investigation would suggest anything else.'

'I'm trying to be objective, Josh, but she's got a track record.

I can't just ignore her intuition. We work our asses off to cultivate leads and I don't want to blow this one off. Citizen input solves lots of cases, and as for Solange Cordray, she's been pretty reliable.'

'Let's keep looking, Q, but let's not let tried-and-true go by the wayside. I won't bring it up again, OK? I'm just asking that we continue to pursue solid investigation techniques. We can't get too caught up in this woo-woo phenomenon. I mean, I've seen it be beneficial but it's a little out there you have to admit. We still have to rely on—'

'I get it, Josh. I get it.'

'Thanks.'

'And thanks for agreeing not to bring it up again.' But Archer knew he would. It was the eight-hundred-pound gorilla in the room. Believing that a voodoo lady could solve a murder case. It was crazy. Since Denise had died, he wanted to be in touch with the spirit world, wanted to have some touch with whatever was out there that a living, breathing human being couldn't fathom. He wanted to know that she was still in his life. And the fact that he was attracted to the one person who seemed to have that spiritual connection made it all that much harder. Life was a bitch. Death was possibly even worse.

FOURTEEN

Late afternoon in Algiers was still relatively calm and Joseph sat on another worn wooden bench, a brown, patchy field of grass surrounding him. The heat and lack of rain had parched the area and the sun had burned the vegetation. Flies buzzed around him as he munched on a leg from Chubbie's Fried Chicken, barely noticing the crisp, juicy texture as he watched the crowd start to warm up.

There were some chants from small groups, 'Black Lives Matter', and some posturing, where twenty of the assembled would raise their fists, then raise their sign with whatever slogan they had been given. It was all very entertaining, but the crowd politely moved off the streets whenever a vehicle approached. Tonight would be the test. A test of the resolve of the law enforcement community. As darkness gave cover, the revelers, the party crowd would be in their faces, never giving in to traffic and waving their crude hand-lettered signs, maybe throwing rocks, bottles or blows. Fueled by alcohol, drugs and the support and rage of hundreds of kindred spirits, the violence would escalate.

The cops would be prepared, defending themselves with shields, helmets, bulletproof vests and tear gas, spraying the caustic fumes into the crowd, temporarily blinding rioters and momentarily preventing them from creating the havoc they desired. There was an excellent chance that the combined forces of law enforcement agencies wouldn't be 100 percent effective. Crowds like the ones he was observing thrived when push came to shove. And they would thrive on camera time, each one hoping for a turn on cable or network television.

A gas station over there, a convenience store over here. The store that Old Joe held up. He was positive that in the next couple of days the Korean family that owned that establishment would pray for a trip back to their native country. The store was assuredly going to be toast. A pile of ashes. A pawnshop and a couple of consignment shops in the dilapidated strip mall, they were all in the line of fire. And tonight would be a wait and see moment. The mayor had gone public, saying he wasn't going to let this be a Ferguson, Missouri, where they just weren't prepared. He'd taken a lesson from Baltimore, Maryland as well. There were some very recent studies on riot control, and the mayor of New Orleans wasn't going to let his city explode. Not like the others. Not if he could help it. And from his protected office, or perhaps his posh home in the Garden District, he would monitor the possible life-and-death situation. Elected officials seemed to have that luxury.

Joseph Brion didn't want to jump the gun. He watched the scene unfold, almost feeling like a director. As the protestors rolled in, so did law enforcement. A bus carrying a small platoon of National Guard soldiers pulled in, fifty feet from where he sat. They piled off the vehicle, each man wearing a camouflage helmet, goggles, bulletproof vest and battle uniform, an M16 assault rifle held tightly against his chest.

Tonight would probably be rough, but Joseph was betting on the next evening. That was when the cops would back off, the National Guard would either downsize or go home. The State Troopers would cut half the force, as long as they felt they had the situation under control. That was the night he wanted for himself. His final hurrah.

So, let hellfire and damnation rule tonight. Cart off fifty people to jail. Bash in a dozen cars, police cruisers, sheriff vehicles, break some merchant's windows and steal the contents. Set street fires and torch businesses. Take the spotlight if you can. Let the world know you are pissed off. Light the shimmering shadows of tomorrow night. Joseph just wanted a small window. In the scope of things, he hoped it wouldn't get in the way of all the chaos tonight. However, he was making a statement and he wanted that statement to be heard.

He'd started this movement, with the cold-blooded killing of Joseph Washington. His godfather. He'd orchestrated that so well. He'd started it, and tomorrow night he wanted to end it. On his terms. A fitting tribute to Pop.

Would his final act be absorbed in the riot? Just another random act of violence? Or would the NOPD or some other organization look a little deeper? He didn't think so.

River's Edge Dementia Center was located as advertised. On the river's edge. A drab gray building that needed no exterior enhancement. The tenants had no sense of decor, inside or out. Their blank stares, their unseeing eyes, never noticed their surroundings.

Solange Cordray knew the grounds well and understood the lack of landscaping, decorations or any other improvement in the look of the establishment. It would have been lost on the inhabitants. She visited four days a week, volunteering her time to be with Ma and her neighbors. A thankless job, since the beneficiaries of her time didn't realize or recognize her effort. The paid staff only gave her and other volunteers a nod, but it was the chance to be with Ma, the former New Orleans queen of voodoo, Clotille Trouville. A lady that once spoke to the power elite of the Big Easy, she also was known for helping the poor, helpless flood victims during the catastrophe known as Katrina. Clotille was a legend in certain circles, but a legend in the past. In recent years, she'd disappeared from the scene. Her advice, her spells, her prayers were sorely missed.

Ma was inside the shell of her former self. Somewhere inside there. Occasionally she spoke to Solange, in brief, muted moments. She would give her one-word answers or for a brief second, shine bright-eyed as if she was engaged. But the moments were fleeting and Solange never knew if her mother truly was aware. Still, the girl shared her innermost thoughts. She asked her wise mother for advice. The woman who raised her, taught her voodoo culture and passed on the gift . . . or curse. She was never sure what it was.

After a breezy ride from the morgue and some deep meditation, she motored to the building that sat on prime real estate on the mighty Mississippi. She'd decided that before she went to her small apartment, before she drank her glass, or multiple glasses of white wine, she wanted to see Ma. She wanted to know if her mother had any insight. Solange was certain that Ma would have a clear vision of what happened with Officer Leroy. It would be a clear vision after you cleared away the clouds. And Solange wasn't sure she could do that. Clear away all the clouds.

She dismounted and entered the lobby, signed in and walked the hall back to Ma's room. She had to sign in, even though the lady at the desk knew her by name. They needed her name and signature, as if she might do harm to a helpless, mindless dementia patient for no reason she could fathom. The next step would be metal detectors, trained dogs and armed guards. They didn't realize her heart was pure, her intentions honorable. There should be a detector for that. There wasn't.

The hall reminded her of where she'd been, the New Orleans City morgue, reeking of an antiseptic combination of alcohol and disinfectant. It always took her a couple of minutes to absorb the smell, then it seemed to dissipate, to leave her system. You could get used to almost anything.

Walking into her ma's room she observed the old woman, staring out of her window. Solange knew she saw nothing.

'Ma.'

Nothing. The lady never turned her head.

'Ma, it's me.'

Nothing.

'I was looking for some advice.'

No acknowledgement.

'I don't know if you've heard, but a cop was killed in Bayou St John. I saw the corpse today.' Drained, worn out, she didn't really wish to discuss it with her mother but there was no choice. She wanted someone to realize what she'd been through. Ma was the one person who would always listen. Maybe never hearing or understanding a single word, but she sat still while Solange spelled out her dilemma.

True to form, Clotille Trouville appeared not to hear anything at all.

'Ma, I picked up some strong vibrations. This cop, an officer Johnny Leroy, has some serious baggage. He wants to escape the consequences. He's got some hidden money somewhere, and I get the impression . . . it's only my impression, that he's taken some-one's life. An innocent person's life.' She hesitated to even tell Ma. An accusation like that shouldn't be shared until there was proof. And she was positive no one was looking into anything that remotely resembled that charge.

Nothing.

'You never saw the body, you never interviewed the corpse,' she always held out the belief that deep inside Ma was still there, 'but some sort of feeling would be helpful.'

She had the impression today wasn't going to be the day. Then, a turn of the head and a whimsical smile. Ma was looking into her eyes.

'Can you help?'

The old lady nodded.

'What do you know?' Still not sure that the old woman really understood the question or even heard her.

'Everyone has a dark side.' Her words were slurred but delib-erate. 'Everyone. Some more than others.' She closed her eyes and Solange knew that the conversation had ended. Still . . . more than she had hoped. Ma was not a fan of Johnny Leroy. Something in his past bothered her and that was a positive. Solange had told Archer he should do another background check. Ma had just reaffirmed that. Everyone had a dark side. That might be true, but Ma was convinced that Officer Leroy had a darker side, darker than most. She knew her mother had just indicted the dead officer.

Solange was convinced of it. She wasn't sure what Ma had indicted him of, but there was something in his past. Something that needed investigating.

FIFTEEN

'I'm calling it, Q. When my eyes start to get blurry, it's time to quit staring at all this print.'

'I'm starting to agree with you, Josh. There doesn't seem to be a lot here. I suppose we can go a little deeper on the actual details, but . . .'

'Look, we know that he shot one armed burglar. The incident was ruled self-defense, and there was no argument. The perp drew on him. All evidence proved that he had no choice. And sure, a couple of collars skated, but he made most of his cases. He was solid, and looking at his record, he was what most patrol officers should aspire to.'

'We'll tackle it tomorrow. I'm staying a little later,' Archer said. 'I just want to review my notes and go through a couple more files.'

'Have at it, my friend.'

'Thanks, Josh.'

Staring at the folders stacked in front of him, he once again read the brief employment history of Johnny Leroy. It didn't appear that his career as an officer of the law had gone sour. No bad marks, no reprimands. He'd been totally cleared on the shooting charge. The robber had drawn on him and he fired in self-defense. No bad marks. None.

Even good cops had blemishes on their record. Archer certainly did. Yet Solange had the distinct impression there was something shady about Leroy. And as little as he really knew about her, he'd grown to trust her instincts. In several cases, she'd surprised him out of the blue with information that she should have no way of knowing. Something in Leroy's history led her to have those feelings. Escape, money and reflection.

Maybe Levy was right. Maybe Archer was letting his interest in the voodoo lady control his investigation of the case. Levy had made the point. His attraction to Solange Cordray might be interfering with good detective work. But what if she did have a glimmer, an inkling of a parallel universe where Leroy used the system. Where he had a past that he was able to hide. God only knew how many cops did abuse the job. From perks like free donuts and coffee and half-price meals to scams. And scams to wholesale manipulation.

He'd read just that week about three cops in East Texas who threatened out-of-town motorists and shook them down for cash and valuables. And the scam had been working for three years before they were caught. As in any profession, there were players who used everything possible to make it work for them. Maybe Leroy was one of them.

Archer stood and stretched, picked up an empty, stained coffee mug and walked to the coffee machine. He poured hot water in the cup. He steeped a bag of green tea in the steamy liquid and walked back to his paperwork.

The arrest records had yet to spark an interest. The twenty-five-year-old background check wasn't stirring any thoughts and no one had seen a young black man with a tattooed necklace. So, when the press called, he ignored the call. He had very little to offer them, except to say there was no news. So why say anything at all. And besides, they now had bigger fish to fry. An unarmed black man had been shot down by an overeager white cop. There was going to be some big news in Algiers tonight no doubt about it. The area was ripe for a riot, and that might just take some heat off him. Temporarily at least.

Archer knew well enough to leave the fireworks alone. He could watch some of them from the banks of the Mississippi, or just put in foam earplugs and go to bed early. It was going to be a wild ride on the other side of the river and he was just as happy to be on this side, where normal crime and violence took place. In Algiers, tonight would be off the charts.

First there had to be an insurgent. And, there had to be a unified resistance, that being the armored National Guard, the state Highway Patrol, the NOPD and the Sheriff's Department. If the enforcement didn't show up, there was no reason for the insurgent.

And the unified resistance did show up. The insurgents attacked with long poles, swinging them at the cops, the enforcement battering back with shields. It was early evening and the offense was somewhat half-hearted. No firebombs yet, no broken windows or looting. No burned-out vehicles . . . yet. Both sides were still testing the water. The darker the sky the more intense the confrontation. There was almost a science to riots.

Once they had begun, the mob, the insurgents, had a life of their own. Deep-seated resentments, repetitive frustrations and long-standing disappointments galvanized people into action. The insurgents provided cover. It became easier to overcome one's usual reticence or moral scruples when a mob mentality was fronting you. You could be immersed in the movement. It was a heady experience, almost joyful. You could release long-suppressed emotions.

And leadership emerged spontaneously. Changing rapidly. Unlike a political climate, a riot changed by the minute, not by the year. The heady environment of violent activity, of a mob rushing to defy authority, was adrenalin to the max and many relatively sane people got caught up in the moment, only to realize later that their actions were not well thought out. They found themselves imprisoned, in hospitals or never found themselves at all. They'd been killed in the conflict.

Joseph walked the streets, sipping coffee from a Styrofoam cup, watching the chemistry of a riot ready to ignite. Let tonight bleed. Let the frustrated and the forgotten have their moment. It was healthy and after tonight, hopefully some of the riotous activity would settle down. Then *his* riotous act would stand out. Tomorrow. His final tribute. In spite of the act to come, in spite of the fact that he'd shot Leroy dead center in the head, he smiled. He'd dreamed of this night for years, payback for his father's untimely death. If you didn't stand up for family, then what was there to live for?

'Dude.' A chocolate-colored man put his hand up, stopping him from continuing his walk.

'I'm just passing through, brother.' His right hand hung low, ready to draw his pistol from the pocket of his cargo shorts.

'Stay for the resistance, my man.'

'That's why you stopped me?'

'No, actually I was attracted to your tat.'

'Attracted?' Immediately his defense was on high alert. It was a guy versus guy thing. Not that he was homophobic, but . . .

'Very telling, my man.'

'Step aside, brother.'

'No, no.' Still holding up his hand, the interloper said, 'Not in that way, man. It's strictly a symbol.'

'Of what?' Very few people even mentioned it, and fewer ventured a guess as to its meaning. He was confrontational. 'Just what do you think this stands for?'

The man turned his head, trying to grasp the visual of the entire piece of art. As Joseph stood still, the observer looked him over. He had an intense glare in his eyes as he walked around him.

'Unity. Has nothing to do with the Jesus thing, does it?' The man nodded, looking into Joseph's eyes. 'It's all connected. Every link unites with the next one. These thorns, they interact, you know? I love this, man. Like our gathering this evening. We're all here for a common cause, dude. That's what it represents. Am I right?'

'Sure. That was the point,' Joseph said, pushing away with his left hand. He just needed to move on.

'I'm glad I got it.' He held his right palm open and gave him a high five. The man shuffled off and Joseph lowered his head and kept on walking. Low profile. He didn't need anyone busting his chops. The whole idea was to be the puppeteer, the man behind the screen. He couldn't afford to be exposed. Not right now.

The event was building. Soon, hopefully, to a riotous peak. He needed it to be off the charts. Then, tomorrow when calm and reason had reentered the equation, he would cause his own sense of chaos. His crowning achievement.

It was going to be one hell of a night.

SIXTEEN

She stripped off her T-shirt, feeling a thin sheen of perspiration covering her lithe, naked body. She'd showered, dried herself and still wasn't refreshed. The heat was relentless and she felt like she could cut the humidity with a knife. The air conditioning at Ma's center was actually preferable, but sleeping there was frowned upon and would be too depressing. She'd stayed with Ma one night, and the wails and suffering in that building convinced her to never spend another evening.

Cranking up the dial on her rattling room air conditioner, she climbed between the thin cotton sheets on her single bed. Solange stared at the plaster ceiling, still stained brown in one corner from a leak on the floor above three years ago. Someone's bathtub had overflowed. The pattern of the stain roughly formed a map of Louisiana. An odd-shaped designer boot with Shreveport in the upper left corner and New Orleans on the toe. The image was often the last sight she had before falling into a troubled sleep.

She looked for symbolism in so many things in her life, trying to read between the lines. That was also a pattern. A pattern of the way her life played out. The boot was probably a coincidence, but she'd printed a map of the Pelican State and after studying it, realized the shape of her ceiling stain was almost an identical replica. She pondered the phenomenon and wondered what to make of it. It was here on the toe that Ma had made a reputation for herself. Here in Louisiana that Solange had been born and raised, had been married and divorced, and was given the skills and spiritual guidance to make a difference in people's lives. And she firmly believed that she had those skills.

There were so many times in her relatively short life that she'd seen results, she'd seen her spells produce miracles. She'd had positive outcomes. And she felt certain that this was where she was meant to be. To take care of Ma and other patients, to help guide her clients through uncharted waters. She made the world, or her tiny part of the world, a better place.

Solange would study the stain, the map, the outline, estimating where rivers and bayous would be. Remembering where cities like Baton Rouge, Lake Charles and Lafayette were located. She got to know the state and its geography very well. The concentration would eventually calm her and she would drift into a dreamless sleep. Not tonight. Her city was at a boiling point, and she prayed that the pot would hold the water. If it boiled out, if the water couldn't be contained, New Orleans was in for a stormy night.

She understood stormy nights. Solange had lived through one of the city's worst catastrophes, where the pot literally couldn't contain the water and when it eventually boiled out it had destroyed hundreds of homes and devastated thousands of people's lives. The catastrophe known as Katrina would haunt this city for twenty lifetimes.

Her head was filled with dozens of thoughts, and sleep wasn't coming anytime soon. She focused on the potential riot in Algiers, just across the river. The civil unrest was bigger than anything she could control, but still she prayed. She asked her living spirit to rid the mob leaders of Agau, the anger god. It was said that when the earth tremors, Agau is angry. There was no question. The earth was set to tremor.

The masses always fell in line, but it was the leaders of the violent protest that were filled with Agau's spirit. That was the danger. Those who were strong enough to keep him in their bodies were puffing with all their strength and sputtering like seals. One had to be very strong to harbor this spirit. If she could defuse, get rid of the spirit of Agau, then she had a chance of tamping down the vehemence. The chance was slim.

Pushing aside the sheets, she stood up and walked naked into the outer shop, and picked a candle from the shelf. A peace candle. The candle of tranquility. Exactly what was needed at this time.

Placing the thick wax cylinder on the candle table, she lit the wick with a purity match. No one was around to smile, assuming she was showing off to the tourists. No one was there to question her sincerity as so many did. She believed, and that was all that mattered. She'd seen evidence of miracles. Maybe not this time. Maybe not for this event, but the prayer went out. The candle flickered and Solange had done what she could do. The fate of the evening, the potential riot, the lives of people were in the hands of the gods. That, she firmly believed. She'd just done her part. This was as much as she could offer.

She prayed fervently that the god of anger and violence left the souls of those people and they were filled with peace and tranquility. That is what she prayed for. But she was very much aware that this was probably bigger than anything she could control. Solange believed in the power of one on one. But when confronted with hundreds, even thousands, then the odds weren't so good. The gods seemed much more comfortable working individually. Cities, countries, continents, they weren't so easy to manipulate.

She shook. She shivered. After an hour, she rose and found the T-shirt. Goosebumps rose on her arms and legs.

Walking back to her bed, she lay down, letting the air conditioning unit chill her almost naked body. She briefly considered taking the ferry and going to Algiers. The traffic coming *back* from the community would be horrendous, but she might be able to read some trends in the participants. Those who were fleeing, fearing for their lives, and those who were going to put their lives on the line. Or . . . find a reason to steal a TV and a six-pack of beer.

The voodoo lady was tempted to turn on the television and watch the riot unfold. But she'd seen her city implode too many times. Maybe the map above her was simply to show her how limited her view of the world was. Possibly it was there to remind her there were forty-nine more states plus an entire planet she could explore.

This city, this microcosm of the universe, was totally unique. The ebb, the flow, the mix of race and ethnicity, the culture, even the food and the spices. The crime and even the types of crime . . . the inventive ways of murdering people, it was inimitable.

When she finally thought her head would explode, Erzulie floated above her, sending healing thoughts and calming messages. Solange couldn't see her, only feel her love, her soothing influence. She whiffed the scent of perfume, she saw the glimmer of sparkling jewelry that flashed in the ceiling stain. There was no question it was the goddess. It was Erzulie.

And as she finally drifted into an unconscious state, she prayed that Erzulie would make her presence known to the unruly mob in Algiers. She was needed. Her loving presence should calm some of the rebellious crazies who intended to blow the city wide open.

She slipped into sleep, far from dreamless. Sometimes the mind causes more problems when at rest than when active. She saw the riots, she felt the pressure that Quentin Archer felt in his search for the cop killer. She heard the voice of the black, unarmed thief, begging for forgiveness for a murder he may have committed. He was the reason for the unrest, yet he had been responsible for killing someone, she was positive.

She heard Ma. Begging for release. Begging for an afterlife where she would be free of her constraints. Free of her silence.

Ma was calling to her, asking for deliverance and that was far beyond Solange's ability. Her skillset was limited. She somehow knew the parameters.

And, asleep, unconscious to the real word, Solange Cordray cried real tears that ran from her eyes and moistened her pillow.

As she slept the events unfolded. Beyond her imagination. Mobs roamed the streets, becoming increasingly violent, incendiary at times. The spirit of the unarmed black man, Joe, was given a new birth. His death spawned a new beginning, or at least a temporary resurgence. But most of the anger, the vitriol, the bile, became personal and the violators took advantage of the situation; stealing, molesting, mugging, they used the protest as a reason to wreak havoc on a mostly stable civilization.

Of course, as much as the civilized population would argue, New Orleans didn't subscribe to a stable civilization. In any area of the city at any time, things were not what they seemed. It was the nature of the beast. Whether natives or people who were drawn there, it made no difference. The Big Easy gave you license to live on the wild side. And tonight was a wide-open pass.

SEVENTEEN

Sixteen-year-old T. J. Bannon heaved the first firebomb of the deadly riot. A high school student whose mother thought he was in his room completing a homework assignment. The young man lit the rag stuffed into a chocolate Yoo-hoo glass-bottle now filled with gasoline, an incendiary device that cost about two dollars total. Throwing it at a blue-and-white SUV, he waited a moment too long to see the results. In retrospect, he should have run like hell.

As the bottle exploded and the NOPD vehicle erupted in flame, two cops rushed him and tackled the young man to the ground. Roughly, a young officer yanked the boy's arms behind his back and snapped his wrists with plastic ties. The first arrest in a long night of incarcerations.

Lines of officers with helmets and protective visors pulled over their faces and riot shields in their hands, advanced on the protestors. Spread in wide formation, they marched, leaving aisles for the defectors to escape. Protestors reached into buckets of rocks and jagged cement pieces, throwing those missiles at the encroaching police officers often with amazing accuracy. The marching force tightened up. In spite of all the defense, body armor, shields and visors, two patrolmen went down, both bleeding from head wounds.

Another Molotov cocktail hit its mark, exploding outside a hardware store, the bright orange flame illuminated in the establishment's front window for a brief moment until the window shattered into a thousand pieces. There was a roar as twenty rioters rushed the store.

The mob kept up a relentless attack on the advancing police force, allowing many of the others to turn their attention to shops and service businesses along the path. Tossing large chunks of concrete at windows, they followed as the glass barriers disintegrated, exposing a large entrance for the intruding throng. And they pushed their way in, grabbing everything in sight. Computers, furniture, building supplies, nothing was sacred.

The invaders seized anything not secured, sprinting out of doors or broken windows. In many cases, cops were there to take them down with stun batons. However, far more ran than were captured.

The riot squad, professional in appearance, terrified in their personal response, regrouped in a square formation, stomping their feet in unison and banging their batons on their shields. The thunderous sound was frightening, and some of the protestors bolted through the escape routes left for them by the squad. The object was to disperse this crowd and the more demonstrators who decided to cut and run the better. Spread out and let them run, but be ready to tighten up at a moment's notice. If the violence escalated again, they were ready.

Two helicopters hovered over the small area, bright spotlights sweeping over the throng. The loud beating sound of their propellers, along with the stomping feet of the police and the rapping of batons on shields on the ground, was deafening. Fighting for attention were two bullhorns from ground crews, instructing the rioters to break up and go home, and two bullhorns from the mob's leaders, telling the crowd to remember Joseph Washington.

Shouting repeatedly that black lives mattered. With all the chaos and confusion, both sides stood their ground.

'People, go home. Please, go home. Break this up and go home or you will spend the night in jail.'

'People, my people,' Reverend Jeremiah Ashley of the Algiers Pentecostal Baptist Church shouted out, 'remember the life of our brother, Joseph Washington. A troubled man, yes, but one who did not deserve to be killed by a white policeman. Black lives matter. Let me hear you say it, people, my people, black lives matter. They truly do.'

And they shouted it out, screaming in defiance of the competing message. 'Black lives matter. Black lives matter.' The ones with slogans on their T-shirts were front line throwing missiles of stone and glass.

'People, please, please go home. We don't want to arrest you. Please, break this up.'

'Roast the pigs, roast the pigs.'

One of the uniformed team collapsed, overcome by the heat, the smothering mask and body armor or the sheer fear of the confrontation.

A handful of people decided they'd had enough. They took advantage of the exits and walked away, having made their presence known. The others, empowered by Reverend Ashley and his message that black lives matter, decided to stay and watch and possibly influence the outcome.

Blue-and-red flashing lights created a purple haze as five men raced toward a police SUV, two of them tossing bricks. As the bricks bounced off the customized vehicle driving down the street, an officer inside put his arm through a customized hole in the door, spraying tear gas. The five rioters turned and ran, holding their arms over their faces, the chemical causing a burning, stinging pain in their eyes. Gas was a driving force in keeping the demonstrators at bay.

Two shots rang out, whether armed protestors or police, but rioters nearby hit the ground.

Across the river, the French Quarter watched and listened, residents and tourists gazing at the flares of orange flames as the homemade bombs exploded. They heard the roar of the crowd, the thunder of stomping feet and the beating of batons on shields.

The odor of burning fuel drifted over the river and it seemed that the entire community of Algiers might explode.

An enraged contingent of thugs and rabble-rousers rushed the Korean-owned convenience store that had been robbed by Joseph Washington. The store that carried a selection of wines, tobacco and sundry food products. Tossing bricks and pieces of concrete, they destroyed the plate-glass window that touted the availability of King Cobra, Colt 45 and Old English. The advertised beers, malt liquors and all the bottles of wine were gone in minutes as the looters ripped the items from the coolers and shelves. Cigarettes, cartons of Newport and Kool were stripped from behind the counter and food items, like bags of chips, processed cookies and crackers, candy and beef jerky, were wiped from the store. In ten minutes, the establishment was bare, with nothing left but a cash register, some shelves, an empty, broken safe and the coolers. When the outlet was totally ransacked, someone pitched a gasoline-filled bottle with *Colt 45* on the label. The irony was lost on everyone as the gas-soaked flaming rag burned down to the neck of the brown bottle which then exploded, lighting up the inside of the store as if it was daylight. Screaming fire trucks fought the angry crowds, but due to the massive amount of people and the rocks and bricks, the blaze was already beyond control by the time they arrived, orange flames and thick black plumes of smoke rising in the sky. The store was ashes when the engines finally broke through the crowds. It was the will of the masses to destroy their own civilization.

EIGHTEEN

Joseph watched from a distance. He could just barely smell the caustic fumes of tear gas and mace, the acrid odor of burning gasoline, and the sweet odor of marijuana. A hot, steamy night in New Orleans had just gotten a whole lot hotter, and he'd been the catalyst. He'd set it up, then waited for it to happen. He wasn't sure how he felt about that.

Dozens of people would be injured, probably a hundred would

be arrested. There was a chance that innocent lives might be taken. Businesses were destroyed. He'd followed the anatomy of riots and always wondered why the marauders destroyed their own neighborhoods. Why they chose to attack the place they lived. If he'd been in charge, he would have started at the NOPD head-quarters in the Quarter. Burn that building down. Or branch out and attack the precincts. Make it a citywide invasion. But it wasn't his decision. He'd only manufactured the reason for the riot. Now the event took on a life of its own.

From his small cottage, a former slave quarter in the French Quarter, Archer could hear the roar of the crowds, the percussive pounding of the riot squads, and the explosions of homemade bombs. The noise competed with the booming bass and screeching of karaoke at the Cat's Meow in front of his apartment. The club revelers were oblivious to the life and death situation across the river.

He hoped the riot would end peacefully and knew it wouldn't. Blood would be shed and unrest would spread to other parts of the city. This wasn't going to be an easy time for the department. There was a target on everyone's back. There might be more cases like the shooting of Officer Johnny Leroy and it was his job to find the perpetrator now.

Solange Cordray drifted in and out of sleep, hearing faint sounds from across the river. At times, she thought it might be a firework display, but she knew what was going on and she prayed again that sanity would eventually rule. Being a sane person herself, she knew she was crazy to believe that would happen. She'd given Archer everything she had. She hoped it would be enough.

The killings of Officer Leroy and Joseph Washington were related, therefore both of them a reason for the riot. Solve the crime, possibly bring some peace to the city. A city that seldom had peace. A city that was always at odds with warring factions. And again, she realized that her utopian dreams made *her* the crazy one.

Joseph heard the ebb and the flow, the ebb stronger early in the morning. Much of the crowd had dispersed and in the morning light the rest of the mob would go home. If the model held form, the situation would stabilize mid-morning. Merchants would survey the damage, call their insurance companies and curse the day they decided to start a business. Some small businesses would realize they were underinsured or had no insurance at all and would simply walk away.

Tonight, the swell would be smaller. The curious, the sideliners had come out last night, to experience the rush, to tell their grand-children they'd participated in a black lives matter event. For them, the rush, the excitement, the raw enthusiasm was over. Let the power hungry carry the torch. Let Reverend Jeremiah Ashley shout into the bullhorn how the downtrodden were being crucified. The part-timers had participated, but one night was enough. Some of them suffered lingering ailments from the gasses, the shock batons, the physical pushback from the officers. Some would spend a night in jail.

But the truth was as Joseph knew it to be. Joseph Washington, the man who held up the Korean convenience store, the devious bastard who all those years ago had found the truck driver with the broken neck, was a crook. A thief, a piece of shit. An oppor-tunist with no talent who lived off the misery of others. He'd signed off on André Brion's death warrant and for that he deserved to die. Joseph, his namesake, only hoped that Washington knew, in the fleeting seconds before the white cop shot him, what a scumbag he was. His life had amounted to nothing positive.

Maybe, in his final moments, Washington said his prayers. Joseph was doubtful Washington had a guiding spirit, doubtful that he believed in an almighty presence, but he wished his personal spirit nothing but pain and torment until time eternal.

Joseph Brion hoped that Joseph Washington would rot in hell.

Tonight, when there was the full attention of the press, and only half the protesters, this was when Joseph would make his defining statement.

CNN, FOX, NBC, CBS, they'd committed to the scene. Handsomely rewarded by last night's display, they weren't going anywhere. News anchors and personalities like NBC's Lester Holt, Fox's Shepard Smith and CNN's Chris Cuomo, they'd be there to cover the limited riot. The toned-down version of what happened several hours ago, was fresh on their viewers' minds. They'd be there tonight. Ratings demanded they'd be there. It was a sick world.

And maybe, just maybe he'd walk away from it all. Maybe in the midst of the confusion, the craziness, the dilemma, he'd walk away, down to the river and the ferry. Along with a couple of hookers and street musicians going to work in the quarter, he'd take the ten-minute boat ride to Canal Street and a bus ride home to Mom. He doubted it, but there was always that possibility.

Algiers had quieted down as the sun rose. There was the occasional shout of an unruly group, or the amplified command of a police officer still breaking the silence, but the leaders had gone home. Home to their everyday lives after disrupting everyone else's. Home to a spouse for a late-night/early-morning dinner. Home to kids who had gone to bed listening to the screaming sirens and police whistles. They left the remains of their night's activities to the fanatics. The drunks, the crazies who hadn't had enough. The leaders knew when to walk away. And they did.

The young man lay on his sleeping bag, watching stars. He knew a little bit about those bright spots in the dark sky. In the history of the universe, with all the chaos and craziness in the world, the stars still shined. Pop had shown him the constellations: the Big Dipper, Orion's belt, Cassiopeia. They were still there. While riots and wars, pestilence and famine, murder and rape rocked the planet, those stars remained constant for millions of years. Compared to the history of those celestial orbs, maybe what he had accomplished, what he was about to do, didn't really matter. Everything in this world paled in comparison. But he still felt it had to be done.

For Pop. To show the world you shouldn't screw around with a good man. And despite what his father might have done outside the family, despite what he might have done to provide *for* his family, Pop was a good man. A family man, a counselor. No one was more loyal. He had your back. If he told you something, you could count on it. No question.

Joseph drifted off, his hand on his pistol. Sleeping under the stars was an amazing experience. One with nature. But in Algiers, you couldn't trust anything or anyone. His pop had once told him, the best way to sleep was with one eye open. He'd literally tried it as a child. Now he knew what it meant. Sleep lightly and be ready for trouble.

He was as ready as he'd ever been.

NINETEEN

Levy hailed him at his desk.

'Morning, Detective Q. We had a sighting last night.'

'A sighting?'

'An officer on riot squad saw a young man with a necklace tattoo last night in Algiers.'

'That would be a huge plus for our side, but I don't know what tats are popular right now, Josh, necklaces might be all the rage and there might be hundreds. I hope not.'

'Except we haven't had any other sighting, Quentin, and this one was supposedly a crown of thorns.'

'And?'

'The officer said this guy was standing just off the street where the riot was exploding. Things were a little dicey and our man was in riot gear, not ready to question a bystander. By the time the officer considered the situation, the guy was gone.'

'I wish he'd approached the man, but I believe those officers over there had more important things on their minds,' Archer said. 'Still . . .'

'You're right. But if your voodoo friend is correct, your case with Leroy is tied to Washington's death. Maybe that's why the guy with the necklace is over there. Maybe there really is something to the connection.'

Archer nodded. 'I'm sure we've got heavy patrol on duty today. I'll put out a bulletin and see if we can find the man.' He took a swallow of green tea. 'We could really use a break, Josh.'

'Hey, Quentin, I was a little harsh yesterday.'

'What?'

'About the young lady Solange. Listen, you never ask about my personal life, and I shouldn't—'

'Hey, Josh, there is no "personal life" between me and the girl. And you weren't too harsh. If you or anyone on this squad thinks I'm not performing up to par, tell me. But it's like I told you. I think she's had some breakthrough ideas and I just want to make sure we follow up on everything in this case.'

'I agree.' Levy nodded.

'I'm still not comfortable with Leroy's past. She believes that something he did or was involved in was responsible for the shooting; yet everything I see and hear says this guy comes off squeaky clean. He's too perfect. I'm sorry, man, but I'm not buying it. He's got some flaws and I think we need to find them. I'm still going to dig. At this point, we've got nothing else.'

'Got it, Detective.'

'In the meantime, I'll look at the arrest records and we'll try to find this guy in Algiers with the necklace of thorns.' He looked down at his stack of papers. 'They've brought in five guys who looked like they might have an axe to grind with Leroy.'

'There are probably fifty or more.'

'Hell, we could bring in everyone on the list. It's like you said, we've got to weed out the weaker candidates. The majority of the fifty are repeat offenders and it looked like there was at least one of them could have been the culprit. Everything seemed perfect except . . .'

'He alibied out.'

'He did.'

'Look, Q, I've got to give the morning up to two of my own cases. Stay in touch, and if you need anything, call me.'

Archer nodded. 'I appreciate all your help, Josh. Seriously. You're a good cop and a good friend. Anything you hear, *you* call me, OK?'

As Levy walked to the exit he turned to Archer and asked, 'Do you know what the national closure rate is on homicide cases? Nationwide? Take into consideration all fifty states.'

Archer smiled and shook his head. 'Come on, Josh. You've always got the facts. You tell me.'

'About 67 percent. That means that 33 percent of all homicides go unsolved.'

'A lot of murderers getting away with murder.' It didn't surprise him.

'And our closure rate, Q, here in New Orleans, was like 27 percent last year. 27 percent.'

'You're kidding me.'

'Swear to you. 73 percent of all homicides go unsolved. Damn. We're the laughing stock of the country. It's like why are we bothering. You want to kill someone and walk away scot-free? Just come on down to Nawlins. Seriously, you can get away with murder.'

'We'll solve this one, Josh. I promise you, we'll get him.'

After Levy left, Archer picked up the employment file for Officer John Leroy. Flipping through the papers he settled on the breaking and entering story at Fox Glass. Possibly a defining moment in Leroy's decision to be a cop. He read the news report again. Not a surprising account. It wasn't filled with much detail. But if that job, that instance when the young security officer apprehended two would-be burglars, defined his career, maybe there was more to the narrative. Maybe that short-lived job needed to be explored. He considered the implications and the circumstances. Certain things happened in your young life that changed it forever. Things that then lived with you possibly into eternity, and there was nothing you could do to change that. There were no second chances.

Every officer in Algiers was looking for a young man with a tattooed neck. A team was reviewing arrest records and interviewing likely suspects. He'd ordered a team of officers to revisit the tattoo shops and widened the territory. Somebody inked this guy. He didn't do his entire neck by himself.

Archer was covering every base he could think of.

Who had a reason to shoot Leroy and what was that reason. Why? It always boiled down to that three-letter question. If you could answer it, you could solve the puzzle. Never failed.

Stacking the manila file folders, he reached for his sport coat. In this scorching heat he almost considered leaving it draped over his desk chair, but he was one of the few detectives who preferred a shoulder holster for his Glock 22 and he preferred a jacket to cover the fact that he was either a cop, or someone about to hold up a liquor store.

Archer grabbed the keys to the Honda Civic from his desk and walked out the door. The detectives drove cars taken from drug dealers and other felons whose vehicle had been impounded.

Sometimes they were beaters, but the Civic at least had an air conditioner that worked. He was ready for a little footwork. Not everything could be found in files and on the Internet. Sometimes you had to meet people face to face.

TWENTY

I t took twenty minutes until he'd crossed the bridge into Algiers. Passing emergency vehicles and law enforcement vehicles going both ways, he thought about the preparation for the rest of the day and this evening. He'd had basic training in riot control, but this was above his pay station. A riot on this scale was frightening. The morning hours seemed much safer.

To his knowledge, no one had been killed. The police had used intimidation, instructing National Guard and State Troopers to let things work themselves out. So far, so good.

If there was an arrest for every infraction, there would have been thousands of people in jail, more than the facilities could handle. In a riot situation, you let the small crimes go. The insurgents throwing rocks, let them throw. The ones tossing bricks at police cars, move on. If they toss a homemade bomb, brandish a gun, those are the ones you want to stop. And if you see a harmless individual with a tattoo around his neck, it just wouldn't seem that important until later in the night.

There were people trying to kill you during a riot and you had to act somewhat passive, which went against anything you ever were taught. He wasn't upset at all that the officer who saw the necklace tattoo didn't register at first. Saving your life and trying to keep a semblance of peace far outweighed reporting a 'sighting.' Except it would have been nice to have a suspect in confinement. As of now, there was no one.

Archer keyed in the Fox Glass address and followed the voice prompts. In another ten minutes, he was there. The brick building was long and low, a one-story structure that appeared to have been a warehouse at some time in its history. The pitted, cracked asphalt parking lot was sparsely populated, only seven cars, a pickup truck and two delivery vans. The large lot could have handled fifty automobiles and trucks easily.

He pulled up by the entrance, next to a white van sporting a cartoon of a smiling brown fox. Stepping from the Honda, he heard a garage door opening further down and two men came walking out, carrying what appeared to be a large, plate-glass window. The glass was covered in brown paper and tape. The van door slid open, and they slipped the window inside.

He walked to the entrance door where the same cartoon fox leered at him from the etched glass.

Inside there was an attempt to make a customer feel comfortable. A worn couch and two faux-leather chairs decorated the lobby. Photos of modern bathrooms with glass-block showers and pictures of elaborate entranceways hung on the walls. You could dream of what your remodeled home would look like. He walked across a soiled gray carpet to the reception desk where an older, gray-haired lady sat bent over her computer. She never once looked up. Archer thought she might be asleep or dead but she occasionally snorted. He'd never heard a dead person snort.

'Excuse me.'

She never raised her eyes.

'Just a minute, hon. I'm a little busy at the moment.'

He waited for a minute, standing there watching her drooping eyes gazing at the screen.

'Ma'am?'

'Not right now, Sonny. Give me a minute.'

Maybe she was playing on-line poker or Candy Crush.

'I would like to talk to Matt Fox.'

Finally she raised her head and studied him for a moment.

'Matty? You want to talk to Matty? What do you want? Is there a problem with a project? Delivery? Installation? Just tell me. I'll route it through the proper channels.'

'No, there's no problem.'

'Then what do you want with Matty?'

Archer pulled the trump card clipped to his belt and held up his gold-plated detective shield.

'NOPD, ma'am. I'm just here to ask Mr Fox some questions.'

'Police?' She seemed to come alive.

'Just a couple of questions,' he said.

'Is he expecting you?'

'I don't think so.' Archer smiled. Ever since he'd met Solange he wasn't always sure that people weren't aware of more than he gave them credit for. Maybe this guy had a premonition that a police officer was going to question him. You never knew.

'Well, I'm quite certain he's busy, Mr—?'

'Detective,' he said. 'Detective Quentin Archer.' He laid heavily on the word *detective*.

'I'll check.' She stood up and stepped out of the area through sliding glass doors. Archer stood and watched as she walked through what appeared to be the factory. Someone with thick safety glasses and gloves was running a high-speed saw, cutting one pane of glass into two. Two men in the rear wearing identical glasses and gloves worked three long tables, buffering, polishing or sanding plates of glass. As the hand-held machines ran along the edges of the glass, a cloud of particles filled the air.

The gray-haired lady approached one of the sanders, and he nodded, shutting down his machine. Lifting his safety glasses, he walked up the room to the reception door.

Archer stood there to greet him.

'Detective Archer?'

'Matt Fox?'

'You sound surprised.'

The young man who stood before him couldn't be more than thirty, probably younger. It was impossible that this was the Matt Fox who hired Johnny Leroy. Totally impossible.

'I expected . . .'

He chuckled. 'You expected my father. It happens all the time, Detective. I should have changed my name years ago, but being a Jr. does have some privileges. Dad has a great reputation, and I get a better table when I call a restaurant using that name. And you know, in New Orleans, restaurant reservations are a great perk. Plus, there are other benefits. The longevity of this company depends on Dad's reputation. It's an interesting phenomenon. So . . .'

'So your father is no longer . . .'

'Alive? Or do you mean associated with the business?' He finished Archer's question.

'Yeah.'

'Quite the contrary on both accounts. Dad still runs things from the business side. I own the company but I keep him on. He's great with the details, the finances and operations, and I stay on the floor. Just works better this way. He is a very savvy businessman. Saved this company a number of years ago when we were going broke.'

The whirring and zinging sound of the saws and sanders leaked through the doors and continued the assault on Archer's ears.

'What brings you here? Is it the rioting? We're just a few blocks down from where that activity was last night. I'm sure you know that,' Fox said. 'We've had no damage, no threats so we're hopeful that will continue. I thought about hiring a security guard but I don't know that a lone guard could—'

'No, I'm not here about the riots.' Archer smiled. 'I'm glad things were peaceful here last night and I sincerely hope you are safe tonight, but I'm here to ask your father about a security guard your company hired twenty-six or so years ago. Johnny Leroy.'

Fox looked surprised. 'Twenty-six years ago?' He seemed genuinely astounded. 'I was two years old so I'm obviously not going to be much help.'

Archer nodded, understanding the absurdity of the situation. 'Is there a chance I can talk to your father?'

'He works from home,' Fox said. 'Sets his own hours. He only shows up here when there's a big order.'

'He lives near here?'

'Oh, God no. Dad wouldn't live in Algiers. After what happened last night I'm surprised anyone lives in this community. The reason we're still here as a business is because this building is paid for. It's an old ammunition storage building, and he bought it for next to nothing over thirty years ago. We've been in business for over forty years, here in Algiers for thirty-one.'

'And you?'

The young man shook his head. 'I wouldn't live here either. We both have homes in the Garden District.'

'So, if I wanted to talk to Dad . . .'

'I'll give you his address. I'm sure he'll talk to you. If I call him, what should I say this is in reference to? A security guard?'

'A cop who was killed a couple of days ago.'

'Oh, Jeez. I heard about that, sure.' He brushed his gloves together and fine particles of glass drifted to the floor.

'He worked for your father before becoming NOPD.'

'No kidding? I hadn't heard.'

'Security guard, worked evenings.'

'Mmmm. You'd think Dad would have mentioned that.'

'It was a long time ago.'

'Still . . .' the young man pulled out a business card and scribbled an address on the back. 'This is where he lives. He's usually home. Has a bad back and knees so he doesn't get out much. I'm sure he'll give you all the information you need. If I can help in any way . . .'

'Thanks,' Archer said.

'And, Detective . . .'

'Yes?'

'If you ever need glass work, even a small bathroom mirror, call that phone number. I'll get you a really good discount and remember, we do quality work. There are a lot of glass companies in this town, but ask anyone. We're the best. You won't be sorry.'

Walking to his car, Archer wondered why Matt the elder never mentioned Johnny Leroy to his son. Two days ago, the officer's death was the talk of New Orleans, and Matt Fox had been one of his first employers.

TWENTY-ONE

The glass business had been good to Matt Sr. His huge white house sat comfortably on a well-manicured, spacious corner lot, its wrap-around porch allowing a wide view of the neighborhood. Archer could see Adirondack chairs and wooden swings hanging from steel chains that adorned the deck as he walked up the flagstone walk from the driveway. He climbed five steps and landed on the spacious porch, a strong reminder of what Southern hospitality must have been like several generations ago.

The solid oak door was answered by a black man in a white jacket and Archer thought he must have stepped back in time.

'I'm here to see Matt Fox.' He flashed the badge. 'Detective Quentin Archer.' You never mentioned homicide unless it was mandatory. Scared the hell out of most people. *Detective* was enough to send shivers down their spine.

'He's expecting you, sir.' He motioned to a chair on the porch. 'He'll see you out here.'

Archer nodded, sitting in the wooden chair. Matty had apparently called ahead as he had said he might. Staring out at the sprawling lawn he admired the four deep-South oaks that shaded the yard, with Spanish moss hanging from their far-reaching limbs. The rich green emerald grass rivaled whatever imagery L. Frank Baum had conjured up in *The Wizard Of Oz*.

'Detective Archer.' A wizened man, stooped and small, stepped out of the door grasping a gnarled wooden cane and he reached out his other hand, whether to shake Archer's or steady himself Archer wasn't sure. 'Matty said you'd stopped by the shop and you wanted to talk. Something about a security issue. Now what is it you want from me?'

He gingerly sat down in the chair next to Archer.

'Thank you for seeing me, Mr Fox.'

The black man in the jacket appeared with a tray, two glasses, and a plate of small white cookies.

'I took the liberty of having Oscar fix some lemonade. If you like, I can have him pour a little vodka in yours?'

'No, no thanks. It's a little early in the day for me, but I appreciate the lemonade. It's a hot day.'

'It is,' Fox said.

'Mr Fox, I'm certain you heard that Officer John Leroy was killed in Bayou St John two days ago.'

The man just nodded and took a sip of his drink. Archer felt certain there was vodka in *that* drink.

'I'm doing some investigating into the officer's background and of course your name and company came up.'

'Quite a few years ago, Detective.'

'Yes, but he did work for your company for at least a year.'

'Sir, that company, Fox Glass, has been in my family for over forty years. A lot of people have come and gone. Of course I remember he worked there. Somebody on my staff reminded me of that fact immediately, but understand, he was employed by a private security company. Not by me. And he worked a night shift when I was home, in bed. So, security officer Leroy was not someone that I knew well. In fact, I'm not certain that I ever met him. A long time ago. I just remember that he worked his shift.'

Archer took a swig of the tart lemonade. He wasn't sure what it was he expected to learn, but it didn't sound like he was going to find out much.

'Mr Fox, Johnny Leroy was responsible for capturing two thieves who were ready to steal several pounds of gold leaf. Do you remember that incident?'

The old man shook his head. 'I don't recall.'

'I was reading a news report about the attempted robbery, and you were interviewed. You told the reporter that Leroy had caught the suspects and wrapped them up in packing tape until the authorities arrived.'

'I may have. I don't remember. We do use tape to protect glass from breaking, so I suppose it's possible.'

'It sounds like Officer Leroy did a good job for you. If those guys had stolen the gold—'

'Son, I don't know what you want, but whatever it is, I don't have it. I'm truly sorry I can't help you. What I know is, he worked as an independent contractor. I'm pretty sure I never met the man and if I did, it was fleeting. I really don't remember isolated incidents that happened that long ago.'

Archer nodded and set his drink on a small table. 'I'm sorry to have wasted your time, sir.'

'Should have had some vodka. Takes the edge off,' Fox said.

He drove out of the paved driveway, watching the large manor house disappear in his rearview mirror. Different people lived different lives. Vastly different. He recalled the conversation with Levy where he told him he'd always wanted to be a cop. There was no other choice. But sometimes, he saw different choices he might have made. He saw other places he might have been. And he wondered. If he weren't a cop, Denise would still be alive. Maybe he could have owned a company, made a small fortune and provided her a different life. If he weren't a cop, maybe his family would still be a family. Just as crooked and dysfunctional, but still a family. It was a crapshoot, and you couldn't replay what had already happened. He was constantly reminded, there were no second chances.

TWENTY-TWO

On the last day of André Brion's life, he was holding up a liquor store. Everything had been peaceful and calm, the clerk telling him he wanted no trouble. He'd do whatever was necessary and Brion told him that all he had to do was clean out the register and everything would go just fine. Collar turned up, gun in his hand he was stoned cool.

'Here's everything I got,' the young man said, handing a wad of cash from the drawer. 'You can just walk away, man. It's not my money, you know what I mean? Not goin' to get shot over that.'

Brion shook his head. 'Now, lest you think I'm stupid, there are some large bills under the tray.' He pointed at the register. 'You, you probably thought that since this is a robbery, I would overlook that possibility and you might just pocket those bills and tell the authorities that I took everything. Even the big bills under the tray. Is that a likelihood? Was that what you thought? That you might have a payday as well?'

The man started shaking. Point a gun at him and he was cool as a cucumber. Accuse him of larceny and he started to panic.

'Just lift that tray and let's see what we've got, OK?'

The clerk's fingers trembled as he slowly lifted the tray and they both saw several hundred-dollar bills and several fifties.

'Ah, you see. I was right. Please, don't ever underestimate me.' He shook his head and pointed his finger at the clueless clerk. 'I'd guess another five hundred dollars,' Brion said. 'What do you think? Usually I'm pretty good at estimating a take. Would you count it for me?' The gun never wavered, the index finger resting on the trigger.

Shaking as he flipped through the bills, the man laid them on the counter. Stepping back, he said, 'Five hundred dollars, sir. Obviously, you were right. I am so sorry. I was a little flustered by the gun and your . . .'

'Would have been a nice bonus for you and no one would have

been wiser. Very nice try. However, since I'm the one putting everything on the line, you can see that the money should be mine. You can see that, can't you? I think you'll agree that I should be rewarded for the effort. I've got everything at risk. You, you're a victim right now. Am I right?'

Tears were in the man's eyes, his right hand on the counter was shaking uncontrollably.

'Yes sir, you're right sir. I'm the victim. Please don't shoot me.'

'I have no intention of shooting you.' Brion drew back in surprise. 'This gun is for show. I'm going to take,' he started peeling off the bills, adding it to the cash the man had handed him, 'four hundred dollars.'

'Four hundred? But sir, there's—'

'You are no longer a victim, my friend.' He smiled at him. 'Now you are an accomplice. Put one hundred in your pocket as a bonus.'

The man looked into the black burglar's eyes, then slipped a Ben Franklin into his pocket, nodding to Brion. Honor among thieves and all that stuff.

'I'm thinking your description of the thief is a heavy-set black man with a backwards Green Bay Packer's cap. He was shaky, carried a little derringer and seemed scared out of his mind. Can you handle that?'

'I can do that.'

'See that you do. Fat, Packer's cap and a derringer. Frightened and shaky. Also, give me three minutes. Please remember, it's you and me, brother. You are now an accomplice.'

'I can do that too.'

'OK. Spend your bonus wisely.' He turned and headed for the door as a customer walked in, the bell hanging on the door ringing loudly.

Brion saw the sign hanging in front of the register.

To be 21 you must have been born November 25th of 1976. The man behind the counter seemed barely twenty-one, yet he was selling alcohol.

He stepped into the street, confident the man wouldn't call anyone for at least three minutes. Change for the customer who walked in the door? That might be a problem since he'd made sure the register was stripped clean.

Truth be told, he missed the days with Jack and Jeff. There were three people to worry the details and even though they very seldom agreed on anything, bases were more easily covered with three. And there was no reason that the three *amigos* couldn't get back together for a couple of really big heists. Heists where the take was in the tens of thousands instead of the hundreds. Life was easier then. Except for the truck driver who'd broken his neck. Bum luck. He often felt he should find a way to tell the young man's family. Give them some closure. Tell them it was all a tragic mistake.

There were times, after a bender, when he thought about just clearing the record. He'd even mentioned it to the boys, but they were quick to point out the consequences. And of course each one of them held that threat over the others' heads.

He picked up the pace, anxious to leave this deteriorating neighborhood and go home to his. The New Orleans he knew tended to be one rotting community morphing into the next.

Brion took a left at the light, the money stuffed into his pockets. Walking was always a preferred way to escape. Cops thought that burglars had getaway cars, and they put out all-point bulletins to stop anyone suspicious. Someone who was walking, just a pedestrian, was someone who didn't deserve a stop-and-search, no matter what their race or ethnicity. He ambled, strolled, just an innocent black man out for a leisurely walk.

André Brion walked down an alley that emptied into a small residential street. The residents lived in substandard shacks, wooden homes that were bleached white from the blazing sun. Houses that probably harbored cheap bottles of liquor from the store he'd just burglarized.

As far as he could tell, he was free and clear. A couple of thousand dollars to the good, enough to get him through another two or three weeks. Over the years, he'd hidden some of his ill-gotten gains and blown through the rest of it. It was still a day-to-day existence, and it made him sad because he owed his family more than that. His suffering wife and his bright-eyed, brilliant son, ten-year-old Joseph. He walked to a bus stop, thankful that once again he'd pulled off the perfect crime. Perfect in his mind meant he hadn't been caught. It was getting harder and harder.

In thirty minutes he'd be home, inside his small house in the

Lower Ninth Ward. Maybe he'd take Joseph down to Jackson Square tomorrow. They would have a po-boy sandwich, watch some entertainment and check out some of the work by local artists. He had a couple of extra bucks and he couldn't think of a better way to spend them than to blow it on his kid. A day they both would relish.

'Andy.'

The voice took Brion by surprise.

'Turn around, man.'

Placing his right hand on the butt of his pocketed pistol, he slowly turned, seeing the patrol officer.

'Jack.' He flashed a weak smile. 'It's been awhile.'

'Sorry, man. I need to see your weapon.'

'What are you talking about?'

'A hold-up at A To Z Liquor. Sounds like your MO.'

'You're kidding, right? I don't know anything about—'

'The robbery, Andy. It has you written all over it.'

'I probably learned that MO from you.'

'A little blame game?'

'Just the truth,' Brion said. 'You know, you were the best teacher I could have asked for.'

'Pull your gun out and drop it on the ground.'

'Jack, it's Andy. You want to arrest me? With all we've been through?' Holding his hands out, he pleaded. 'Come on, man. I can't afford to take a hit on this. Besides, I could bury you, man. You know that.'

'I do.' The officer nodded. 'I surely do.' The gun was steady, pointed at his midsection. 'We all understand you could bury us. Been thinking about that for some time.'

'You think I'm gonna rat? After all this time?'

'Yeah, we think if anyone is going to ruin it, it would be you.'

'That's why are you doing this? Let well enough alone. I'm telling you, Jack, this isn't a good idea for any of us. I'm never going to tell that story.'

'Pull your weapon where I can see it, then drop it on the ground.'

'Jack . . .'

'Do it,' he screamed.

'Man, you are going to be so sorry.' Brion glanced around but there was no one to give evidence.

'I won't tell you again, Andy.'

'I'll have your ass.' Slowly André Brion pulled the pistol from his pocket. He probably shouldn't have threatened an officer of the law. Especially Jack. Probably should have just walked away. There was no way Jack was going to shoot him in the back. When his weapon had cleared, he nodded to the officer. At that exact moment, the patrolman pulled the trigger, putting a bullet clean through Brion's heart. The officer fired again and again. The final examination showed seven wounds to Brion's body. But after all, the thief had drawn his weapon. A man had to defend himself.

TWENTY-THREE

If you believed in spirits and ghosts that traveled the planet, and she did, then you understood shape-shifters. Spirits who were able to take on other forms, their only opportunity to physically assert themselves. Spirits normally drifted under the radar, causing havoc, righting wrongs. Sometimes making people pay for their sins or helping people through turbulent times. But almost always quietly. Almost always they worked through supernatural forces. But there were times when the spirits needed to be a little more demonstrative. And that's when they took physical shapes. They became shape-shifters.

She'd seen them appear as various animate objects. Eschu Carrefour was the god of mischief. He was often used to test the character of a man, and she'd offered many prayers and supplications to him, asking for insight into her clients or people who wanted to love them or harm them.

Solange was certain beyond a reasonable doubt that Eschu often shape-shifted into a mournful Labrador retriever that sat with a homeless man in the doorway twenty steps down from her shop. Therianthropy, when a spirit shaped into an animal. She only noticed the sad-eyed dog when she had recently prayed for Eschu's guidance. Covered by his matted coat, the canine would be sitting there, giving her a whine or sharp bark when she walked by. She knew the sounds were answers to her questions. She didn't share that observation with anyone else. Not even the thin man with braided hair, dressed in rags, who sat next to the dog and petted her when the animal became somewhat emotional. Solange was very much aware that she was already perceived as a little crazy.

A shape-shifting spirit could take over almost anything that was alive. A dog, a fish, even a frog, like the prince who could only be changed back by the kiss of a princess. Once in a great while, she was aware of a spirit taking over *her*. Using her to speak, to give advice or warn someone. It wasn't something she was at all comfortable with, just as her voodoo gift was most often a curse, but it had happened with the detective. She'd been overpowered with the sense of a spirit. That spirit had told Archer that Joseph Washington had killed someone in his past. A fact she was totally unaware of. Baron Gede had entered her body and stolen her soul and voice for a brief moment. The shape-shifting thief had used her.

She could pray weeks on end for a breakthrough, make dozens of gris-gris bags with sacred stones, twigs and lavender inside. She could do a dance, burn a candle and get no answer. And then, without any fanfare, a spirit could enter her, speak his piece and move on. Her entire being would be personally violated, and so easily.

The actions of these voodoo gods, these supernatural creatures, were unpredictable at best. They spoke to her in all kinds of ways, and that was fine. She could interpret signs, read cast bones, see messages in fire, but when they spoke *through* her, she was frightened. She didn't like to think she was that easy to access. There was a vulnerability she had trouble admitting to. Solange felt that she was a strong woman. Standing up to an abusive husband, now an ex, and dealing with some very strong customers while she held her ground. But spirits who took control of her body and her soul, that was something totally different. That phenomenon shook her to the core.

Now she prayed to that same god who took her voice for a moment, she asked Baron Gede to give her an insight into who Joseph Washington had killed. If it was worth stealing her voice, then at least tell her who the victim was. She could share that with Archer and possibly help solve the murder of Officer Johnny Leroy. So she prayed and lit a candle in a glass vase. Who was the victim? She simply asked Baron Gede to finish the process. It seemed only fair.

The girl let the candle burn, safely surrounded by the vase. If her prayer wasn't answered, she didn't want the building to go up in flames. Laying her head on the pillow, she closed her eyes and wished for an answer. She just wanted a nap. And a dreamless sleep. The two wishes were incongruous. She needed the answer. She drifted, on a boat, on the air, a free-floating experience that defied explanation. Suspended animation, hearing words and voices that made no sense. The girl was adrift in a fantasyland, unable to understand her surroundings. She was thankful for an unconscious experience, yet frightened by the spirits that seemed to inhabit it.

She heard the store's bell ring. Someone had entered her business. A nap that had barely begun was interrupted. Walking out from her quarters into the small shop, she looked for the intruder.

'Can I help you?'

A white-haired old man stood in the entranceway. His weathered face was burned and wrinkled and he blinked, as if disoriented. He wore white linen pants and a collared white shirt, with brown leather sandals. Not an unusual look for the French Quarter.

'Yes, sir, what can I do for you?'

He again blinked and shook his head. Maybe a meth addict or someone who had recently ingested some heroin.

Finally, he seemed to focus and he spoke.

'It's what I can do for you.' His piercing green eyes stared into hers. His leathery skin glowed, a faint aura, maybe just the glisten from perspiration. Possibly from a mystic presence.

She crossed her arms and hugged the thin T-shirt across her thin frame. It suddenly occurred to her she was barely covered and barefoot. In front of a total stranger.

'What can you do for me?'

'I can give you the information you seek.' Dripping with sweat, he shuddered as if chilled. In this weather, that was impossible.

'You can do this?' If this was true it was the first time her prayers had been answered this quickly. And never in her memory, so directly. The gods and goddesses usually forced her to work for the answers. They would ask for sacrifices, for prayers and supplications. If this person, this spirit who had shape-shifted, could give her an answer . . .

'You asked for it. I can do it. I can lead you.'

'There are so many times I ask for . . .'

'Solange, be thankful for what you get. Everything can't be granted, please understand. And answers aren't always available on your timetable. There are reasons far beyond your understanding. But this request, this I can help you with.'

'Whatever you can tell me is appreciated.' She stared intently, now realizing that she was floating, maybe twelve inches off the ground, looking down at this man.

'One man was killed in a series of truck hijackings, twenty-five years ago. He would love to have closure. It's been a long, long time.'

Fitfully she tossed on the mattress, dealing with the revelation. Suddenly she opened her eyes. For a second she shook, realizing it had only been a dream. A dream, but an eye-opening experience.

She closed her eyes and thanked Damballa. The snake god had given her an answer from a shape-shifter. She was sure of that. If the old man of her dream were actually real, he would stumble out the door and after some disorientation would never remember a thing about this confrontation. He was simply a vessel to be used by a spirit.

And she thought she was stronger than that. But in truth, everyone was under the influence of a higher power who could bend the body, the mind, the spirit and if even for a brief moment, change the course of that person's history. No one was entirely in charge of their own destiny.

In the flickering candlelight, she saw the shadowy figures of her sparse furniture. A dresser, chair, nightstand and a shelf. Standing up, she walked through her shop and unlocked the front door. Looking left, looking right, there was no one. A dream. A strange, creepy dream.

The girl closed the door and set the lock. The second it was secure she heard a soft knocking.

'Who's there?'

'Please . . . I need to talk to someone.'

'Who are you?' she asked.

'Please.'

It was broad daylight, no real danger.

Unlocking the door, she cracked it open.

'Do we know each other?' he said. 'Have we talked before?'

The white-haired green-eyed man with the weathered face was standing there, a confused look on his face. Her nightmare had come to life.

Archer called the office from his car and got Beeman.

'Sergeant, if you read my notes, you know Officer Leroy apprehended two men in conjunction with a gold robbery when he was a private security dick. He worked at a place called Fox Glass in Algiers.'

'I saw it in your report last night. Do you think a background check on Leroy's previous employment is relevant?'

'I don't know, but it's the way I want to conduct the investigation. I want to explore this. Can you have archives dig a little deeper? I want to know who the two men were and what sentences they received. Should be grand theft.'

'I'll try to track it down and call you back.'

'As soon as possible, Sergeant.' Archer was worried that time was running out and he didn't want to blow the biggest case he'd ever worked.

'Priority, Detective.'

He called a distracted Levy.

'Q, I'm up to my ass right now. I just got handed our latest shooting. A road-rage incident. The victim is a rookie for the New Orleans Saints. It's like we need another high-profile case, right?'

'Damn. Who was it?'

'Twenty-three-year-old kid named Dante Jameson, recruit from Ole Miss. Never even got to play in the show. I don't know much about him, but we just keep substituting one front-page headline for another one, don't we?'

'Sorry you drew it, man.'

'Sorry we draw any cases. Maybe it *is* time to get out of this game. It's starting to get to me, Q.'

'Let me bounce something off you regarding Johnny Leroy.'

'Shoot.'

'Not a good word. I visited Fox Glass today.'

'You still think there's a possibility that Leroy's previous job is going to give you a break?'

'Matt Fox's kid runs the show. He's young and doesn't remember the incident where Leroy captured the two thieves, but . . . he put me in touch with his old man. I drove out to the Garden District and paid him a visit. I had about a ten-minute conversation with the patriarch.'

'And?'

'He's a crusty old guy, lives in a gorgeous house, butler and the whole nine yards. The business has been good to him. Basically, he told me he doesn't remember anything about it.'

'A little forgetful?'

'Maybe. But he was very defensive. I just called Beeman and asked him to get me the names of the robbers that Leroy detained. We've been looking at arrest records. This goes back a ways, but it was almost like an arrest. Right? He busted two burglars, and if they had an axe to grind, we need to investigate them as well. Maybe one of them wanted him dead.

'It took them a long time to make that decision.' The sarcasm was strong in his statement.

'Josh, I just wanted a sounding board.'

'Sorry, Q, you've got it. I just think that's a long time to hold a grudge, then act on it. Hey, my friend, go for it. I think you need to chase down every possible link. You know I've got your back.'

'I know. And while I appreciate it,' Archer smiled, 'that doesn't get me squat, does it?'

'Well, I may be the best friend you have, Detective. A gunfight? I'm there, partner. A brawl, I'll weigh in. A hearing from the big guys in the department . . . I'll be busy fishing. I can't have your back all the time.'

'No, I know you too well.' Archer laughed. 'You'd be there.' And he knew Josh would be there. 'Thanks, man, and good luck with your rookie case. Hate to hear some young kid snuffed out.'

'This city takes out the good and the bad, Q. And I once again go on record, John Leroy is one of the good guys. While I admit I didn't know him well, I looked up to him. I admired what he did, the fact that he stayed a street cop. It's part of the record, Archer, this man saved lives. Don't go after him. Go after the person who shot him. That's who we need to concentrate on. Find this guy with the tattooed necklace. Find someone who had a grudge. Leroy was just following the rules and as you pointed out, getting the bad guys off the street. Anything else, personally speaking, I think is bullshit.'

TWENTY-FOUR

'Archer, I've got the names of the two burglars.'

'That was quick, Sarge.'

'If it speeds up the process, I'll get whatever you need. You know the intensity of this case.'

'No promises. I am exploring every avenue, and I just want to track down these two guys.'

'I've got a very brief history on the two suspects. You won't be interviewing them any time soon, that's a guarantee.'

'They're dead?'

'Bingo.'

His heart skipped a beat. Dead men told no tales. Silent as a grave. The chances of these two men having any influence on the case was drastically diminished. Archer took a deep breath. He had been hoping for access. Apparently, that was out of the question.

'Give me their names.'

'Two lowlifes. Both had priors for petty theft,' Beeman said. 'Hang on to your hat, Archer. One was André Brion. Sound familiar? Brion had several . . .'

'Wait a minute. Brion?'

'Exactly.'

'André Brion?'

'That's the name.'

'Well, Sergeant, as I'm sure you know, that's the name of the man that John Leroy shot twenty some years ago. The only black mark on his record. Brion drew his weapon and Leroy shot him. And the officer was exonerated. Self-defense. You're telling me that this Brion was one of the burglars at Fox Glass?'

Beeman took an audible breath, then paused and there was silence on both sides. Finally, the officer spoke.

'I did run this name and I'm sure it's the same guy. Do you think it's a coincidence?'

'Highly unlikely,' Archer said, 'but tell me the second name.'

'This is going to come as a shock, Q. If this were a coincidence as well,' Beeman said, 'it would be the strangest set of coincidences I've ever run across on this beat. We all were a little shocked when his name came up.'

'Just give me the name, Sergeant.'

'Joseph Washington.'

'No.'

'Yes. We couldn't believe it.'

'Damn. Joseph Washington? Really?' Archer shook his head. It didn't make any sense.

'I'm not making this shit up, Detective.'

'I think we're trying to defuse a riot because this man, this Joseph Washington was gunned down. Any chance this is a different Joseph Washington? There are probably several.'

'I've got people looking into it. We're also checking on all André Brions, but my guess is he is probably the same guy who Officer Leroy shot. Seven times. Not a lot of André Brions in the white pages. Where does it lead, Archer? Is there a correlation? There must be something.'

'I wish I knew.'

'Anything else I can offer, let me know.'

'Leroy detains two criminals on his security gig. Brion and Washington. They're both thieves with a background.'

'Exactly.'

'In his police career, Officer John Leroy confronts a burglar who draws on him, and he shoots André Brion in the line of duty. Same guy he detained a number of years ago. What are the chances he finds this guy for a second time? It's got to be the same guy, right?'

'As I said, it appears so,' Beeman said.

'Then John Leroy is killed by an unknown gunman and within forty-eight hours the second burglar, Joseph Washington, is killed by one of our officers.'

'It's crazy, Q. If all the names check out, it's just plain crazy. Like a jigsaw puzzle where the pieces don't seem to fit.'

'The second you know if it's a positive on Washington and Brion, call me,' Archer said. 'I don't know how it's connected to Leroy's death, but if we can make those pieces fit, it's going to be a huge step toward solving this murder and maybe keeping this city from exploding. Thanks, Sergeant. As you know, every bit of information helps.'

He wasn't sure what that huge step was, but his gut instinct told him this was the biggest lead he'd had. Truth be told, the only real lead. The rest was all just voodoo magic.

Archer thought about the situation. A cop had been murdered in cold blood. An unarmed burglar had been killed by a white cop. And there were tentacles. Possibly every act was connected. It was up to him to find those connections. There was a reason the process was called 'detecting'.

And he wondered what else he could be doing? What other profession was he suited for? Anything else. The strain was stressing him. Archer wondered what bartenders started at. He could mix drinks for a living. With tips he'd probably make more than he did now. Maybe a plumber, a carpenter. An insurance salesman? Anything that didn't come with guilt, with heavy baggage. He'd known from the start of his career, he would be judged for everything he did. Part of the territory. It was a crazy world he lived in. A universe where every minute made you prove you deserved to exist. You were forced to persevere. And sometimes you just wanted to throw your hands up and say, 'Fuck it.'

He acknowledged, deep down inside, he wasn't wired that way. He wasn't capable of accepting a menial job. Archer needed to be challenged. When his back was to the wall, he became stronger. He came out swinging. And maybe that time would be now. He needed to find out who killed Johnny Leroy. Number one priority and he was going to have the answer to that question very soon.

TWENTY-FIVE

Officer Johnny 'Jack' Leroy had it coming for two reasons. He'd killed Pop. Taken away the most important person in Joseph's life. The second grievous sin he'd committed was he'd left Mom a widow. Mom had withdrawn into a small, hard shell and never fully reappeared.

Loretta Brion had been a strong woman, strict where his father was lenient, yet loving. She kept a good home, saw to it that a hot meal was served once a day, and was adamant that the boy followed her to church every Sunday. When he asked why his father didn't adhere to that rule, she simply shrugged and told him the Lord dealt with different people in different ways. He took that to mean that Pop had his own way of worshiping. Pop and God were on a different level. Joseph vowed that as an adult, he'd find that relationship as well, and skip all the ceremony, the shouting about hellfire and brimstone, the fervent screaming of parishioners as the spirit moved them. Every Sunday morning, he cringed, knowing he was going to be confronted with people he considered a little crazy. Frankly, church scared the hell out of him.

As a child, he sometimes prayed that God wasn't a vengeful creator. He didn't want to burn in hell for the small transgressions that he had committed. And he sometimes offered that prayer now, because his small transgressions had escalated into much bigger ones.

Joseph knew his father worked strange hours, sometimes only one night a week. In his spare time, he frequented some sort of club. He'd often come home smelling of alcohol and tobacco, but if anything, the drinking and the smoke seemed to make him mellow. Joseph remembered fondly, the man always kissed his wife when he left and when he returned. The ritual warmed Joseph's heart. He knew from a young age he was part of a loving family.

Mom read the Bible religiously and sometimes late at night Joseph could hear her reciting a verse from 1 Peter.

Above everything, love one another earnestly, because love covers over many sins.

Over and over again she would repeat it, like a mantra. And she prayed for him, for Joseph, he could hear her loud and clear . . . and for his father. Asking for forgiveness for sins she wasn't quite sure had been committed. It was as if she took no chances.

Looking back, he knew she was a bright woman. She obviously knew that André 'Andy' Brion lived a life of crime, but she chose not to be confrontational. The man provided, and provided quite well. They had a fine home in Marigny, just northeast of the French Quarter. There was a yard and trees he could climb. That was his earliest memory. Shortly before the murder of his father, and he knew it had been a murder, not self-defense, they'd had a financial crisis. Something had happened and Pop wasn't bringing in the money he once had. Somewhere the 'business' had fallen off, gone south.

His father had lost the spacious three-bedroom home and they had moved to the Lower Ninth. It was a traumatic time in his life. His mother had tried to make a game of it, the move, the downsizing, but the adventure didn't last long and that's when she started losing it. When Pop was killed, murdered, she never recovered. And neither did Joseph.

Mom was now protected. By her church affiliation, by the congregation. Joseph was certain of that. The young preacher would ask for donations and she would be sheltered and fed. And Joseph knew that she was in God's hands as well. Someone as deeply religious as she was had to have God's blessing. She was Joseph's biggest concern, but he felt somewhat relieved knowing that she believed in the Savior and by his grace alone, his mother would be saved.

All these thoughts clouded his mind as he rolled his sleeping bag, loaded his pack and went in search of a cup of coffee. He could wire himself on caffeine today because he seriously needed to be alert. No drugs, no alcohol. Today was his day. Pop's day. And again, he sent out a prayer for Mom.

She paddled the kayak down the Pearl, named by the French settlers who found the shells and pearls left by the Indians who shucked the oysters. By historic accounts the French had discovered piles and piles of pearls, three or four feet high. The natives could eat the slimy oysters. The white, opaque abnormalities they occasionally found in the shells, they couldn't. These were left behind. The Frenchmen must have thought they had found a treasure trove.

Ma's friend Matebo, the old man of the swamps, had moved to the Pearl River and in very private areas he harvested herbs, swamp grass and other things that were used in voodoo spells and potions. He sold them to a regular group of practitioners and made a modest living. Solange's regular trips guaranteed fresh produce and the octogenarian was always glad to see her. Before the dementia, before the slide into the vacuous state she now inhabited, Ma used to visit and often Solange was invited along. There was a closeness between Ma and Matebo that seemed to transcend friendship, but she'd been a little girl and possibly a little too impressionable. Still, she often thought that the swamp dweller might be the mysterious father that she'd never known.

Through a swamp of trees dripping with Spanish moss she traveled, passing the heads of two alligators who lay submerged, only their eyes above water, dully watching as she slid by. Tall stakes dotted the shore where permit holders would string lines and hooks with dead chickens as bait, hoping to catch the reptiles and sell the meat, the skins, even the organs and head.

Breathing in the smoky, musty odor of the marsh, she watched three feral black hogs rooting around the base of a tree and she smiled when she saw a blacksnake swimming next to her. Possibly a relative of Damballa the snake god, sent to keep her safe. The murky water in front of her swirled as some underwater creature stirred up the bottom.

A green-slime-covered fishing boat was beached on the far side of the shallow river, it's bottom rotted out, and she knew that she was close. A landmark.

And there he was, waving at her, his long, stark-white hair contrasting sharply with his deep brown skin. Looking thin and frail, he helped her pull the kayak up on the shore.

'You're a sight for sore eyes, Solange. How's Ma?'

'Once in a while there's a glimmer,' she said. 'Other than that . . .'

'All the potions, all the spells, all the herbs that are available,' the old man shook his head, 'and we can't find one that works.'

She shook her head.

'Speaking of spells, potions and remedies, I see you have your devil's wood root in the red flannel bag.'

She pointed to the small red bag tied to his waist.

'*Ça va bien.*' He smiled. 'And observe.' Holding up his hands, he made two fists, then raised his arms high.

'Amazing. The last time you couldn't do that at all. And your back?'

'Well, I have my days, but remember, girl, I'm eighty-five. The root has given me some motion back and for that I am thankful.'

She followed him as he walked to a rustic campsite, a protected fire burning and a black pot hanging over the coals.

'So over the years you've taught me that roots are the most powerful of the natural medicines, because—'

'Because the root is the anchor. The root is the source of nutrition. All things start with a root.'

He motioned her to sit in a canvas sling-back chair, while he circled the fire.

'I know,' she said. 'I've heard you and Ma both say, "Channel what the root stands for and make it work for you."'

'Devil's wood root, despite its name,' he grasped the red pouch, 'is based in a calming, healing aura. Inflammation, the cause of arthritis, retreats when I wear the bag.'

'So I have a question.'

'You always have a question. And another and another.' He laughed. 'Little girl, when you *were* a little girl, you asked me a ton of questions every time Ma brought you. *Joie de vivre.*'

'I should have asked how strong the relationship was between you and Ma. I never had the courage.'

The old man shook his head, the fine white hair moving with the shake. She understood he wasn't going to answer the question about Ma.

'What's your *other* question?'

'Two, actually.'

'I'm not surprised.'

'I'm in touch with the spirit of a dead cop. He was killed for a reason, and if I can find the reason, I am reasonably sure that the homicide detective—'

'Archer,' Matebo said. 'Quentin Archer, the man you are somewhat interested in.'

'Maybe.' She rolled her eyes. 'Anyway, I need to find more specifics. His spirit has spoken to me, but as usual, the terms are vague. Do you have any suggestions? I could use some help.'

'Girl, there are hundreds of questions I should ask, and hundreds of possible solutions as you know. But, here's something you might try. I'll include this in your package.'

'You have something new?'

'Something old. Thirty million years old, originating in Eurasia.'

'Have I heard of this?'

'Of course. It is used for digestive problems, heart ailments, bone strength and dozens of other remedies. But in this case, dandelions increase the possibility of clairvoyance.'

'The lion's tooth?'

'In French, yes. And maybe being a little bit psychic, seeing into the past and the future, will help you find what you need.'

'I never knew.'

'As a tea, as an herb, in salads it can be a health food. But people ignore the spiritual aspect. When you pray to the gods then ingest the essence of the plant, miracles can happen. You can unlock secrets of the universe. I believe this would work for you.'

He squatted in his linen pants and shirt, picking up a long branch and stirring whatever was in the pot. The smell interested her.

'Rattlesnake soup,' he said. 'I included some snake-shed in your package. Powder it, and it gets rid of bad spirits.'

'Thank you. I need to pick up and be going.'

'Stay for lunch?'

'No, but I appreciate the offer. My last question, and this may not be the one you are prepared to answer.'

'Solange, I've always felt like . . .' he hesitated, 'like a father figure to you. You can ask me anything. And then if it's totally uncomfortable, I'll pretend I'm hard of hearing and we can forget it ever happened.'

She smiled and clapped her hands.

'I have been involved in three murder cases with this Quentin Archer. Each time I've been drawn in and I've had some interesting insight. I can modestly say that my input has helped solve the crime.'

'You've made a statement, my dear. No question. No need for any help. What's happened has happened.'

'The question is yet to come,' she said.

'Is there some jeopardy in entering into a personal relationship with this detective?'

'You knew?'

He settled back, stirring the pot. 'I have no way of knowing how far you've gone, but there is one thing you need to understand in any relationship. You need to know the difference between when someone is speaking to you during their free time . . . and when they are freeing up their time to speak to you. I'm not sure I can give you better advice.'

'You're saying . . .'

'I'm saying what I said. Solange, I love you like a daughter. I was devastated when your last relationship didn't work. I was torn between wanting it to be healed, and wanting that terrible man out of your life. I pray that if you do become involved again with anyone, that there is a deep-seated commitment.

'You said it only works if someone frees up their time because they want or need to communicate? Not if they just want to pass the time?'

'Have some soup with me. With the proper spices, the snake is delicious.' He sniffed the steam arising from his creation.

'He's asked for some free time. I declined for now. Quentin wanted to take me out for dinner but I was hesitant. There are stressful moments in this case and I thought the situation was much too serious.'

'That and he still mourns for his deceased wife.'

'That too,' she said, somewhat embarrassed that Matebo knew so much about the detective.

'I told you what I can tell you,' Matebo said.

'The package,' she said.

He handed it to her along with a small bouquet of dandelions, and she handed him fifty dollars, cash.

'There's some High John root and dried toadstool tops in there as well.'

She nodded. Always a little surprise from the old man.

'Solange, be careful. You are a young woman and you have a lot of life to live. I don't want you to ruin that life.'

'I don't intend to.'

'So many young people ignore what is important. The gods, the spirits are watching. If you, especially you, give the dream up . . . ignore your legacy—'

'Matebo,' she shouted, 'what I want is out. Please show me a way.'

The man stared at her, his mouth wide open.

'Well, I certainly didn't see that coming.'

'How do I move on from the spirit world?'

'I'm not sure you do.' He calmly continued to stir the pot.

'Sometimes I think that this is what drove Ma crazy. This calling, this obsession with the voodoo gods, the voodoo community, it caused her to lose her mind. I don't want to end up like that.'

He smiled at her, the wrinkled face creasing.

'Even in the mindless state she seems to inhabit, you have admitted there are moments when your mother shows she's still connected.'

Solange took a deep breath, then slowly let it out.

'I'm sorry for the outburst. It's just that the frustration wears on me and there are times—'

'Nothing to be sorry about. Don't you think that I've had moments of doubts in all these years. When people yelled at me on the streets of the Quarter that I was a damned hoodoo man. I've been called Diablo, and Beelzebub. They said worse. And there were times when I wanted to walk away. But the spirits wouldn't let go. And you know, they can be a persistent bunch. Besides, there were too many people who needed me. They needed me to build the bridge, to communicate for them. And people depend on you.'

'And of course you are correct. I do have a sizable following of people who depend on me. I understand that.'

Matebo walked from the fire and took her hand. He stared into her eyes, and she felt all her troubles fly away.

'Then go, do your work. Make Ma proud of you. And when you see her, tell her I think of her. Always.'

TWENTY-SIX

Joseph Washington had to die. For two reasons. The first reason was that Old Joe had betrayed Pop. The petty criminal had walked out on an unlawful but lucrative business. Piecing together his father's checkered past, Brion understood the deeds his father had committed. However, but for one instance, as far as he was able to ascertain, there had never been anyone seriously hurt. The only black mark was the accidental death of an innocent man. A death due to the crime involving his father, but it was accidental.

For all of his crimes, and there appeared to be many, his father was not solely responsible for that death. It wasn't something he was proud of, but he had come to terms with that.

There were others who were more intimately involved. Joseph Washington had commiserated with Jack Leroy. They'd both been afraid that Andy Brion was going to go soft and announce to everyone what had happened and who was involved. Brion nodded to himself, confident that was the reason for Pop's death. For that, Joseph Washington had to die. The man had obviously agreed that André had to be killed. Why else had Old Joe been allowed to live? And he had to die for a second reason, as well. Joseph Brion needed a catalyst, and Joseph Washington was the perfect stimulus.

Something had to happen to spark a riot. He wanted a full-blown revolt to celebrate his old man and Washington was the perfect foil. Oh, there were other ways to get his desired outcome. Joseph Brion had his minions who were not above killing someone for him, but as much as he feared the fallout, a large scale riot, this had been a perfect storm. A rare combination of circumstances that aggravates a situation drastically. A little inside information, some well-planted seeds of doubt. Besides, he knew Joseph. Joseph Washington was his godfather. Andy Brion's kid knew just how Joseph thought and acted. And he was true to form. No disappointment.

From what Brion had read about the shooting, Joseph had been a little on the dramatic side. The robbery money blowing in the wind, and the pause before he pulled his other hand out of his pocket. Perfect Washington. He had always been a drama queen. He patterned his actions after Hollywood characters. Loved the classics. And maybe it had been suicide by cop. Possibly Old Joe had decided this was a time to check out. If so, he took the cowards way and let a cop do it for him. Anyway, it was going to be a spectacular celebration.

Brion had never planned for the kid, this rookie officer Jethro Montgomery, to actually shoot Washington. But if it had to be, Joseph Washington was always one to go out with flair. So Joseph had to die.

Now there was just one to go. He sat on the concrete bench, watching a paddlewheel steamer crawl up the Mighty Miss.

The slow laziness of the craft made him melancholy for those days with Pop. He'd told him stories of Mark Twain, and some of the famous early steamboats. *The New Orleans*, *The Comet*, *The Enterprise* and *The Washington*. Stories about their captains and obviously made-up heroic stories about their endeavors. Gamblers, shady ladies and other people of ill-repute. Stories of rollin' on the river.

Pop was a criminal, and his small family had made peace with that. But to be gunned down by one of his own, to be brutally murdered in the streets of his own city, to have his life taken at such an early age was inexcusable. The sentence for the person who took his life, causing him to leave behind a child and an inconsolable wife, could only be execution. There was no other way to pay for the crime. And Joseph played that over and over in his head. The only way he could live with himself. He'd killed a man who deserved to die. He tried to erase the image of shooting the man in the face with the conviction that the gruesome, hideous deed was one that had to happen.

Joseph Brion closed his eyes and pictured a simpler time. Sitting on the steps of Jackson Square. A calliope coming down the street, the *oompah-pahs* booming from its tinny speakers, and the colorful wagon zigzagging in front of the square. Horse-drawn carriages, vendors hawking their wares and artists selling portraits and paintings depicting the tackiness of the Quarter. He slowly drifted into a much-needed sleep, his hand positioned perfectly over the pocket of his cargo-shorts. The next best thing to sleeping with one eye open was to be ready at a moment's notice with your pistol.

Archer grabbed his buzzing phone.

'Quentin, it's Solange.'

Back to first names.

'Hey, surprise. Did you think of something else?'

'I have an idea for you. You told me that Officer Leroy shot a man named André Brion.'

'Totally exonerated.' Very strange that she would bring that story up. And he was surprised at his immediate defense of the officer. He was simply echoing Levy's adamant concerns.

'I told you I thought that Leroy's death and Joseph Washington's death were tied together.'

'You also said that you thought Washington had killed someone and went out of his way to make sure he wouldn't kill again. That's why he didn't carry a weapon. Am I right?'

'Yes, I apparently said that, although at the time, I didn't remember making that statement.'

'So,' Archer took a breath, already puzzled by the call, 'you've got another idea?'

'Quentin, it is so hard to explain the complexity of some of my thoughts. Most of the time I don't understand them myself. Seriously. There are spirits that speak to me, there are some things that, like your process, are just deductions. And there are often things that are just happenstance. Like you, I can make an educated guess, or make a huge blunder.'

He laughed out loud.

'I assume you've made several?'

'Oh, yes.'

'Please, bear with me while I tell you this.'

'I don't pretend to understand, but just tell me. I promise you I'll at least explore whatever you've got.'

'There's another thought. Someone who died, possibly by Joseph Washington's hand.'

'That's the one death that he struggled with?'

'Maybe, but I've had a strange feeling since seeing Officer Leroy's corpse. I think that Johnny Leroy may have been responsible for another killing.'

'Leroy?' He had one killing to his record. She had to be wrong. 'Solange, he's totally clean. If there was anyone else he'd killed, we'd have a record of it. When an officer is involved in a death, it doesn't go unreported. There would be paperwork like you can't believe, and—'

'Not if it happened off duty. Not if it happened in a different universe, Quentin. Explore just a little with me.'

He was quiet for a moment, wondering what other universe she could possibly be referencing. He couldn't explore what he didn't understand.

'Quentin, most people live a dual life. We have two faces. Be honest with yourself. You know there's the one we show to the world, hopefully a positive one, and the face that we wear at night, in the deepest of shadows, when no one is watching. That is our disguise. In many cases, in most cases, the second face is a darker side that we don't want others to see. I have this feeling that Officer Johnny Leroy lived two lives, had two faces. You and I have had this conversation before. I'm asking you to look into the death of a man killed during a series of truck hijackings. I know that the science of keeping records wasn't necessarily perfect back then, but this should be easy. One driver was killed. Who was it?'

A darker side? God knew he had one. He wanted vengeance for the death of his wife. He wanted retribution for the crimes his brothers had committed, hooking hundreds of people on drugs. He wanted some reckoning with his family, mother and father, who had shunned him for turning on his brothers.

'The truck hijackings. It's sketchy. I can look it up, but that's hard to say that he was responsible for the driver's death.'

'I think he was . . .' she hesitated as if getting her thoughts together. 'I get it. This is a very sketchy lead, but I believe that Leroy and Washington were involved in the death of this driver. That death ties them together.'

'Wow.' He considered for a moment telling the woman what he knew. 'I will share something with you,' he said, 'but in the strictest of confidence. Please, you can't tell anyone about this.'

'Who am I going to tell, Detective? We don't exactly run in the same social circles.'

He realized the absurdity of his request.

'Officer Johnny Leroy worked as a security guard at a business in Algiers, before he joined the force.'

'That's secret information?'

'No. The secret information is what happened during his employment. During the year he worked the night shift, he stopped two would-be thieves and detained them until the cops arrived.'

'You've got some names of those thieves?'

'I do. Confidential.'

'Tell me.'

'Joseph Washington and Andy Brion. And now you bring up the truck driver. I have no knowledge of him, but damn, this whole thing seems to be dovetailing.'

'It's like all the stars are converging to one point,' she said. 'Detective, I've given you as much information as I can. It's all I know. I seriously believe that if you track this driver, you may very well find why your Johnny Leroy was killed.'

'Solange, do you ever feel like your brain is aching? Too much information? Sensory overload?' he asked.

'Are you truly asking me for an answer, or are you just commenting on the current situation?'

'No,' he said, 'I'm asking. There are so many avenues to explore in this case. I'm still working with fellow officers in Detroit on Denise's murder, I've got four other cases that I'm actively involved with and we're on our second night of riots in Algiers. My brain is about ready to explode. Sometimes I wonder why—'

'I'm sorry, Quentin.'

'And I shouldn't lay that all out on you. But do you ever feel that?'

'Every day, Detective. Every hour, every minute.'

TWENTY-SEVEN

Nick Martin. The records, as old as they were, spit up the name. He had no knowledge of the man, but any lead was a positive so he called the office and asked them to run records. And he tried to grasp all the information he had in his head. The cell phone buzzed again and he answered. Detroit calling.

'Archer.'

'Q, good news, my friend. Really good news.'

Tom Lyons sounded very positive.

'I could use any good news, Tom. On a number of levels. There's a lot of shit going on.'

'United States Marshalls, they found Bobby Mercer.'

Officer Bobby Mercer, until recently a member of the DPD. At one time one of Archer's comrades in blue. This was the man who had recruited his brothers into the drug ring. The man who had walked out on the force and traveled down to New Orleans, threatening Archer. The man who killed Denise, his wife. He'd run her down with a stolen car to send a message to Archer. He was the one person he'd kill in a heartbeat. His darkest enemy. He had hoped, dreamed and prayed that he could spend fifteen minutes with Mercer. He wanted to choke the confession out of him, endlessly kick him in the balls, torture the motherfucker. The man who killed Denise. The damned motherfucker. Archer was shaking.

'Details, my friend. Please, details.'

'Two hours ago, Q. That's all I know. And I've already been informed there are some very scared cops on our force at this moment. For some reason, I think some of the "participants" thought that Mercer was an untouchable. We've already had some sudden defections.'

'Where? Where did they find him?'

'Dallas, Texas.'

'Doing what?'

'What do you think? Selling opioids. You'd think he'd be a lot smarter, but he was trying to move some H to an undercover cop. *We're* cops. He was a cop. Can't we usually spot a narc?' Lyons took a breath. 'Bobby Mercer was smart enough to set up the ring, but he got a little too cocky. That's my take on it, Q.'

Archer almost smiled. 'As long as they nail the son of a bitch, Tom. I hope he gets life. The absolute worst for our former friend.'

'Death would be nice,' Lyons said, 'but that hasn't happened since the 1800s.'

The death sentence had been abolished in the late 1800s in Michigan, and most cops wished it would come back.

'Tom, right now I'm tied up in this shooting of a New Orleans cop, a black-lives-matter riot in Algiers, and a number of other cases but—'

'We've all got a lot on our table, Quentin. Trust me. How does that play into the arrest of Mercer?'

'Look, I'm just saying, in spite of a full schedule, you have to know how desperately important this is to me. If the prosecutor needs me to come back, no matter when, I'm there.'

'I know. As I said, this just happened two hours ago,' Lyons said. 'So, at the moment I don't know any more than that. I could speculate, but for now I'm just keeping you up to date, my man. We've finally got some traction. You know what I mean?'

'I do. And you did a whole lot more than that. No, Tom, it goes way beyond friendship. You and your handful of cohorts, if it hadn't been for your work behind the scenes, that son of a bitch would still be running the business from his squad car. You guys drove him out. I couldn't be any happier. We are now in family status. *Capisce*?'

Lyons chuckled. 'I know your family, my friend. I'm not certain I want to be a part of that dysfunctional group. We're all extremely happy that Bobby Mercer has been captured. The family up here in the frozen tundra is happy. Not *your* family of misfits.'

Archer laid the phone down and drawing a breath put his head in his hands. Dad, once a cop, was now vocally disappointed in his son. His brothers, at one time friends, were now sworn enemies who had both been salesmen in Mercer's drug cartel. Dad was first and foremost a family man, and Archer had betrayed the family. That was always forefront in his mind. But Denise, the naïve nurse, had been the love of his life. His *best* friend. They'd shared dreams, talked about kids and planned a life. It was hard to deal with the sadness of losing family, but harder still, losing his love. Archer tried to pull it together.

'Q? Are you there?'

He picked up the phone. 'Thanks, Tom. Needed a moment. I guess I just wait for the next step?'

'I'm sure they're working on extradition. My uneducated guess is they will ask you to return to Detroit sometime in the near . . . oh hell, Quentin, you know that it won't be pleasant.'

'Unlike it's been since she was run down?' He closed his eyes and took a breath. '*Won't be pleasant* seems to be a watered-down phrase from what it's actually been, Tom.'

'I can't imagine, my friend. I have no idea what you're going through. But we want to nail him. Make the conviction stick. You know that. Doing everything possible here to make that happen. And you? You're working on the cop killing . . . I imagine you are going through a new kind of personal hell. An officer down is a scary situation.'

'I am.' He was.

'Quentin, I told you there are some cops looking over their shoulders. There are also some resignations up here and some cops who have just disappeared.'

Just like cops had disappeared right after Katrina. Cops with stolen cars and weapons. No one knew where they'd gone.

'The writing's on the wall, Q. I believe this drug thing may be deeper than any of us thought.'

'Deeper?' Archer asked. He was somewhat incredulous. 'They ran me out of town, Tom. Destroyed my life, and took Denise's. I *always* thought it was deep. Hopefully this arrest will bring the house down.'

'I get it.'

'So keep me informed. No chance he can skate on this?'

There was a long silence on the other end. Finally, 'Hey, you know the way the justice system works. Anyone, anywhere can skate. If someone oils the skids. If someone greases the wheels. You know that as well as I do. Every minute, someone in power is screwing with the system. It can happen, pal. But I think we've got some solid evidence. A video that almost nails Mercer stealing the car and then another one that shows the hit-and-run.'

'We're going to get him, Tom. We're going to get him.'

The phone buzzed again, and this time Beeman was on the other end.

'OK, Q, I don't know where you got the name Nick Martin, but here's a thumbnail of what we've found so far. A Nick Martin was a truck driver for the Lane Freight Company about twenty-five years ago.'

'There must be dozens if not hundreds of Nick Martins who died in the last twenty-five years. You're sure you've got the guy who died during the hijacking?'

'Patience, my son. A lot of manpower, a lot of investigation went on in the last half hour. You're working on a cop killing and there are no limits as to time and effort. You know that. Overtime be damned.'

Archer was quiet.

'On the night in question, Martin was hauling a load of cigarettes to a wholesale warehouse in New Iberia. There's a record of a

CB broadcast he made asking about a detour on I-90. Highway Department isn't sure they have records that go that far back to verify, but for whatever reason, he got off the highway, driving his rig onto some jerk-water country road. He went off the road, the truck jackknifed and skidded down an embankment. When the cab flipped, he broke his neck and died on the scene.'

'Wow. That's a tragic story.' He still wasn't sure how it all fit together. 'Sarge, what does a truck accident have to do with the case?'

'I'm not sure, Q. But at the time, there were maybe seven truck hijackings in the area. Almost every other week. Possibly a mob thing. No other drivers were killed, but they were forced off the highway and when they stopped, a band of robbers unloaded their trailers. Almost an epidemic. Liquor and tobacco seemed to be the preferred cargo.'

'Easy to unload, easy to sell. But I'm still confused Sergeant. What does all this have to do with Johnny Leroy?'

'By the time a hiker saw the wrecked truck and called it in, the man's, this Nicky Martin's load of cigarettes, had been stolen. The trailer was empty. Stripped bare. Because we,' he paused, 'well, *they* assumed it was probably the work of the hijackers, our department sent a team of officers to the scene. The first responder was Officer Johnny Leroy.'

Archer shook his head. 'We've got over one thousand law enforcement agents in the department,' he said. 'One thousand plus, but one officer's name keeps surfacing.'

'John Leroy.'

'Coincidence?'

'Keep digging, Archer. We're going to get to the bottom of this. And do you have any more reports about the guy with the tattooed necklace?'

'We've got everyone in Algiers on alert.'

'We'll do whatever it takes from this end.'

'Keep looking at the Nick Martin case. If anything else pops up, let me know. Sooner or later we're going to put the pieces together.'

'Make it sooner, Detective Archer. Please, make it sooner.'

TWENTY-EIGHT

He sipped a cola, seated at a table in the shade of a faded, ragged yellow awning hanging out four feet from a storefront that was in desperate need of a new paint job. The peeling facade gave proof to the blistering sun and relentless heat that smothered New Orleans. The restaurant had survived neighborhood attacks from the mob last night.

It was two blocks from Fox Glass. Two blocks from his evening destination. His focus was solid. As much as he wanted to drift, his mind wouldn't allow it to happen.

'Would you like to order, hon?'

The pudgy waitress surprised him with her deep, husky voice. Standing there with a stained white apron and a bored look on her face, her pencil was poised to write the information on the pad she held.

'No, the Coke is fine,' he said. He was just killing time.

The black girl shook her head, obviously not pleased that her tip might be hinged on a two-dollar soft drink.

Looking out on the street, he watched two Crescent City cop cars that had pulled up next to each other. The uniformed officers had stepped out and now stood beside their vehicles, deep in conversation, their sunglasses sporting body cams, mounted to the frames. Brion realized he actually owned one of those cameras. He hadn't decided to destroy it just yet. Probably should have. If he survived tonight, he didn't want any evidence of his past crimes.

The young man considered his possibilities. Once he was finished with his business, he could try to blend in and just walk away. If he was caught, he could use his Smith and Wesson 9mm pistol and try to fight his way out. With a clip of sixteen rounds, he could attempt an escape. The cops used Glock 22s with only fifteen rounds, but he'd be down by at least one once he was finished with his task. And possibly he'd be down by seven rounds. And the police had riot weapons that he had no access to. No question he was going to be outgunned. Brion realized there was no correct answer. He had to play it by ear.

And his other option, the toughest one of all. He'd proved to himself he could kill another human being. Could he kill himself? Could he put the gun to his heart and pull the trigger? To decide that you had given all you had and there was no more purpose, that was a tough call. Or were most suicides just a cowardly way out of a bad situation? He realized he might have to face that dilemma.

A siren wailed down the street getting closer and he heard the loud blast of a semi truck's horn, echoing off the buildings. The siren got louder, the shrill whine piercing the neighborhood peace. As the rescue vehicle passed with lights flashing, he put his fingers in his ears, slightly muffling the penetrating noise. He noticed the two cops barely looked up. They were conditioned to tense situations. And maybe he was starting to be conditioned as well.

He'd killed someone. Shot them point blank in the face. Brion had expected to be a little shocked, but it never happened. He didn't feel as bad as he thought he would. Maybe if he'd killed someone who didn't deserve to die, someone who just happened to show up at the wrong time, like . . . he hated to think about it . . . like Nick Martin, the truck driver, maybe then he'd feel bad.

He still wasn't sure who was responsible for Nick Martin's death. He had a strong suspicion, and it wasn't Joseph, Jack, or his father. His father had hinted at it, but young Joseph didn't want to know back then. What boy wants to go through life knowing his dad was a criminal? Possibly a killer? No, his father was in commerce. The acquisition of goods and the selling of these goods. That's what he knew, what he wanted to believe.

But stories crept out. And one night he'd heard Joseph and Pop, on the back stoop of the big house. They'd been drinking Four Roses single-barrel bourbon, quite a bit of it, and the voices got a little loud. He could still remember the brief conversation.

'It was the circumstances, Joe. Nobody saw it coming, nobody planned it. The circumstances.'

'We made it happen, Andy. No one else to blame.'

'Oh, I beg to differ.' His father had sounded somewhat indignant.

He then continued. 'We may have instigated it, but you know damned well that it wasn't our idea.'

'No, it wasn't our idea to get the driver killed. But this guy, Nick Martin, he panicked. And that was our fault, Andy.'

'I blame the guy who hired us and set the whole thing up. That's who I blame,' his father said.

Joseph was quiet for a moment.

'Andy,' he mused, 'think about it, my friend, we could have been sitting in jail if it wasn't for him.'

'And the driver would still be alive.'

'Yeah. I think that sometimes.'

'So do I, Joe. I'm trying to pass the guilt and the pain, OK. I try every day. And sometimes I'm successful and sometimes I'm not. And sometimes I think about just telling them the whole story. Just putting it out there and letting the chips fall where they may. Don't you feel that way too?'

'No. Jesus, no. Don't you ever say that out loud. Jesus Christ, Andy, don't let Jack or anybody else hear you say that.'

And that was the moment his mother grabbed him by the collar and pulled him from his crouch by the door.

'Don't you eavesdrop on your pop and Uncle Joe. What kind of manners did I teach you?'

She lightly slapped him upside his head.

'You march upstairs and get ready for bed and I never want to see you spy on anyone again. Do you understand me, boy?'

He mumbled a 'yes, ma'am', and ran up the stairs. Admonished, embarrassed, chastised, but he'd heard a conversation he played over and over in his head. He twisted and turned the words and phrases and still couldn't figure out exactly what had happened and who was at fault.

Two weeks later, when the two men drank their Four Roses beneath the dark of a New Orleans sky, Joseph's mother was at a prayer meeting, one she hadn't dragged him to. This was a holy meeting of the women of the church, where he understood they talked about the rigors of child-rearing, and the strange behavior of their spouses. And he huddled by the door, sure that this time his mother wouldn't interfere. And again, after several drinks, the conversation drifted back to who was to blame.

It was that night that he heard a name, a situation, and even though he still didn't understand the complexity of the situation, he had more to work with. A very confused young boy went to bed that evening, determined to work it out. It took a long time, but in the last several weeks, he finally thought he had.

It was all supposition. Still, he was pretty damned sure. Just shy of positive, and he was basing tonight on definitely positive. He just wanted a little more assurance. Then he could, in the business world verbiage, pull the trigger. The phrase seemed perfect.

Sipping his beverage through the straw, he was totally unaware that the sweet drink had lost all of its carbonation. It was flat as a pancake. He wanted a moment of freedom, of bliss, where his mind wasn't cluttered with all the crap that was going on. So Brion stared blankly into the afternoon sky, trying to become one with the drifting clouds.

Archer's phone was busier than he could remember. He stopped the buzz with the push of a button. The caller initiated the conversation.

'Detective Archer?'

'I'm here.' Somewhat irritated.

'Officer Ron Ricard calling. I have some information on the man with a tattooed necklace, sir.'

Archer figured him to be former military. No one called him sir. Asshole, idiot, lamebrain, but never sir.

'What do you have, Officer. Believe me, I could use some good information right about now.'

'We have a tattoo artist. Guy has been out sick for two weeks and just got back to work. He didn't get the bulletin, but when he showed up today, he read it. He remembers giving a man the necklace tattoo about eighteen months ago. He's got some records.'

'Where is the parlor?'

'It's N.O. Tattoo on Frenchman Street. His name is Enrico.'

'Officer Ricard, are you on premise?'

'I am.'

'Can you stay there with Enrico? I'll be there in,' he looked at his watch, 'twenty-five minutes, tops.'

'I'll be here, sir. Enrico can give you all the information.'

*   *   *

'Detective, I have maybe the information you need.' The man spoke with a thick Spanish accent.

'Officer Ricard says you may know the man with the thorn-of-crowns tattoo around his neck.'

'No, I don't know him personally, but I obviously spent some time with him. A couple of hours at least to do the art. A beautiful piece. Listen, Mr Archer, we run a clean shop here. We keep our needles clean, we keep our records clean.' The little man, smiled, displaying stained yellow teeth. 'I hope this is the man you are looking for and that I can help you catch such a dastardly criminal, Detective.'

'So you have records on your clients?'

'We want to know if they have any problems, with the work, with any problems in healing, so we stay in touch. Yes. The slightest complaint, and we respond. We are a very responsible business.' He smiled again, selling himself to the law. Archer wondered if he'd been in trouble before.

'And, to be honest with you, Detective Archer, it helps us to resell.'

'Resell?'

'I want their contact so I can resell.' He stared at Archer. 'You understand? Resell?'

Archer shook his head.

'OK, let's say you want a skull and crossbones on your arm or thigh. We give you a skull and crossbones. Very reasonable price, by the way. Six months later, we email you and suggest a small pirate ship or maybe a tattoo of Captain Jack Sparrow to go with your skull. If we give you a heart, we contact you in six months suggesting a bouquet of flowers. You ask for a hula girl, we email you suggesting a palm tree. Resell.'

'Keeping records is good for business.'

'You bet. We resell 15 percent of our clients. A nice, tidy income and all it takes is an email.'

'Tell me about the man with the necklace.'

'A year and a half ago he came to see me. I'm positive it is him. I had done a bracelet for a friend of his, a series of skulls around his wrist. He described the necklace he wanted. Here, I printed out the information.' He handed Archer the papers. 'There is no physical address, but his email and name are right here. And here is the photograph of the necklace. Pretty good work for a custom job if I do say so myself.'

'Did you ever contact or resell this man?'

'Yes. You can see right here we've sent two emails to him. The second email, we sent a graphic of our suggested follow up. It's just good business.'

Archer studied the paper.

'OK, what did you suggest he do? What comes after a crown-of-thorn necklace?'

'Oh, Detective Archer, it was spectacular. When we contacted him again, our suggestion, which he never responded to, was a cross with the body of Jesus Christ, our Lord and Savior hanging from it. We suggested it would be a perfect match, and that we put it right on the center of his chest. Trust me, it would have been a masterpiece.'

Archer glanced at the name and took a deep breath.

Joseph Brion. The name on the paper was Joseph Brion. To his knowledge, Johnny Leroy had only killed one man. An armed robber named André Brion. Probably the same man Leroy had detained at Fox Glass. Now the name Brion popped up again. Joseph. Possibly related to André? Almost assuredly related. So whoever this Joseph was, *if* he was related, the *why* was answered.

Revenge.

If André Brion had done time because he was captured by the security guard Johnny Leroy, if André Brion had been killed by Officer Leroy, then whoever this Joseph Brion was, he killed Officer Johnny Leroy out of vengeance. But now, this tattoo-necklaced suspect was spotted in Algiers. Was he just a participant in the riots, or was there even a more sinister motive?

He did not want to visit Algiers again. Especially not in the evening. There would be fewer rioters but the radical element would still be out. It usually took them two or three nights to finally cease activities. Unless something else set off another spark. He stared at the papers in his hand, lost in his thoughts. Archer's head was seriously about to explode.

TWENTY-NINE

S he opened the paper sack, sorting out the herbs, the plants, and carefully placing the shed snake skin on a table at the back of her shop. Powdering the thin skin would take some extra work.

She saw the small bouquet of dandelions, and wondered why she'd never used the flower and root before. The plant, normally considered a weed, was also a cleansing herb, opening passages. She should have realized there were possibly psychic powers in the spongy yellow flower. The voodoo lady studied the wilting flower and decided to try something new.

Lighting a purity candle, she waited for the flame to heat, then rinsed the roots in cold water, using a towel to dry them. Carefully, Solange held the flowers and rotated the roots over the flame. She turned them over and over like toasting a marshmallow. Like cooking a chicken on a rotisserie. A rich, dark-chocolaty aroma rose from the flame, with hints of spice and vanilla. Careful not to burn the stems, she waited until the roots were a deep dark brown.

Carrying them to the sink, she pulled a cutting board from the drawer and with a sharp paring knife, she cut the roots into half-inch sections, inspecting them to make certain they were roasted all the way through. Satisfied that the roast was complete, she boiled water on the stove. Once the water was bubbling, Solange dropped the root pieces in the roiling liquid and waited for five minutes. As the sections steeped in the water, she considered the effects of what she wanted to accomplish.

If she drank the tea and had no purpose, no goal, the experiment was useless. She was looking for some insight into the past, into the future. Matebo had said the properties of the plant would possibly give her some clairvoyance. She wanted to see into the past, to gaze through the haze of time and view the connection between Johnny Leroy and Joseph Washington.

And that connection, a shared murder, would possibly be enough to offer Archer and give him a lead that would solve his crime. Or at least answer the question 'why'.

She also wanted to see into the future, and find out what the killer had planned next. If anything. The voodoo lady doubted that all her wishes, her desires would be granted, but if she had even a brief moment of insight, it could make a huge difference.

Five minutes passed and she waited two more, savoring the smell. Not her normal herbal tea. She turned off the gas, the jets hissing as the flames died, and Solange poured the water through a sieve, straining out the roots and letting the brown-colored water run into an antique pot. From the pot, she poured the tea into an old ceramic cup, the blue finish cracked due to heat and age.

Quietly she prayed for insight. Into the past, into the future. This was uncharted territory, taking something that was much like a drug. An herb that possibly gave her powers. If the dandelion tea was successful, then the spirits knew what she wanted. To know if Quentin Archer would be successful in his search for the person who killed Johnny Leroy.

They would also know she wanted to look into the future, to see if her mother would recover. She knew better, but there was still the ability to pray for a miracle. And she did so, every morning, noon and night.

As with every potion, as with every spell she cast, with every gris-gris bag that she filled and every voodoo doll she designed, she closed her eyes and prayed that the creation would have its desired effect. She prayed that the dandelion tea would give her some vision. There was always some degree of skepticism, and she often wondered if ministers of competing faiths had the same feelings.

When a Christian minister, a Catholic priest, a bishop or pastor, when a Hindu holy man or a Buddhist monk, when those holy figures prayed, asked for intercession . . . did they have doubts. Did those esteemed men and women ever question whether they were just charlatans? Did they ever wonder if there was any help on the other end? She couldn't be the only practitioner of a faith that sometimes had doubts. Could she?

Asking again for vision, she took a sip of the liquid. Bitter, a little chocolate, the beverage warmed her as it settled in her stomach. Solange moved to the rear of the building, sitting down on her small bed. She closed her eyes and felt the room start to move. Either the tea was tainted or she was about to have an epiphany.

The day dragged on, the sun cooking the heart out of the afternoon. He'd stowed his sleeping bag and backpack behind an old shed at the rear of an empty parking lot. Except for his Smith and Wesson, Brion wanted to be unencumbered. His pistol was the same make and model his father had owned. The gun that André Brion was accused of drawing when Jack Leroy shot him. Seven times.

Joseph wandered the streets, ending up on the banks of the Mississippi. He passed by police on every corner, red-and-blue lights flashing on top of their cars as if that was enough to keep the rioters away. Officers, either sitting in their cars ready to respond at a moment's notice, or standing stoically beside their cruiser, daring someone to hurl a brick, pull a gun or pick a fight.

The riot squads were nowhere to be seen, probably regrouping for tonight's possible unrest. The evidence of last night was everywhere. Shards of plate-glass windows, burned-out stores smelling of wet ash, cars that had been destroyed with chunks of concrete and tire irons. Couches and chairs had been pulled to the street, soaked in kerosene and set ablaze. The pungent odor of a gas-fed fire and the smoky smell of burned upholstery lingered in the air.

Beer bottles, empty bourbon bottles and red plastic cups littered the pavement, and the cheap, hand-lettered cardboard signs were tossed into vacant lots and people's front yards. One of them in big block letters read, *SAVE OUR HOOD*. A couple of mangy dogs roamed that same neighborhood, looking for a kind neighbor who might offer them a bite to eat. Most of the residents were either hiding inside or they had left the neighborhood after last night, preferring to stay somewhere else until the trouble blew over.

On the river, they partied. A paddlewheel steamer moved down the Mighty Miss, a Dixieland band playing standards, and drunken revelers shouting out lyrics to the songs. Across the river, every bar in the French Quarter was packed with people looking for release, a little debauchery, something different from the humdrum existence of their dreary, ordinary lives.

Pop had been shot by a cop, a business colleague. Mom was confined to a wheelchair, imprisoned in her body and her mind. Their son was now hunted, a cop killer who had never explored the party experience. He'd never understood the need to abandon sanity, to wallow in the depths of self-gratification. Joseph Brion raised a middle finger, a 'fuck you' to all of them. His mission was established, his focus laser sharp.

'Excuse me, sir.'

He turned and looked into the pale face of a uniformed police officer.

'Please, raise your hands.'

His eyes traveled down this man's body. Waist level, the belt carried a Taser, heavy steel handcuffs, a baton, pepper spray, a radio and an empty holster. The cop's gun was aimed at his head.

THIRTY

He called Beeman.

'Sarge, I'm going to Algiers. I think this guy is over there. But can we run a check, see where he lives and get a couple squad cars over there, assuming he's in our jurisdiction?'

'If we can find his home, Archer, we'll dispatch immediately. I don't know how many Joseph Brions we're going to find.'

Algiers wasn't a large area, but he was totally unfamiliar with the terrain. Looking for the proverbial needle in a haystack. That was pretty much what he was doing. Finding a black man with a tattoo around his neck. It was a crapshoot. Late afternoon presented a better chance than exploring in the dark of night. And the dark of night was going to be filled with force and fires.

It had come down to homicide detectives actually running traffic control during Mardi Gras, Jazz Fest and other major events. The force was slim and every officer in the department was called on for a number of jobs. At this time, he'd actually prefer traffic control to this case, but there was a cop killer in Algiers and he couldn't let that go.

The riot took place over a two-block area. Walking that area, he figured he would see a number of people. Joseph Brion, if that was his real name, would try to blend in. Ball cap, cargo shorts, a T-shirt and a necklace tattoo. He knew the type. Head down, hands in his pockets. Probably half the pedestrians fit that description minus the tattoo, but Archer had a hunch. A feeling that this guy would try too hard.

He checked his peripherals, walking through the devastated district, sidestepping sharp slabs of glass, the charred remains of vehicles and furniture. There were few pedestrians, most of them staying inside, but the majority of walkers were just like him. Curious onlookers who had come out in the relative safety of daylight. They'd hid in the dark of night, under bedding or crouched in the corner of a room in their home. Now, in the brightness of a new day, they braved the sunlight and assessed the damage, wondering if tonight was going to be another evening of terror.

There were young men, heads hung down, ball caps on backwards. But none of them fit the description. He just had the feeling. And after half an hour's walk, he expanded his area, working his way to the river. Archer studied a hundred people, especially those whose shirts exposed their necks. Sometimes he got a little too close, causing people to stare at him, wondering what his motive was. A man with a sport jacket and a tie, walking through a dangerous neighborhood, where blood had been shed the night before. He was definitely out of place.

The detective felt the tight strap and holster that hugged his chest, some comfort in a strange environment. There was never a threat, but knowing he had protection was somewhat reassuring. And then he could see the Mississippi. And the French Quarter on the other side. Somewhere over there was his small, insignificant apartment and Solange Cordray's voodoo shop and home. The dementia center where her mother lived was just around the bend. He'd become attached to certain areas of the Quarter, and obviously to certain people.

The metal bench was inviting, a chance to sit down and take stock of the situation. A chance to survey the river and survey what a hair-brained idea it was to drive to Algiers to see if he could single-handedly catch the cop killer. An act of desperation. He was sure that the thorn-necklaced man was the murderer, but with a huge squad of New Orleans cops checking everyone out, what did he think one lone homicide detective could accomplish?

Andy Brion, Joseph Washington, and now Joseph Brion, who may have killed Leroy. It was all crazy. Two of them arrested twenty some years ago. Then one of them shot by Johnny Leroy and one killed in a robbery. There was a missing link. Had to be. He didn't have enough information. Somehow they were tied together. As Solange had suggested, there must have been a parallel universe. Another life that no one was aware of. Except maybe for Joseph Brion.

He pulled out his cell phone and called the precinct. In a minute, Beeman answered the phone.

'Sergeant, you gave me the names of the two guys who tried to steal the gold from Fox Glass.'

'No question, Q. Those were the guys.'

'Grand theft. Right?'

'I don't see how it could be anything else.'

'Just a crazy thought. They were charged, right?'

'As far as I could tell. Hell yes. I'm sure they were charged. The story made the paper.'

'OK, were they convicted?'

'What?'

'Were they convicted? Just because someone is charged . . .'

'Well, of course they were convicted. I mean, I didn't go that far but Leroy caught them red-handed. Grand theft. So of course they were.'

'Can you check? And if they were convicted, I need to know how long they served.'

'Archer, whatever it takes. But they were trying to heist thousands of dollars worth of gold. I'm certain they did some serious time.'

'Look, Sarge, I need to know. There are way too many coincidences. Way too many ways that these people are interacting. I want to know what the consequences were. I'm trying to tie up a lot of loose ends, OK?'

'I'll call you back, Archer. Actually it shouldn't take too long.

However, I think on that situation you're on a useless fishing expedition.'

'At least my line's still in the water, Sergeant Beeman. I'm not going to stop until I catch something.'

'Quentin, I've got some other news. Saved the best for last.'

Oh, yeah. There was the question of where did Joseph Brion live.

'We found a Brion family living in the Ninth Ward.'

'And?'

'Ownership in the name of André Brion, Detective. I think we've got him.'

'Great. But I'll bet anything he's over here.'

'We're sending a team to find out. I'll get back to you. In the meantime, be safe and good luck.'

Brion smiled at the officer. A disarming smile, although the policeman didn't seem interested at all in disarming.

'Is this because I'm black and you've got a riot on your hands? Believe me, Officer, I have no interest in the riot. I used to come over here with my father on the ferry and I was just reminiscing and thinking . . .'

'Raise your hands, son.'

'Seriously, sir, I'm not going to be a problem.'

'That tattoo around your neck. The necklace of thorns. I've got orders. You need to raise those hands.'

And then he knew. That's how they were going to convict him. A customized piece of art. Of all the things. He could and did blend into any community in New Orleans, be right at home, fade into the backgrounds like a piece of camouflage. Except for his crown of thorns. Shit. He was so proud of it, admired it every morning in the mirror. And that was going to be his downfall. No, he wasn't going to let that happen. Not yet. Tonight, when the fireworks went off, maybe. But he wasn't quite finished. There was work to be done.

'Sir,' the officer was now reaching for his Taser. He couldn't shoot what appeared to be an unarmed black man. That would spark a riot far worse than the one in progress. So, he'd probably taser him. Except, except that the officer didn't know Joseph wasn't exactly unarmed.

'Officer, I am carrying a gun.'

The policeman squinted, not quite sure he'd heard the man right and not sure what to make of the confession.

'I have a carry license, so it's all aboveboard.'

Of course he didn't, but it sounded right. Defuse the situation.

'You have a gun?'

'I'm going to pull it out.' Brion slowly reached into his pocket. Looking the officer directly in the eye.

'Sir . . .'

'And I'm just going to drop it on the ground.' He imagined this was almost exactly what happened to his father. Jack Leroy told Pop to reach for his weapon and drop it, and as André Brion drew the Smith and Wesson from his pocket, Officer Jack had shot him. Pop would not have pulled a gun on Jack. His business partner, his friend. Joseph was sure of it. But by all appearances, Pop had drawn down on the officer.

'So, please, don't shoot, don't tase me. Let's not start another riot, Officer. Wouldn't be a smart move.' He was pretty sure the cop hadn't radioed the information. The instrument was still on his belt. That was the one positive thing in this interaction. Protocol said he should radio for backup. This was a maverick who thought he could pull it off by himself.

He pulled the Smith and Wesson from his pocket with his right hand, his left hand held high in surrender.

The police officer had one hand on his Taser and held his Glock 22 in the other when Joseph fired his first shot. The round went through the policeman's throat and he dropped the Glock. Brion saw the shock and recognition on the man's face. The second bullet caught him in the forehead and he staggered, blindly trying to fire the Taser before he stumbled and crumpled to the ground.

And now Joseph felt truly sorry. Devastated. The others had deserved to die. Evil men, the two of them. This man was just doing his job. Some average guy who was just doing what he was told. Leaning down, he ripped off the small body cam from the officer's lapel. Now he owned two of them for all the good it would do him. For all the good it would do the police.

Brion walked briskly, just as he had when he'd shot Leroy. Not too fast, but fast enough to distance himself from the dead body.

This time was different. An innocent person had been in the line of fire, and Joseph felt the hot tears running down his cheeks. Pop most assuredly wouldn't be happy.

THIRTY-ONE

She'd been with Ma when she took the powerful dementia drugs. Sometimes her mother was delusional, and often she would hallucinate, shouting out incoherent diatribes. It was often as if she spoke in tongues although Solange couldn't make out the language. In lucid moments, Ma would tell her it wasn't the medication or dementia. It was just the spirits speaking to her, but the doctors assured Solange that those side effects were common. The medical professionals didn't outwardly believe in spiritual intervention, so they gave no credence to the older lady's crazy dreams. And as her condition worsened, they took her off the medication. The drugs had made her irrational, not the voodoo spirits.

Solange had never taken drugs. Never even smoked a joint. Her ex-husband had experimented, but she'd never been tempted. Not even pain medication, so the feeling she was now experiencing was unexpected. It was not so much dizziness, but a sensation as if she was floating. Not like when the spirits used her to speak, shape-shifting her petite figure to become their spokesperson, but almost a carefree, effortless feeling of flying. She could look down and see herself, huddled on the bed. And the euphoric sense almost released her from her mission. This entire experience, the dandelion tea, the prayers for clairvoyance, all were to lead to a better understanding of who killed Officer Johnny Leroy. Matebo told her this should work, told her that the potent tea would help give her clairvoyance, and she was enjoying the freedom, maybe a little too much. But she was still unsure how to find the answer, the vision the . . .

And then she saw it. Floating above the scene, she watched the semi truck turn down the winding road, never meant for an eighteen-wheeler. In a dream, you might see a scene like this. You might wake up and try to understand the reason it came to you. This wasn't a dream. Solange was positive of that. She was wide-awake, alert as she had ever been, and yet the vision was totally real. Over twenty years ago, but as current as today.

She watched the vehicle as it braked, dodged into the left lane, then jerked back to the right, sliding off the road into a pine forest. The truck tumbled down the embankment and slid to a stop. It happened so fast, maybe in thirty seconds, and all the while she considered the circumstances. The driver might have been high or drunk, spinning the wheel, going left, going right. It could have been a blown tire, or a malfunctioning steering system, but she was certain there was nothing in front of him, nothing behind him. His erratic driving was unexplained. Almost as if another vehicle was heading toward him, taunting him, daring this Nick Martin to meet him face to face. And Martin twisted and turned, yet there was nothing.

From her perch, her high-in-the-sky perspective, she had a bird's-eye view of the entire area. The driver, Nick Martin, defi-nitely drove erratically, wildly over the two-lane road. No reason, no excuse. She knew he'd died in the crash, and as far as she could see, no one was responsible for his crazy antics except for him. The moment was brief and when she silently asked for a replay, it was granted. She viewed the entire scene again.

She noticed a brief flash of light on the windshield of the truck, as if the moon or a spotlight was reflecting off the glass, but other than that, it was cast in stone. What had happened, had happened. No seconds, no revision of history. There was clairvoyance, yet no new evidence to offer to Detective Archer.

She would offer him her vision, but there was no new revela-tion. No 'ah-ha' moment where she could uncover the killer.

And as soon as the vision had come to her, it disappeared. She sat there, bathed in sweat. She knew everything and knew nothing. Not much good to a man who made his living solving crimes. And she so wanted to give him some new information.

Twenty minutes after the shooting, after Joseph Brion had walked away from the officer's body, Archer got a call on his cell phone.

'Q, where the hell are you.'

'I'm in Algiers, Josh. I'm determined to find this guy.'

'Be careful, my friend. Message just came in. Somebody shot an officer down by the river.'

Archer paused. He was by the river. A little scary.

'In Algiers?'

'They found the body about ten minutes ago. Bulletin says it was current. Maybe twenty minutes ago. For God's sake, be careful.'

'The second officer in a week.'

'Yeah. My guess is a daylight rioter.'

'Josh, I'm not wearing a uniform. I mean . . .'

'Sport coat, tie, glancing over your shoulder. It shouldn't take anyone too long to figure out you're a cop.'

'Good point.' He thought about losing the jacket and tie. But the tie was uniform, so . . .

'So, what do you think is going to come from this? You're going to stumble on the killer with the necklace? Out of the blue? Come on, Detective. You wandering around that cesspool is not good police work.'

'We've got people working every angle, Josh. I could sit back and let all of those ideas come together and do nothing. Or I can come here and hope this guy is still in Algiers. Hope that he has some other business to accomplish. Don't you ever back up against a brick wall? Figure out you've had enough? Don't you ever decide to get a little more involved? Come out swinging?'

'Right now, Algiers is the most treacherous place in New Orleans, Quentin. As you're standing there. I really think we need you back on the mainland. Listen to me, *amigo*. You are in some grave danger.'

'Tonight, maybe. But right now, I'm going to continue to look.'

'Twenty minutes ago, someone shot blue, Archer. You do understand that? Officer down. The numbers are stacking up, man. Don't be next, OK? You're one of the good guys.'

'Eyes wide open, Josh. It's relatively calm.'

'It's not calm. Did you hear me? Twenty minute ago, Q. Believe me, you are a target.'

He knew that. Didn't want to believe it. Invincible, bulletproof. However, he'd lost Denise. He'd assumed she was bulletproof as well and that hadn't worked out so well.

'I'm going to find him, Josh. I'm out of ideas. I'll get back to you once that's accomplished.'

'Good luck, Q. And don't get involved in this evening's festivities. Promise me you won't do that.'

'No riot gear, no protection, Josh. I'm not the brightest guy in the world, but I won't go near the riot. I promise you.'

'Our numbers are dwindling, Quentin. We can't afford to lose any more.'

He walked along the bank, staring at the muddy water until he saw the commotion up ahead. An ambulance and two police cars, lights flashing. Jogging, he reached the scene and recognized Detective Rory James.

'Detective James, is this the officer that was shot?' He motioned to the ambulance.

'Detective Q. It is. We're just wrapping up. He had his Glock and Taser out so he was either trying to defend himself or arrest someone.'

'Either of them fired?'

'No. Didn't appear to be.'

'And no sign of—'

'I've got some men out scouring the area, but there's not much here. Most people are laying low until this thing settles down. I sincerely doubt we'll find anyone who saw the shooting, and if we do, well, this isn't a very sympathetic neighborhood when it comes to the police. Especially when it involves a white officer.'

The two men watched the white-and-gold EMS vehicle with the gold fleur-de-lys on the side as it slowly drove away. Another officer down. Homicide's worst nightmare.

'What are you doing over here?'

'Working Johnny Leroy's murder.'

'Over here? That was Bayou St John, right?'

'Story is the man who killed him was spotted at the riot last night.'

'You don't think—'

'That my guy is your guy? I don't think much anymore. Anything is possible, Detective. Who was the officer?'

'Young guy, Bob Durand. On the force for two years.'

'Chances are slim it was Leroy's killer, but there have been a lot of strange things involving this case. We're looking for a black man, fond of cargo shorts, a baseball cap on backwards and a pistol, apparently in his pocket.'

'Hundreds of those guys down here right now.'

'Apparently he has one distinguishing characteristic. He has an original crown-of-thorns tattoo around his neck. A necklace.'

'One of a kind?'

'I talked to the artist who designed it. He says the shooter is a man named Joseph Brion.'

'Any lead on exactly where he might be?'

'No, just here in Algiers. It appears he lives in the Ninth, and we've got a team who is going there now. But my guess is he's watching this riot from the sidelines. I would imagine he's left his home for good. He's over here now, just waiting. I just don't know what he has planned next.'

James gazed out at the river, the distraction of a mostly peaceful body of water flowing gently down to the ocean. He wiped the sweat from his brow.

'Maybe he had this killing planned next. It would be nice if they'd give us one day off, Quentin. Everybody just take a break. Don't kill somebody today. Don't *plan* on killing somebody today. Everybody take a deep breath.'

Archer nodded.

'You're going back to the office?'

'After we've canvassed the area. I doubt we'll turn up anything but you know the drill.'

'Rory, you see a kid with a tattooed necklace, crown of thorns, call backup. You'll probably need it.'

THIRTY-TWO

She relived the moment behind her eyelids, squeezing them tight. She'd seen something, sensed something, yet she couldn't find it. The scene had been played for her so she would have some sense of the killing, the death of the young man. She was too blind to know what it was. Ma wouldn't understand, and Matebo was too far down the river this late in the afternoon.

The old man had once told her that clairvoyance, seeing into the past and future, had to be accompanied by wisdom. The wisdom to interpret the vision. And she tried to apply that to the casting of bones, the reading of tarot cards, even tea leaves or images in candle flames. And she often did interpret the message. She had the wisdom to find the answer, the solution. But this time was different. She'd been given the entire vision. As if her own film company shot the complete episode and handed her the reel. The truck, the road, the forest of pine trees. How was it she could read pieces of bones on a canvas map, very mumbo-jumbo with no specific direction, yet when given the movie version with every detail clearly defined, she couldn't figure it out?

There was a flash of light. Brilliant, she recalled. And the flash was brief, during a nighttime scene. She was surprised she could see everything so clearly during a dark evening. The scene was so clean, so vivid. Had the moon been that bright, or was this just a cinematic effect. To let her see the vision? But that bright spark on the windshield, as if the glass had briefly reflected a golden fire. Then as the truck twisted and turned, the flash was gone. It all happened so fast, yet the impact was so strong. She shouldn't have been surprised. Death happened in an instant. One moment you were there, and the next moment you weren't.

Solange breathed deeply and opened her eyes. The loud beating of a bass drum and the shrill blare of horns from the street told her a funeral procession was marching by. Possibly the spirits giving a nod to the passing of the truck driver many years ago. She walked to the entrance and opened the creaking door.

Four pall-bearers carried the polished wood coffin, and a ten-piece, red-and-gold uniformed brass band trailed behind, playing a mournful version of St Louis Blues. The trombones and wailing trumpets echoed off the brick-and-stucco shops, their metallic harmonies telling a tale of despair. Leading the parade was the professional mourner, decked out in a top hat, long-tailed coat and cane. He waved the wand, encouraging the onlookers to join him in singing.

> *Been to da gypsy, to get my fortune tole*
> *Cause I'm most wile bout my jelly roll.*
> *Ashes to ashes, dust to dust*
> *If my blues don't get you*
> *Then my grievin' must.*

Without thinking she closed her eyes and said a prayer that the deceased would pass peacefully into the next life. Her intercession with the spirit world. It was part of her makeup, in her blood. Somewhere in the distant future, someone would test her DNA and shout out, 'Voodoo. She is part voodoo.' There would be a celebration, and maybe even Ma would be there, celebrating that Matebo was right. Her connection to the spirit world would never end. Never, ever end. The spirits wouldn't allow it.

Joseph Brion spent fifteen dollars, buying a cheap souvenir T-shirt that sported the slogan *New Orleans Voodoo* with a smiling skull dead center. It didn't matter what it said. He needed a piece of cloth he could tie around his neck, and the extra-large shirt did the trick. He told the questioning clerk it was for his extra-large brother-in-law. And it tied around his neck like a scarf. He was almost embarrassed that he was afraid to show off his unity confirmation. The necklace he'd designed to show how close he was to family and friends. Right now, it was safer to hide the ink, so the shirt performed the task. Occasionally a very subtle breeze stirred and blew the cloth up, but he was relatively sure no one would notice.

Timing was everything now. It was still three and a half hours before the appointed time. His meeting was scheduled at seven, and even the threat of the riot wasn't going to stop this summit.

Now that another officer had been killed, they'd be scouring the streets, the sidewalks and back alleys even more thoroughly. Brion was fairly positive they wouldn't have a description of him on that shooting, but security being what it was, you never knew. There could have been a witness, there could have been a camera.

Three squad cars pulled up to the shotgun house. The narrow wooden home, partly hidden by tall grass and weeds, was deep in the Ninth, and nobody liked to make calls in the Lower Ninth. Four officers stepped out, two staying in their car in case the suspect tried to make a run for it. Three approached the porch, one headed for the rear of the home. Warily they climbed the steps, afraid the rotting wood would collapse, and afraid of what might be on the other side of the door.

The three officers activated their body cams, and one knocked loudly on the door with his baton. The other two stood there, Glocks pointed at the entrance.

'Joseph Brion, open the door. Police.'

There was no response.

'One more try, Sam.'

'Open up, Joseph, we've got the house surrounded.' He beat on the old wooden door again, the battering baton sounding almost like pistol shots.

Finally, it creaked open, and the officers were looking at a small, wizened lady in a wheelchair. Curled up in her lap was a gray cat. A far cry from the cop killer they'd expected to confront. Her sunken eyes took them in, obviously noticing the drawn pistols.

'He's not here. Went to help his pa.'

'Can you tell us where he went?' Their eyes swept the living area.

'Wherever his pa is. And that I couldn't tell you.'

'Ma'am, we'll have to come in and check the premises.' He flashed a warrant, and she nodded.

'You come ahead.' She rolled the chair out of their way. 'He's not here and I sincerely doubt he's ever coming back.'

They stepped over the faded welcome mat, walking into the house with modest furnishings and sparse decorations.

'You,' Sam pointed to the smaller of the three, 'take the kitchen. Kevin, the lady's room. I'll do Joseph's room.'

Down the hall, one door to the right. The suspect's iron frame bed was made tight, almost like a cot in an army barracks. Sam had been a Marine and recognized the style, sheets and bedspread pulled taut. A nightstand stood by the bed and one chest of drawers against the wall. The only decoration in the room was a faded poster tacked to the wall. The artwork featured a clown riding a huge elephant. The ad for Ringling Brothers Barnum and Bailey Circus boasted *200 years of circus in America.*

Sam pulled the single drawer on the nightstand open and for a moment, stopped breathing.

'Guys, come in here.'

The two officers walked in, looking into the drawer where Sam was pointing.

'Jesus. Sunglasses and a cam. I think we've got our man.'

'No,' Sam said. 'We know who he is, but we haven't got him.

He could be anywhere and could be killing another officer as we speak.'

THIRTY-THREE

A rcher's phone rang and he answered immediately.
'Archer, it's Beeman.'
'Sergeant, you know we've got another officer down, here in Algiers? A Bob Durand.'

'I do. Detective James has a team out there. Any ideas?'

'I'm pretty sure we've got Leroy's killer over here. Could be him.'

'And we've got sunglasses and a body cam from Brion's house. I'm certain we'll have proof they belonged to Leroy.'

'Great news.'

'I don't think there's much doubt about who Officer Leroy's killer is. We had him in lock-up several years ago for battery. That picture, minus the necklace, is now circulating. Hopefully someone will recognize him. Now the idea is to bring him in. Damn, be careful. This guy is one dangerous dude.'

'So we've got a positive.' Archer swallowed a bite of his chicken sandwich from the Dry Dock Cafe on the point. 'I think almost everyone in Algiers is looking for him, Sarge. And I think there's a good chance he killed the officer here. If this Officer Durand recognized Brion and approached him, it just makes sense that Brion shot him.'

'If that's true, this guy has two cop killings under his belt. There's no reason to think he won't go for three. Things are fucked up, Q. It's like we're sitting ducks for this guy.'

Archer took a sip of his coffee in the paper cup. Sitting on a bench by the river he realized he had no appetite for the sandwich and onion rings. Things were just a little too crazy at the moment. As the Sergeant had said, things were 'fucked up'.

'Sarge, do you have anything else?'

'Yeah, and it's not going to make much sense. We did some digging on the two thieves who tried to steal the gold at Fox Glass.

André Brion and Joseph Washington. I don't know why you asked the questions about if they were charged and convicted, but the answer to the first half is yes, they were charged. We were able to find some records that indicated they were arrested and booked that night.'

'Sounds right.'

'So, it should also sound right that they would be arraigned the next morning. Agreed?'

'Agreed.'

'They were. They both pled not guilty.'

'No surprise there.'

'Not guilty, that's never a surprise. The surprise, however, is that there was no conviction that we can find.'

'What?'

'No conviction. We can't find any record that the two of them ever did any time for the crime.'

Archer was quiet for a moment. 'That's impossible. That should have been grand theft. It must just be a result of poor record-keeping back then. I mean, it sounds like everything was done by the book.'

'Quentin, you asked the question. You must have some suspicions.'

'Not really. There were just too many situations where these people intersected. I wanted to start at the beginning and get all the information. The beginning seemed to be the attempted gold robbery. I didn't expect this.'

'I don't have the answer, Detective.'

'It makes no sense. Leroy caught them red-handed. Keep looking. They didn't just walk away from this crime.'

'Stranger things have happened, but we're checking into it, Quentin. I don't know if the answer has ties to the murder of Leroy or not, but we're digging. You found out, it's all paper shoved into file folders. Christ, I don't know how the old timers found anything.'

Archer remembered. Going to the precinct with his father in Detroit and hearing the clacking of manual typewriters, the banging and ringing of the carriages as detectives typed up their reports. He remembered the thick, stale smell of cheap tobacco from smoldering unfiltered cigarettes and what appeared to a young boy to be miles of metal file cabinets. The entire scene had seemed romantic to him. A total departure from his childhood at six years old. This was real adult stuff. The atmosphere was heady.

Every desk had a stained coffee mug, half full of full-strength caffeine, and every desk had five or six manila file folders piled on them. No keyboards, no screens, no immediate background checks. He'd heard his dad say it, and he'd witnessed it. Hard police work. And no voodoo. If his father knew that he was relying on the spirit world for some of his information—

'It's just tough since we've never put all this information on digital files. Digitizing old records never made priority status. Too few officers were working too many cases in the here and now. There was never time to transfer information. Still isn't.'

'Sarge, when we get up to full capacity, and we have funding for all our projects, including raises for everyone—'

'Yeah, when pigs fly.'

'When that happens, we ought to look into that. Digital files.'

'I'll be sure and bring that up to them, Detective. I'll tell them it was your suggestion. I'm sure it will then be a high priority.'

'Until then, Sarge, I'm looking for Joseph Brion. My number one priority right now.'

'Find that son of a bitch and make our lives a lot easier.'

He got up from the metal bench, spotted a trash container down the way and pitched most of the sandwich, all the onion rings and the rest of his coffee. Find this guy, this Joseph Brion, arrest him, get him in the New Orleans jail and then worry about a decent meal.

He'd seen this happen in Detroit. A gangster, a high-profile criminal would walk away from a charge due to intimidation of a witness. Somebody would threaten their family, or they would suffer an unfortunate accident. More than once a witness would disappear or end up dead. It was hard to convict someone when no one would help the prosecution. But these two petty thieves had been caught red-handed. There was no question they had paid for the crime and Archer seriously doubted that they had muscle on the outside to intimidate Leroy. That just didn't seem likely. So where was the information?

He felt certain that it was just sloppy record-keeping. Beeman would call him back after a thorough check and let him know the charges and convictions.

In the meantime, he needed to walk and take advantage of the daylight. He was searching for a cop killer and someone with a tattooed necklace of thorns. The constant ringing of his phone kept distracting him from that mission.

'Archer.'

'Quentin, do you have a minute?'

Solange sounded as if she worried she was intruding and it couldn't be further from his truth. Archer found that her voice, no matter what the message, seemed to calm him down.

'Sure. What have you got?'

'You're going to think I'm crazy.'

'I'm the one going crazy.'

'Here's what I know. Or I think I know. Nick Martin died almost twenty-six years ago.'

'In a truck accident. Officer Johnny Leroy was the first one on the scene,' Archer said.

'Nick Martin was on a backwoods road,' Solange continued, 'where he was going, I have no idea, but his driving was erratic. He was swerving right, then left, finally going hard right and the truck tipped and slid down a slope.'

'Could have been,' Archer said.

'I'm fairly certain that's exactly what happened. But it appeared that someone was either chasing him, or heading right toward him. Please, don't ask me how I know this, but it is very clear to me that either the driver was high on something, or trying to avoid an accident.'

'So you saw the incident? Twenty-six years ago?'

'Please, Quentin.'

'You saw someone chasing him or heading toward him?'

'There was no one chasing him. No one in front of him. So, I assume he was either high or drunk. However, I did observe—'

'So you *did* see this accident?'

'Well, of course I didn't see it in real time. I would have been four years old. But I can tell you there was a brilliant reflection on the truck's windshield, just before the truck went off the road.'

'Something blinded the driver?'

'I thought the same thing,' she said. 'There was a glare on the windshield. I don't know if that added to the confusion.'

'It was in the evening,' Archer said.

'Dark night, but I had the impression there was some light,' she said. 'Either the moon, or maybe a city nearby, the lights casting a halo. Regardless, a light bounced off the windshield and Nick Martin turned into the trees and the truck slid down the hill.'

Archer mulled over the information. He wasn't at all sure how it fit into Leroy's murder. If anything, it seemed to muddy the already murky waters. The only thing that worked was that Leroy had arrived on the scene first. He was the one who would have radioed the information back to the precinct. Leroy would have had first access to the cab, the body, the empty trailer.

And with the record-keeping back then, it could take days to find if there were still files regarding the incident.

THIRTY-FOUR

There was an act on Jackson Square that defied any other act he'd seen. Joseph knew from an early age that he loved sleight of hand. He loved tricks that baffled his mind. From the steps of the Square he watched a magician sawing a woman in two. He saw illusionists levitating people right in front of him. Then there was the floating crystal ball. Oh, he knew they were tricks. But his curiosity demanded that it be satisfied. Magic was a hoax but he wanted to find the solution and with much research he figured out almost all of the illusions. It was never his intention to perform the acts. Brion never pictured himself as the illusionist. He just wanted to know that he was as smart as the performer.

He knew that two people were used in the sawing trick. One was the head, the other the feet, and he figured out how they stuffed half their bodies into either side of the magician's contraption. The levitating woman had to be done with a metal device that was hidden by the conjurer. As he stood there, running his hoop over the floating girl's body, he simply followed the hidden contours of the S shaped bend in the metal. With a little bit of concentration, he could figure out almost anything.

There was one deception that confused him, baffled him, made him doubt his own sanity. The magician walked in front of the concrete steps pulling a red wagon. He was dressed in ordinary street clothes, jeans and a T-shirt and he topped off the outfit with a tuxedo jacket. Equipped with a microphone and a loud speaker attached to his belt, he began a conversation with his audience. Joseph and Pop were immediately taken in with his smooth talk and gentle persuasion.

'Ladies and gentlemen, it takes most people years to build their dreams. To build their castles in the sky. In many cases, wasted time, trying to achieve the impossible.'

He stood there, the statue of Andrew Jackson in the background, looking out at the sparse crowd sitting on the cement rows.

'Whatever you want, you can have it now. Now, not in twenty years. Not when you are old and retired. Tell me something you want. A vacation, a dream home, a pony?'

Reaching into his wagon he pulled out a package of canvas and aluminum poles. In a matter of seconds, he had created a sizable tent with a red velvet curtain hanging in front. The audience applauded, the rapid creation of the tent being a pretty surprising feat in itself. The magician bowed, and peaked behind the curtain. He nodded and pulled the material aside. A small white pony with a bushy brown mane came strolling out. Joseph's jaw dropped.

The magician petted the miniature animal, held out his hand with sugar cubes for the horse to eat, then slapped the pony on its flank and the horse walked back into the tent.

'Do you need a couple of thousand dollars to pay the rent? You should have invested in my magic tent.'

With a flourish, the magician once again looked behind the red curtain, then pulled it aside. Out pranced the pony, this time harnessed and pulling a small wagon. Bundles of bills were inside, stacked high. The man reached for one package and tore the paper binding. Walking to the edge of the seats, he suddenly tossed the money into the crowd, and people scrambled to pick up what appeared to be loose one dollar bills.

Joseph remembered the magician kept this up for twenty minutes.

'Do you want a car?' Out came a miniature clown car, a midget clown driving and waving to the assembled.

For his final presentation, the magician pulled aside the curtain and reached inside, his hand returning with two huge, overblown tickets to the Cole Brothers Circus that was coming to town the next week. The pieces of cardboard were as big as Joseph was.

He turned to Pop and hugged him, but the tickets weren't for them. The performer walked up the steps and stopped one row from the father and son. He grabbed a little girl and her mother and presented them with tickets to the event. At a young, tender age, Joseph knew the whole show had been a sham, staged, to advertise the circus. Even the fake dollar bills were nothing but a printed advertisement for the circus. But how that man made things appear still baffled him. For months he played various scenarios in his mind, eventually discounting every one of them. There was no way that the magic tent could produce what it did.

He and Pop didn't ever go to the circus because of 'business' obligations. Joseph remembered thinking that Pop didn't really want to take him to the circus. It would be a self-defeating act. Pop had built the circus up as a once in a lifetime event, with the elephants, the big cats and the high-wire acts. It would be an experience that could never be replicated, and everything that he and Pop did after that would pale in comparison. So he deduced that his father made an excuse. And the small times they had together had more impact, more importance. The circus remained just that unattainable dream, and Pop would create his own series of circus acts, like the bands, the acrobats, the musicians and magicians at Jackson Square. And as a young boy who loved his father, that was OK. It was still him and Pop.

But Joseph never forgot the man who made things appear out of thin air. The magician, who made a pony and a car appear from nowhere.

It was years later that he discovered how his father played magician in *his* line of work. Making things appear out of thin air. Pop was able to perform his magic on an even grander scale.

Joseph ran his own small-time businesses, ran his cadre of minions, bagmen and drug runners who did his dirty work, but he never measured up to the size of his pop's short-time business venture. Pop had perfected the system. Pop and his cohorts were the Jackson Square magician, on steroids. For a brief time. Until the truck driver broke his neck. He'd listened to the conversations, late at night, as Pop and Joseph Washington drank their whiskey and tongues loosened up. He heard stories he didn't understand.

Joseph Brion became more and more sceptical about his father's moral compass. And as an impressionable youth, he wondered if there was really a need for that compass. A man had to do what a man had to do. To support himself, his family, to make his mark in the world. He heard contrition in his father's conversations. He detected a note of sorrow, but for the brief time that Pop was bringing in the bucks, making a life for his young family, Joseph knew that André Brion was proud. Proud that he'd found a way to live the good life. For the brief time that he was financially sound, his father had stood with his head held high. After the fall, there was a lot of head shaking and tears. The Lower Ninth was the lowest anyone could go.

THIRTY-FIVE

He felt certain the man with the tattooed necklace was down here. Parading around Algiers. By now that man knew he was being hunted because of his necklace. Archer felt confident that the young officer shot to death had identified Joseph Brion, and Brion had shot him to stop an arrest. If that was true, the killer could have gone to ground or tried to hide the necklace.

To go to ground meant he was in a safe house or hovering in a restaurant or bar, hiding in a corner. He may have friends in Algiers, but Archer had a strong feeling the man was still wandering. He was waiting for something, and cowering in a public place didn't seem to fit his profile. He needed to be out and about, free at a moment's notice. The detective just wished he knew what Brion was waiting for. He needed to find this guy, and stop the bloodshed.

So, in the oppressive heat of a New Orleans September, Archer watched for young men who wore excessive clothing. Anyone who wore a jacket – there were none – or a scarf – there were none; anyone with any sign of covering up the neck, he wanted to confront them. But the heat and humidity prohibited the outdoor population from wearing any extra layers.

Another idea crossed his mind. He'd been intrigued by the truck accident involving Nick Martin. In the initial investigation, there had been a mention of seven or eight other truck hijackings and the fact that maybe the mob was behind the robberies. Archer had read stories about the Mafia godfather Carlos Marcello. The chieftan was rumored to have been involved in President John Kennedy's assassination thirty years before the hijackings, but Marcello ran New Orleans and the French Quarter with an iron fist when the trucks were robbed. The truck thefts sounded like a mob operation. He hadn't yet heard how the trucks were robbed, but Solange's version of Martin's accident was intriguing. Precisely what she saw, or how she saw it, eluded him but he somehow believed her. She'd had a glimpse of Martin's last ride. While the young man could have been under the influence of substance abuse, the wild, chaotic ride sounded more like he was evading another vehicle. Yet the voodoo lady had said that she saw no other vehicle.

Since Sergeant Beeman was insisting on being at his disposal, he may as well take him up on the offer. He dialed Beeman's cell.

'Archer, tell me you've got Joseph Brion.'

'I wish, but it's not a one-hour TV show, Sarge. What I have is another question.'

'Give it to me.'

'I've been thinking about Nick Martin's death. There was talk about several other hijackings during that same time period. I never heard how those trucks were stopped and then robbed. I mean, what reports did the truck drivers volunteer? Supposedly there were seven or eight robberies, so there has to be some information, right?'

'I'll get right on it, Q. Again, we're dealing with reports done on typewriters and stuffed into files, twenty-five, twenty-six years ago. Documents from then weren't catalogued properly, and some have been damaged or destroyed. With everything we are experiencing, it could take a while. Give me some time, OK?'

'Time is one thing we don't have, Sergeant. I also need to know what kind of time Washington and Brion served for the attempted gold heist. We've got to speed things up, Sarge. If this guy kills someone else, we are all in for some serious hell.'

'Not that we aren't there now, Detective.'

* * *

The late afternoon sun cast shadows on the street outside her shop. The funeral had passed by an hour ago. Now the traffic was pedestrian tourists who wanted to buy a souvenir voodoo doll, a gris-gris bag with no concern what it would do. Thank God for the tourists, but they dumbed down the faith.

She had no idea what they did with the knick-knacks they purchased, and she often told the purchasers that without the prayers, without the knowledge of the gods, the items they bought were useless. Still, she sold thousands of items a year. People wanted to participate in the voodoo culture. If voodoo worked for someone, it could work for them.

Solange went to the sink and splashed water on her face. She'd been through a self-induced out-of-body experience. She'd said prayers to all the spirits she could conjure up. Then she played voodoo queen to the tourists. And she'd tried to convey her concerns to the detective. She was exhausted. As she did every hour of every day, she wished that Ma would come back. She wished that Ma would give her infinite wisdom, the confidence she sometimes lacked.

But it always struck her that Ma was probably as insecure as she was. She put on a strong front, telling her little girl 'don't be afraid', when the older lady was probably the one who was afraid. There was some comfort in thinking that. No one had all the answers. The successful were the ones who forged ahead anyway, assuming the answers would come. True strength was the ability to continue on. Have faith that there was a light at the end of the tunnel. You had to lead people through that tunnel, full of bluff and bravado. And when you finally emerged into the blinding sunshine, when you saw that proverbial light, you would turn to the faithful and say, 'See? I told you so.'

Small groups of men and a few women stood on street corners, smoking tobacco, smoking weed. Shuffling their feet, kicking aluminum cans, candy wrappers and empty cigarette packs to the gutter, they milled in growing numbers. Much too early for full-scale riot mode, they watched squad cars, cops on every corner, glowering at the officers with a sinister look in their eyes. Later tonight, under the influence of drugs, alcohol or peer pressure, these people would be a lot more confident. A lot more boisterous.

A lot more dangerous. Later tonight there would be outright rebellion. Algiers would again be burning.

Archer watched, considering where Joseph Brion might be. Any of these corners would be a perfect hiding place, mixing with the masses. There were plenty of young men with caps, with wool hats pulled low on their foreheads, some wearing green army fatigues, some with khaki cargo shorts. He could be anywhere, and it was probably a useless search. Still, nothing else seemed to be working.

His phone rang and he grabbed it, hopeful for any information at all.

'Archer, it's Beeman.'

'What have you got, Sarge?'

'It's what I don't have. For whatever reason, it appears that Washington and Brion didn't do time after being arrested at Fox Glass.'

'No one could prove that it was grand theft? Attempted grand theft?'

'No. I say it appears, because the reports are sketchy. You'll have to read them for yourself. It appears that Matt Fox refused to press charges.'

'What?'

'That's what the report says. The case was dropped when Matthew Fox refused to press charges. At that time.'

'What does that mean? Somebody got to him.'

'Could be. But the report says that he refused to press charges *at that time*.'

'He was hedging? Maybe he'd press charges later?'

'It's cryptic. I mean, I've seen charges pressed close to the date of the statute of limitations. Charges pressed just before some criminal thinks he or she is going to get away with their crime. But this one I don't understand.'

'What are the limitations on grand theft?'

'The DA has four years to charge someone.'

'So Fox refuses to press charges, and that gives him four years to decide if he wants to nail these two guys.'

'It appears that's the case,' Beeman said. 'The reason it's sketchy is that we don't know for sure if he did press charges. Two or three years later possibly he tried to reopen the case. We haven't found any record of that happening yet, but he left himself open. Maybe they leaned on him, got him to back off, but why didn't he just fold? Instead, he says he won't press charges "at this time".'

'You haven't helped at all, you realize that, right?'

'If you figure out why Fox backed off,' Beeman paused, 'you might be closer to your solution.'

'It was twenty-six years ago, so it might mean nothing at all. I just find it strange that when I interviewed Fox, he had no recollection of the incident. I can't believe that the department didn't give him a hard time about that. We responded, these two guys were wrapped in tape, they were put in jail and the next morning they were arraigned. It sounds like it should have been a slam dunk. They attempted a robbery, and we need convictions, it's what we live for. Our entire job is built on how many arrests and convictions we have. Yet, there was no prosecution. Without a charge . . .'

'No question about it. Fox should have been all over this case.'

Archer pictured the situation. Private security officer Johnny Leroy, in some remote location inside Fox Glass, with two suspects wrapped in packing tape. The police show up and he announces the reason that he's bound these suspects. Washington and Brion are arrested, taken to headquarters and put in jail, and charged the next morning. Obviously, they plead not guilty.

All of a sudden, the business owner, Matt Fox, decides not to press charges. But he reserves the right to press charges within the next four years. It made no sense. Unless one of the suspects had threatened Fox. Yet if that had happened, Fox would have backed off. He wouldn't have kept open the threat of pressing charges sometime in the next four years. If his life and the safety of his family had been threatened, the business owner would have walked away entirely. But no, he kept his options open. Why?

'So after four years, the DA can't prosecute, right?'

'As I read it,' Beeman said.

'And if the criminals had walked off with the gold and no charges had been brought, the gold would be theirs free and clear.'

'Louisiana law, Detective.'

For some criminals, it paid to take their chances.

'We're still pouring over records, Q. I'll get back to you.'

A roar went up in the next block. Archer could see smoke and watched as a straw scarecrow in a police uniform went up in flame. Nothing worth an arrest at this point, but the troublemakers were starting a little early. He checked his watch. Not that it meant anything, but there were six hours until the newly imposed curfew. Today could be explosive.

'Call me, Sarge. I've got a feeling I'm going to be here for a while.'

THIRTY-SIX

Time moved slowly. Not if you had plotting to do, then it raced by. If you schemed and planned, time rushed along. But if you set your clock, waiting to meet a final antici-pated event, then seconds turned into minutes, the minutes turned into hours, and the hours seemed to take forever. He'd checked his watch fifty times and it was still several hours before the appointed time. He just wanted it to be over. Right now. He was tired of waiting.

Brion was pleased by the early arrival of the crowd. He needed some distraction, and it would have been nice to know they were there for the common cause, but he was a realist. He knew they weren't all there because of the cause. He'd studied several essays on the anatomy of a race riot, and learned that the second-day revelers were often there just because they wanted to rumble. Any cause was a reason. He was never quite comfortable with those people. A lot of rabble-rousers just looking for a fight.

With the XL T-shirt wrapped around his neck like a superhero's cape, he stood outside a café, smoking a cigarette and trying his best to look like a part of the crowd, instead of being the reason the crowd existed. It was somewhat of a heady experience, having brought this entire experience to a peak. Without his direction, none of this would be happening.

He imagined each cop giving him a look. He was certain that his photo was available to every law enforcement agent in the state by now. He'd killed two first responders. His life as he knew it was over. There was no way out. His name, his reputation, his father's reputation was going to be front-page news. Mom had surely heard by now. He was positive they'd been to the house, and certainly confronted her. He was truly sorry about Mom. She didn't deserve any of this. But he wasn't going to back out of his commitment. Not now. The buildup, the momentum had been too strong. The end result was now imminent. He had to finish the mission. He snuffed out the cigarette and gazed around.

Just like him, the bystanders were nervous, waiting for the action to begin. Here, friendships were forged by strangers, a little apprehensive, but emboldened by harsh rhetoric. There were a handful of whites that had shown up to support the protest and they talked tough too. There were intricate handshakes, fist bumps and the names Trayvon Martin, Walter Scott and Michael Brown were thrown around. Unarmed blacks who had been shot. One by a neighborhood watch volunteer and two by police officers.

The department had been forced to release the name of Jethro Montgomery as the officer who gunned down unarmed Joseph Washington. It was as if a death warrant had been signed for the officer. In the last three hours, signs started popping up with his name prominent in the hand lettering.

Kill Jethro Montgomery. Jethro Belongs on Death Row.

Brion knew they'd moved the young police officer out of the city. Maybe even out of state. He would never ever be safe in New Orleans again. His life would always be in danger, and even if he walked on the shooting, he'd be better off to give up law enforcement as a career choice. But Montgomery had taken Joseph Washington off the streets, and that made him a hero in Brion's book.

He wanted to walk. The few blocks to Fox Glass. They didn't know him there, and the location was out of the central riot district, so there was a pretty good chance he would not be recognized. The ball cap was pulled almost to his eyes and he wore the voodoo shirt around his neck, hiding any sign of the necklace tattoo. Brion felt his gun, resting against his thigh.

He moved off the corner, and walked down the street, figuring he'd see the old warehouse in about five or six minutes. He just wanted a visual. Not trying to rush anything. He was just what his mother used to refer to as *antsy*. Nervously awaiting the next step.

*   *   *

Archer walked past the burned-out Korean grocer's store, the strong musty smell of wet ashes and accelerant still in the air. Four young black men stood on the walk, hands thrust into their pockets, as if protecting their turf. He walked on, ignoring their menacing looks. None of them matched Brion's description.

Pulling his cell phone from his pocket he studied the photo, taken two years ago when Joseph Brion had been arrested for assault. Nice looking kid, clean-shaven, a buzz cut. There was a smirk on his face, but other than that just a clean-cut kid. By now he could have a beard. Long braided hair. The lady who identified the necklace only saw him from the back. He could be wearing sunglasses, hiding the brown eyes that stared back from his mug shot.

By now, every law enforcement officer in the State of Louisiana, maybe the country, had this photo on their phone. Every newspaper and every television news program had the ability to carry the picture. It would be almost impossible for the cop killer to hide. Any minute the department would announce an award for information leading to his capture. As soon as the dollar amount reached ten thousand or up, the calls would come pouring in. Crime Stoppers and private citizens always stepped up. And the public input helped solve a lot of crimes.

Almost stumbling on a man lying fetal position in a doorway, Archer glanced down, checking to see if the vagrant had a necklace. Negative. He kept walking. For some reason, he was drawn to Fox Glass. He would like to talk to Matty Fox one more time, just to get a sense of the truthfulness of the son. There was something missing in the Fox Glass story. Why hadn't the old man pushed his advantage and pressed charges on the two would-be thieves? What did they have on him that steered Matt Fox away from putting them in prison?

At the next intersection, he waited for the light, ready to cross the street. That's when he saw the man, head down, cap pulled low on his head. What caught his attention was the cloth tied around his neck, billowing up in the back. Why would someone wear a cape in this heat and humidity? It struck him as odd. But, he rationalized, people seeing him in a sport coat and tie probably thought he was a little crazy as well.

Archer liked the jacket because it hid his gun. Why would

someone wear a cloth around their neck? To hide a crown-of-thorns tattoo. The man was crossing with the light on the other side of the street, and Archer crossed on his side, keeping a view of the man with the cape. He was now dead even with the suspect walking across the street. A dash across the pavement would put him in danger from passing automobiles, and even if there were no cars or trucks it would still be a fifteen-second jog. By then, the man could put fifteen or twenty seconds of running time between them. And, if this was the cop killer, he had a gun. He could spin around at any time and take Archer out. Archer didn't have the luxury of shooting first. He couldn't be sure it was Brion and no one benefited from the shooting of another unarmed suspect. He needed backup.

Pulling his phone from an inside pocket he rang Beeman, dropping back so it didn't appear he was trying to keep up.

'Sarge, I may have spotted Brion. Corner of Pelican and Bermuda. He's walking toward the river and I'm across the street keeping pace. Baseball cap and a piece of cloth tied around his neck. Can you get a squad car and some backup?'

'Sure, we've got half the force over there right now, but he sees the car he's going to run. You've got a plan for that?'

'If we get two cars, one on Pelican, one on Bermuda, and I'm available from the third angle, we've just about got him boxed in.'

'I'm on it, Detective, but if we lose him he's going to go into hiding. And hiding may mean innocent people could get hurt.'

'Hey, if you've got a better idea . . .' Archer truly wished the sergeant did have a better idea, but the possibilities were slim. 'It's a chance we've got to take. The problem is I can't tell you for sure it's our guy.'

'Well then, we'll give an innocent guy one hell of a scare. Be careful. If it is him, he doesn't care about shooting officers.'

Archer slipped the phone back in his pocket and glanced at the suspect, now about twenty feet ahead. The kid glanced back, and Archer tried to avert his gaze. If the guy even suspected he was being followed, Brion would bolt. There were houses and businesses in the neighborhood, and he could go anywhere. Innocent people could be involved, but he couldn't afford to wait. If this was their man, they had to pull him off the street.

He passed an aging Chevy, its hood open as if waiting for a

mechanic. Two small children chased each other in a dirt, weed-infested front yard. A heavy-set woman perched on the steps of her cement front porch, wearing a loose dress of pastel greens and blues, fanning herself with a magazine. This situation couldn't escalate to gun play. Too many things could go wrong. He caught the suspect out of the corner of his eye. He'd stepped up his pace, and Archer was losing ground.

The cars couldn't be far behind. Archer and the suspect were just a few blocks from where the riot had started and the police were still thick in the area. As the thought went through his mind he saw the blue-and-white, slowly driving up the street. The driver was deliberately staying behind the two pedestrians on either side of the pavement, but that couldn't go on for long. Eventually Brion, if that's who it was, would realize he was being stalked.

The number two car approached from the other direction, head on toward Archer and the man. The suspect spun around, now aware of the car behind him. He was passing a long green house with stark white shutters. The man stopped, looking at the house, then with another spin, he ran up three wooden steps, hit the porch and went through the front door as if he'd been an invited guest.

The two police cars pulled to the curb and three officers jumped out as Archer ran across the street. The driver of one of the vehicles remained behind the wheel as Archer motioned the officers to loop behind the house as he leaped onto the porch and knocked on the open screen door. There was no answer. It was less than a minute since the suspect entered the house, but no one was responding. He prayed the occupants weren't hurt. It could be a volatile situation. Pulling open the door he walked in, gun drawn.

'Anyone home?'

'I am,' an angry voice answered. 'Just minding my own business. Just getting myself an ice tea when your friend runs into my home, shoves me out of the way and bolts out the back door.' An old black man in a T-shirt and overalls walked out from the kitchen. 'Now *you* just waltz in like you own the place. This is my house and I am calling the *po*lice,' leaning hard on the po.

'I don't blame you,' Archer said as he reached the back door. 'To make it easy for you, they're right outside.'

THIRTY-SEVEN

The three officers were in back, shaking their heads.

'Did you see him?'

'Nothing, Detective,' the tallest of the men spoke. 'Ground is rock hard so no sign of footprints and if he went left there are two alleys. To the right, it's wide open. Straight ahead is the backyard of the house on the next street. Hell, he could be anywhere.'

'And he could have a hostage. Could be holed up in one of these houses. Split up and canvass the neighborhood. Anything suspicious, anything at all, call for backup. He's killed two officers and won't even blink before he pulls the trigger on you. You've all got your vests?'

They nodded.

'I'll get the driver from the second squad car and have him cruise the next street while you talk to the residents. Added cover. Go in with your guns drawn. It will scare the hell out of people but you want to be able to defend yourself at a moment's notice.'

'What happens if we shoot him, Detective? What happens if one of us kills him? Are you positive this is the guy?'

He took a deep breath.

'It's like any other confrontation, Officer. You use your instinct. It's part of the job, right?' He looked at the three uniforms. 'I'm leveling with you. No, I'm not one hundred percent positive this is our suspect. But everything so far has led me to that guess.'

'Still, it's a guess,' the officer said. 'We're working off of your guess. You know, Officer Jethro Montgomery *guessed* that his suspect had a gun. Wasn't a good call, was it? Wasn't a good guess.'

Archer shook his head.

'We're cops. We take chances every day. When you sign on, Officer, that's what you do.'

They would never understand. Even your family was at risk. Your immediate family and even your wife. It wasn't just about *your* vulnerability. It was about everyone in your orbit.

As they fanned out, he called Levy.

'Hey, Q. You got your guy?'

'So close, Josh. So damned close.'

'But you'll get him, right?'

'There's going to be another riot tonight. You know that.'

'I do.'

'Remember our conversation? Unless it's a meeting with the brass, you've got my back?'

'I do. You've got a meeting with headquarters? I'm planning on a fishing expedition.'

'No meeting with the brass, Josh. Something else entirely. I wish I wasn't making this call but . . .'

'Well, I didn't expect you to pick a riot, but . . .'

'I understand how busy you are. I also know I could use your help. I don't have a true game plan, but our two heads tend to be better than one. I think you could make a difference.'

There wasn't a hesitation.

'I'll tie up any loose ends in the next hour. Probably a bad time to show up with the craziness tonight, but we'll weather this together, my friend.'

'Thanks, Josh. The guy is here. We've just got to figure out where, and find a way to avoid any more bloodshed.'

One of the good guys. The man had an overflowing plate, but Levy understood the severity of the situation. And in the back of his mind, Archer wondered if he was looking for a fellow scapegoat. Someone to share this responsibility. Because if he failed, and was unable to apprehend Joseph Brion, he could always share the blame with Josh Levy. But it wasn't that. He felt certain that bringing Levy into the case would open things up. Archer knew himself well enough to admit he was willing to go out on a limb, take a flying chance. Levy tended to play by the book, using solid police procedures. And he'd proven something else. Josh Levy had his back.

He crouched down in a dank, musty tool shed with a power mower, a can of gasoline and assorted lawn tools. A rake, a shovel and God knew what else. So he'd figured it out. The suit across the street, the blue-and-white cruising that same street, then the second car. You could show the neck, or hide the neck. But hiding it was apparently almost as dangerous as going naked.

The next step was a drugstore. Find some makeup that would temporarily cover the tattoo. But right now, in this defensive position, finding a Walgreens wasn't in the cards. He should have built that into his plans.

Brion listened intensely. A dog barked in the distance and cars drove by, a couple with bad mufflers. The roar of a motorcycle broke through the afternoon air, but he heard no one walking nearby, no sounds of footsteps or murmured voices. He may have been mistaken. Maybe those signs that he saw were perfectly innocent. After all, Algiers was on lockdown and there could be hundreds of reasons that 5-0 was on the street. But he'd killed not one, but two police officers. Two. He may be the most hunted man in the country. In the world. He wasn't sure how to deal with that concept.

He thought about the brothers who bombed the Boston Marathon. After the incident, one had hidden inside a boat stored in a shed. They'd turned up that brother in a matter of hours. Yet, here Joseph was. Safe, somewhat secure, and prepared for the next step. As long as no one decided, at this late hour, to mow the lawn.

THIRTY-EIGHT

Levy met him at Congregation Coffee on Pelican Avenue.

'We've gone public with a reward, Q. It's currently twenty-five thousand for information leading to the arrest of Joseph Brion.'

'A good start.'

With one to-go cup of green tea, one of coffee in hand, they stepped into Archer's car.

'For thirty-four years, Crime Stoppers and the public and private sector have been stepping up. Over two million dollars have been distributed for leads.' Levy and his facts.

'So how many successes?' Archer asked. He stepped on the gas, heading for the search area.

'Over fifteen thousand arrests and convictions based on people responding to rewards.'

'OK, I have no head for math. How much per year?'

'About fifty-nine thousand dollars a year is given away by Crime Stoppers. Most of the time individuals add a lot more. Twenty-five thousand is a good figure. It will go up if we don't catch the son of a bitch. That's almost four-hundred fifty arrests per year. Without that—'

'And our conviction rate is the lowest in the country?'

'Damn close,' Levy said.

'We're still fighting a losing battle, Josh.'

'But we're still in the ring, Q. And as long as we're swinging, there's a chance we might win. Let's find this guy.'

Six officers had struck out. They'd pounded on doors, frightening law-abiding citizens and some that probably weren't. After explaining why they were there, they'd asked the pertinent questions.

'Has anyone approached you for refuge?'

'Are you being held by force?'

'Is anyone in your household being held captive?'

An elderly woman had told an officer that her daughter-in law beat her on a regular basis, and a ten-year old girl said that her mother had grounded her. She wanted to know her rights. Two men answered the door with their arms around each other's waist and complained to the officer that the neighbor's dog kept them up most nights. Other than frightening the neighborhood half to death, they'd found no evidence that Joseph Brion was hiding in the area.

Archer stood by his car, sipping the tea and talking to one of the first responding officers.

'Everyone's been warned to stay inside and not answer the door? That's first and foremost, right?'

'Of course, but come on, Detective. After we show up with a drawn weapon, the last thing they are going to do is answer the next knock.'

'Let's expand the area. He's got to be somewhere.'

The officer nodded. 'We'll move block to block. It's probably better than riot duty. Less chance of getting our asses handed to us.'

'Don't be too sure. Vacant buildings?'

'The guys are checking garages, sheds, storage buildings.'

'Can we spare someone to recheck those? Our guy could be under a tarp, pressed into a corner, maybe hiding in the rafters.'

'Detective, whatever it takes to find this guy. We all take it very personally. You know that.'

Back in the car, he turned to Levy.

'You're Joseph Brion. You know that we've identified you. You know we've got your picture, we know about the tattoo and now we are aware of the shirt around your neck. We are canvassing the neighborhood where you were last seen. What's your next move, Detective?'

Levy paused and sipped his black coffee. He starred out the window, watching the fading hours of a warm September afternoon.

'The law enforcement numbers here are impressive. They may have dwindled for tonight, but the police are still here in force. State Troopers are here, the Sheriff's Department has a significant number of their staff on the ground. Even the National Guard still has armed soldiers in the riot zone.'

'All true,' Archer said. 'So what are you going to do?'

'There is one element that has more numbers than you do.'

Archer studied him.

'The rioters, Q. They outnumber all the uniforms.'

'And?'

'I'd use them. If I can get the rioters riled up, in a frenzy, you have to pull your cops off the search detail. No one in law enforcement is going to be looking for me. They'll be trying their damnedest to minimize the damage, quell the tide if you will. What good is a riot if you can't use it for personal reasons?'

'How would you do that? The crowd is already up for a good riot. Maybe a little less crazy than last night, but . . .'

'Q, I'm winging this. No idea if this has any validity. This Joseph Brion has been arrested and did time, am I right?'

'He beat up a drug runner who worked for him. We never got him on drug charges, but apparently the guy was one of his runners.'

'I'm a small-time dealer with a couple of guys who work for me. They do what I tell them, because I pay them, *and* they know I have a history of violence. If you don't do what I ask, you stand the risk of bodily harm.'

Archer smiled and slapped his hands on the steering wheel.

'So, you call your boys and tell them to rile the crowd.'

'That's what I would do.' Levy nodded. 'A few more incendiary devices thrown at the riot squad, maybe some gun shots. Let the cops know that this time it's serious. If you're responsible for a couple more officers' deaths, it doesn't really matter. The punishment for two is the same as it is for four.'

'It makes sense, Josh. But I don't think this is going on just to cover your tracks. You're not trying to escape. Based on the fact that you are *here*, in the heart of the riot, I think you have one more mission to accomplish. I think you've got one more job to do, then you don't care what happens to you. I just don't know what that mission is. You need one more thing to happen to finish the puzzle. If we figure that out, we can take this guy off the street and stop any more destruction he may have planned.'

'Why did Brion decide to show up in Algiers of all places?' Levy placed his coffee in the cup holder. 'Here, where he had to defend himself. Before we knew who he was he could have been miles, states away. Hell, he could have traveled to Cuba. He could have escaped to Jackson, Mississippi. No one would know him and it's 80 percent black. Or your hometown, Q. Detroit's 80 percent black. He could have blended in very well. He could, should, be long gone. Without another mission he should have been on the road. Instead, he stayed here, in his home town where people know him very well, and chose the most dangerous neighborhood in the entire state of Louisiana right now. Something is going down. You know that.'

Archer felt the buzz in his pocket before he heard the ring. Grabbing it, he answered.

'Archer.'

'Q, it's Beeman. I hope you are safe. I've got another piece of news for you. Do with it what you will.'

'What is it?'

'We found two reports on truck hijackings that took place around the same time that Nick Martin died. Both witnesses, drivers in this case, told the identical story. Another truck ran them off the road. One was on a side road and one was at a detour.'

'Were there any signs of another truck interfering when we did the investigation? Anyone who saw the confrontation?'

'No. There were no signs that any trucks were in the vicinity. No witness saw any sign of anger, road rage or reckless operation.'

'Any tire tracks from an oncoming vehicle?'

'I read both reports. They were brief, to the point, but apparently no one could find proof that there was another vehicle involved in the hijacking.'

Solange had seen the evasive action of Martin. She claimed she was witness to the zigzagging performance of his driving. He felt foolish believing her vision, but she was under the impression that the driver was avoiding someone. Or, as she had suggested, the driver was under the influence. Now Beeman was telling him that two other victims reported the same thing. It wasn't drugs or alcohol, of that he was now sure. Somebody, twenty-five years ago, had found a way to run trucks off the road, then steal their loads. And those somebodies had never been apprehended.

How it mattered to his Johnny Leroy case he had no idea. Except that Leroy had been the first responder to Nick Martin's death. He was the first to explore the evidence and make determinations that would affect the final results. And Solange Cordray seemed to think this was an important link to the murder of Officer Leroy.

Instead of the case tightening, it just seemed to spread out. The main objective was to find Joseph Brion. First step. Most important step. And with Levy and the support of every cop on the force, that was going to happen.

'Thanks, Sarge. I'll get back to you if we have any questions.'

'Archer, it's always dangerous out there, but tonight is off the charts. You know that. The riot, a cop killer . . .'

'I'll be safe, Sergeant.'

'You'd damned well better be. You get killed tonight, it means we've got to go out and find somebody else to take your place. Apparently cops don't grow on trees. Human resources wants you alive, Archer.'

'Thanks for the sentiment.'

THIRTY-NINE

Brion was pretty sure he knew the routine. They would check residences first. Assure the neighborhood residents that they were on top of the situation and make sure all citizens were safe. That made sense. Then, they would start with parked cars, garages, empty buildings and sheds. Tool sheds. So his time was limited. He felt certain they'd be barging in any moment now. He wasn't keen on shooting another policeman or having them shoot him. Still, he touched his gun for reassurance.

He pushed on the shed door, opening it two inches. Peering out he could see the neighborhood seemed quiet. He tried to get his bearings, gauging where he was and how he could get back the crowds. Considering everything, that seemed like the best idea. He'd find a way to get to Fox Glass by seven, forget going there now. His immediate problem was finding cover.

The shed was behind a yellow frame shotgun house. From his position he could see that the carport out front was empty and there was no sign of a vehicle parked on the street. He could take a chance that no one was home. But the husband might have the car, the wife might be inside. A kid could be looking out through a bedroom window. Damn. There had to be a way. He couldn't just walk outside with the shirt around his neck because they were looking for that, but he couldn't walk around with the tattoo exposed either. Cops would be swarming this neighborhood. There had to be a better disguise, some sort of diversion.

Tying the voodoo shirt around his waist, Brion opened the door, tugged on the lawnmower and pulled it into the yard. He furtively glanced around the area and saw no one. Nobody was sounding the alarm. He pushed the door shut and started pushing the lawn mower toward the sidewalk. Just a young man going home from mowing some lawns. A guy had to make a living doing something, right? It might just be the best disguise he'd ever come up with.

*   *   *

The crowd was growing. Five o'clock and workers were getting off. This was a great place to let off a little or a lot of steam. The unemployed had finally gotten out of bed and were heading down to the riot-torn area for a look around, to see the remains of the mess they'd made the night before.

Air horns blared in the early evening, followed by shouts and chants. Drivers in rusted autos laid on their horns, threatening people to keep them from driving on the area streets. It was the job of a few to clog the traffic. The after-five hour was warming up fast. No riot squads yet. They were preparing, several blocks away, hoping some early craziness would wear a few of the protestors out.

An empty blue-and-white car was the target for ten young men, who rocked it, five on a side. No Molotov cocktails, no bricks through the windshield. Not yet. Just a rocking, back and forth, back and forth until the car went over on its side. A cheer arose from the surrounding spectators as the window glass shattered and the car crunched against pavement.

The rockers all gathered on the bottom side and started pushing. Armed officers stood back, guns drawn but only watching. It took all of forty seconds before the vehicle was completely turned over, resting on its top.

A dumpster that had hidden behind a sandwich shop had been rolled to the street and someone had set the greasy residue of French fry oil and remnants of meat sandwiches on fire. The orange flames crackled and reached for the sky as the smell of roasted beef and pork permeated the air.

Disguised as a humble lawn guy, Brion saw the commotion and rejoiced at the fact that he'd traversed the path back to the zone. A policeman had actually nodded to him as he walked down the sidewalk, scared out of his mind. Maybe the cop admired a little ingenuity, some entrepreneurship. He'd nodded back, ready to go for the gun in a moment's notice. It struck him that the officer was fortunate to still be alive. The last two law enforcement officials he'd confronted hadn't been so lucky.

A loud cheer erupted as someone tossed a torch onto the belly of the cop car and the gas tank erupted into a towering flame with thick black smoke blotting the sky.

Still the armed officers stayed back. Still the riot squad stayed several blocks away. Cameras were recording the incidents, and even with their faces masked, there would be some who would be identified.

The squad car's sudden explosion was surprising and deafening, shards of hot metal hurling through the air, spraying the bystanders. Those close by fell to the ground, scrambling to get as far away as possible.

Brion left the mower on the sidewalk and jogged to the nearest gathering, joining in the high-fiving, the exuberance of defiance against the establishment. Damn. Black lives mattered. Of course they did.

She sat on the edge of her bed, staring up at the ceiling stain, seeing nothing. She was an emotional wreck. Ma, Quentin, Matebo, the spirits, sometimes it seemed too much to deal with. And she was reminded of something a Christian friend of hers had once said: 'God will never give you more than you can handle.' She wasn't Christian and neither was she quite sure that there was any truth to that statement. Right now she was overwhelmed, about at a breaking point. If there was a god of the Christians, what he had laid on her was just about over the limit.

People depended on her strength. They looked to her for their own peace of mind, and that was a lot to lay on someone. When they looked in her eyes, they wanted to see themselves reflected, but with her strong sensibilities, her determination, her morality and inner beauty. And she doubted if she had any of those characteristics. Was she a charlatan, a scam artist who made a living by fooling the public? All she wanted was to be relieved of obligations. She wanted the spirits to leave her alone. Yet she was engaged with them. They floated through her thoughts. Her job was to tend to the needy.

She weighed the matters over in her troubled mind, but as much as Ma was her main concern, she kept coming back to Quentin's problem. Finding why officer Johnny Leroy was killed, and where the killer was now. Leroy had some serious problems. His spirit had spoken to her. And she knew it had something to do with the death of the truck driver Nick Martin, whose life had been snuffed out at twenty-nine. Leroy had something to do with that death, and not just because he was the first responder.

Like Quentin Archer felt chased by the haunting memory of his time in Detroit and the death of his wife, like she felt chased by the demons and spirits she encountered on a daily basis, Nick Martin had been chased the night his truck crashed. She was positive. Yet she had seen nothing except a bright reflection off his windshield. Distracting, but no sign of something chasing him.

Solange closed her eyes and one more time relived the vision she'd seen after drinking the root-of-dandelion tea. Her clairvoyant moment. It was nighttime. From the driver's perspective the trees would have hidden even the moon. Her view was from above. Like a movie shot from high above the action. The only light on that dark, desolate road was from the headlights of Nick Martin's truck. And then it hit her. He'd been chased by himself.

Archer stepped back into the car. He and Levy checked dozens of vacant cars, trucks, the empty garages and sheds. So far, they'd found no one. It was nerve-wracking, hoping no one would leap from a dark space, from the rafters, a shadowed corner. The riot hour was getting close and he prayed that they would find the killer before everything went crazy. Archer believed they would find him. As he waited for Levy, exploring a small tool shed in the next property, he considered Solange and her stress on Nick Martin's accident twenty-five years ago.

She insisted that she'd seen the wreck, and insisted that the truck seemed to be chased. And in the dark of night she saw a reflection in the windshield. A bounce of light where there was no light. Except from Nick Martin's headlights. And all of a sudden it hit him. He knew who was chasing the Peterbilt, twenty-five years ago. It had to be.

Levy got into the car, shaking his head.

'No luck, Q. By now, he could be anywhere.'

'I know where he's going, Josh. Maybe now, maybe in the next hour. I'm not sure why, but I'm pretty sure he's headed to Fox Glass.'

'Why would Joseph Brion visit a glass company?'

'Do you remember that Solange suggested that—'

'Jesus, Quentin, you're still strong on the voodoo bit?'

'She suggested that,' ignoring his partner's disbelief, 'reflection was a part of the story.'

'Yeah, I remember. Listen, you've got to give this up.'

'Twenty-five years ago, Nick Martin wrecked his truck due to a reflection in his windshield. What reflects light in the dark of night? Tell me, Josh.'

'A shiny surface.' Levy was now somewhat subdued.

'What constitutes a shiny surface in the middle of a pine forest on a desolate road in the middle of the night? Any ideas?'

Levy shook his head, and gazed straight ahead.

'I think I know.'

'Archer, what difference does it make? How does this little game you are playing have anything to do with the capture of Officer Leroy's killer? It's insane. Don't make me sorry I came over here to help you, OK?'

'If I'm wrong, Josh, get me kicked off the force. It's not like that hasn't happened before. But I believe that I know how that murder and theft happened. And I have a very strong idea that Johnny Leroy played a part in it.'

'Because Solange says so?'

'Josh, there are too many paths that are intersecting.'

Levy looked him in the face for the third time.

'OK. What caused the reflection?'

'The reflection, the erratic driving, it's all tied to one thing.'

'Archer, no melodrama.'

'I'm saying it for the first time, Josh. I need to hear myself say it.' Archer closed his eyes, realizing how this all sounded. Unbelievable. But he was finally putting the pieces of the puzzle together.

He started the engine, setting the air conditioning on high.

'I don't know that Nick Martin, or his death, had anything to do with the death of Leroy, but let's assume it did. Let's agree that something drove him off the road. If he was driving erratically, wildly changing lanes as Solange suggests—'

Levy subtly rolled his eyes.

'Then he was driving under the influence, *or* under the impression someone was chasing him. Or, maybe, driving toward him in something that was substantial. My guess is that whatever scared him was equal in size and stature. Possibly another truck, but there was no sign of another vehicle. We've got reports on two other hijackings during that time, same neighborhood, and the drivers told a story about another truck trying to run them down. Again, no skid marks, no tire tracks off the road, no sign of another truck chasing them.'

'So your theory is there wasn't anyone else?'

'Oh, no. There were other players, but they weren't chasing him with a truck. What reflects the headlights? You said, a shiny surface. Josh, what if it was a mirror?'

'What?'

'A mirror. Reflecting his headlights back at him. What he saw was a truck coming at him. But what if it was just the reflection of his own headlights, mimicking every move he made?'

'So who could . . .' Levy stopped in mid-sentence.

'You know who could.'

'That would have to be one big mirror.'

'Put it on rollers, carry it in another semi.'

'So Fox Glass is a glass manufacturer. They make windows and mirrors, right?'

'Right.'

'You've got this all worked out?'

'All worked out? Are you crazy?' Archer asked. 'I'm just now putting it together. It's the only thing that makes sense.

'I thought—'

'A large, large mirror, one that covered the road, would reflect what appears as an approaching vehicle.'

'Archer, that might be a brilliant deduction, but how does this change anything? We're trying to find Joseph Brion.'

'Whose father tried to rob Fox Glass. Whose father was apprehended by Johnny Leroy. Who also apprehended Joseph Washington, whose death is the reason we're all over here in Algiers. And the owner, Matt Fox, refused to press charges.'

'It's crazy. I know I'm not the brightest Jew in the neighborhood, Q, so put it together for me, please.'

'I don't have the answer, but if we're working on the idea that reflection had something to do with it, and we know Fox Glass is somehow involved, then it starts to make sense that Brion is going to end up at Fox. We can scour all of Algiers and never find him again. But my best guess is he's headed to Fox Glass.'

'OK. We've got patrol still looking for him. Every law-enforcement agent in Louisiana has his photo and a drawing of the tattoo. Even though you can't tell me why this guy might visit the glass factory, let's do a stakeout. I'm game if you are.'

FORTY

One hour to go. They would meet him in the lobby and there would be a major surprise. He pictured the look on their faces.

Brion had called his two minions, and told them to fire up the crowd. As if those rowdy groups weren't fired enough already. He'd provided De Shea and Grady with firebombs, smoke bombs and a couple cans of gasoline. Fuel for the second night riots. Starting at six thirty, the two young men were to lead the assault, then they were allowed to disappear. They were the catalyst. The shit would happen because of the momentum. That's all he wanted. Get the cops, the Guard, State Troopers and Sheriff's Department focusing on the main event. He would take care of the rest. Maybe he didn't need to add fuel to the fire, but the more agitated the crowd became the more cover he had for his final act.

On what became a weekly visit, he'd listened to the conversations between Pop and Joseph. In whispered voices, they discussed the death of the truck driver Nick Martin. When Brion finally figured out that the trio was somewhat responsible, he was fascinated and found a way to hear more. His bedroom in the big house was above the den where they talked. Once Mom started curtailing his eavesdropping, he went to bed early, listening to the echoing conversation through the laundry shoot that descended from the upstairs hallway. Although he couldn't catch everything, he caught enough. And he figured out their magic trick of making a truck appear out of thin air. Smoke and mirrors. Today he would reveal his knowledge of the trick. It was a good thing he wasn't a magician because a true magician never reveals his trick.

In fifteen minutes the fireworks would begin. Half an hour later he would appear before his audience.

She called him, but only got voicemail.

'Quentin, I think I've figured out the reflection I saw on the windshield. As cryptic as it sounds, I believe the man was chasing himself. Please call me.'

As she hung up, she knew he'd think she was even stranger than he already did, but she wasn't going to explain her idea over voicemail. She wanted to talk to him personally. And maybe he'd already figured it out himself. She hoped he had.

Solange considered getting on her motorbike and driving to Algiers. She was certain he was there, and she felt her presence might give him some protection. But, exactly what a young, single, black voodoo practitioner was going to really accomplish, she wasn't sure. She hoped he would call back and they could have a meaningful conversation. She was becoming more focused on the crime and the criminal. Solange wanted to share that with the detective. And she was considering some more personal conversation. A chance to share their misfortunes. Some companionship would be welcome. More than welcome. Maybe over a drink or a meal. She couldn't believe she was actually entertaining that thought. After she'd thrown cold water on the idea just the other day.

'Consider this.' They had parked across the street from Fox Glass, even though the parking lot could hold dozens of cars. This was a stakeout, not a proclamation that 'the cops were in the house'. 'No charges were ever filed against Brion or Washington.'

'You've made that case. Something happened.'

'Normally you'd think that the suspects had threatened the people leveling the charges. Maybe André Brion and Joseph Washington warned Fox that they would get even if he had them jailed.'

'That's a possibility,' Levy said, sipping his Tout de Suite take-out coffee.

'But, what if *Fox* threatened Washington and Brion—?'

'With what?' interrupted Levy. 'Matt Fox didn't even know these guys. Or at least I don't think he did.'

'Matt Fox had the power of life and death in his hands. He

could press the charges and put those two away for years. But he didn't. And just to play devil's advocate, let's assume that they didn't have anything to hold against Fox. So why did he decide *not* to press charges? Why?'

'Your favorite question, Q. Why?'

'Here's a scenario. Fox *did* have something on these two suspects besides this robbery.'

'What?' Levy sounded exasperated.

'Nothing in the past. He didn't have a clue who they were or why they targeted his company. Actually, let's assume it didn't really matter.'

'So how did he have anything on them?'

'What he had on them regarded their future. What they were to become.'

Levy shook his head. 'You are a headcase, Archer.'

'If he refused to press charges *not* because they threatened him, then he must have promised them something in the future.'

'Honest to God, Q . . .'

'Stay with me, Josh. It's the process of elimination. He says to them, "I could have you arrested. But, if you do me a favor, I'll let you off the hook."'

'And what was that favor?'

'"I've got a great idea how to hijack trucks. I want you to be the guys on the front line."'

'You're saying,' the look of disbelief was all over Levy's face, 'you're saying that Matt Fox actually hired these two thieves as partners in crime.'

'I'm suggesting that it is highly probable. I can come up with no other reason for him to not file charges.'

'What about Johnny Leroy? How was he going to process the fact that after capturing these two guys, Fox was letting them go free? That should have pissed him off.'

Looking out over the parking lot, Archer took a sharp breath. A Bentley convertible, top up, turned in off the street. Parking next to the entrance, the driver's door opened and a hunched over Matt Fox slowly exited, cane in hand.

'Wow. Surprise. Old man Fox is here. This must be a serious meeting,' Archer said.

'That's Matt Fox?'

'Senior. He works from home. His kid said he doesn't ever show up here. Now, he appears on the most dangerous night in years?'

In the distance, they could hear firearms being discharged, the *pop-pop-pop* of guns being fired. Then a roar from the crowd and an explosion. A smoky fire lit up the sky, and more gunfire.

'This just gets more and more interesting,' Archer said.

Joseph Brion retrieved his backpack, and ducked behind a service station to pull on the carefully rolled trousers and jacket. Not much camouflage, but a rumpled attempt to cover his entrance for a few minutes. All he needed was those few minutes. Just a moment to make his case. Let them all know what was going on. The explanation, making them aware that he'd figured it all out, was crucial. After all, when someone is going to die, it would be nice to know why. A courtesy that they hadn't offered his father. He was pretty sure that Johnny 'Jack' Leroy got the message, ever so briefly.

His concern had become more personal. Minute by minute, he wondered how he would deal with the consequences. Would he be able to go out in a hail of gunfire if it came to that? Would he have the courage to take his own life . . . or was that the coward's way to escape? Could he seriously do that?

The jacket and long pants were already too much. He was perspiring as he walked the sidewalk, then into the street when the pedestrian walkway ended. He'd transferred the Smith and Wesson to his waist, hidden by the sport coat. The noise three blocks away let him know that the commotion and confusion were paying off. By all accounts, he should have this moment to himself.

FORTY-ONE

Two cars were in the spacious parking lot, a Bentley and a late-model Corvette. It figured. High-end cars for people who knew how to manipulate the system. He'd taken a streetcar to see the homes they lived in, and the opulence was astounding. Business must have been very good for the past twenty-five years. Before that—

Brion glanced at the car across the street, strangely out of place at this time of the afternoon, in this neighborhood. Opening the door with the etched fox on the glass, he walked in, nodding at the two men standing at the reception desk.

'Mr Bardo?' The younger man looked puzzled.

'Is there an office where we can talk?'

'Of course.'

Matty Fox motioned for him to follow and the three of them walked down a hall to a spacious office with a glass desk, acrylic chairs and a brush-brown rug.

The younger Fox sat down behind the desk, his father on one of the uncomfortable-looking chairs. Brion reached into his belt and pulled out the gun.

'Gentlemen, please put your hands in front of you so I can see them at all times.'

The old man squinted his eyes, staring at Brion.

'So you got me here on the pretense of a multi-million-dollar project and all you want to do is rob the business? Jesus Christ, take what you want.'

'No, Mr Fox, it's more than that. You see, I'm André Brion's son. And I understand you instructed Jack Leroy to kill my father.'

The color evaporated from the old man's face.

'You're going to kill me?'

'Oh, no.' Brion shook his head. 'That isn't what this is about at all. First of all I wanted to tell you that I've figured out the entire chain of events.'

Matty Fox was shaking. His hands folded in front of him, his body quivering.

'I don't know what the hell you are talking about.'

'Maybe you do,' Brion said, 'maybe you don't. But here's how I see it.'

Matt Fox started to rise.

'Yes, I will kill you if you make one more move, Mr Fox. I want you to sit still while I make my case. Do you understand? Just nod or I will blow you to kingdom come.'

The elderly gentleman nodded.

'Jack Leroy caught my father and Joseph Washington when they attempted a robbery at this establishment. Is that correct.'

The old man nodded.

'Very good. The two of them were attempting the theft of a shipment of gold. That should have been a felony, but you refused to press charges. I want you to tell me why.'

The elder Fox shook his head.

'Tell me,' Brion shouted. Using his full force he struck the forehead of the man with the barrel of his gun. 'Don't make me do that again.'

Reaching up and wiping blood from his head, the man lowered his gaze.

'I wanted to hire them for a job.'

'What job, Mr Fox?'

'Hijacking trucks.'

The younger Fox looked confused, his gaze switching from his father to Brion.

'So, you used Joseph Washington and my father to steal loads of liquor and cigarettes.'

'They made out very well, young man. It was a very lucrative business until—'

'Until Nick Martin was killed.'

Matty Fox studied his father.

'Dad?'

'Our business was going through some hard times. It was easy money and—'

'Somebody died,' Brion said. 'You were using your giant mirror, and your three henchmen. They would park their semi up the road, roll out the giant mirror, run the trucks off the road and steal the merchandise. But somebody, Nick Martin, was killed. Right?'

'What do you want?'

'A confession.'

'I'm an old man. I didn't kill your father, so why don't you—'

'I want a confession. And I want it now.'

'Yes, it happened, as you say.'

'Your contribution?'

'I placed detour signs on the road,' he glanced at his son, tears now streaming down his cheeks, 'and picked them up after the hijackings.'

'You do yourself a disservice. It was your entire idea. You manufactured the mirror to run trucks off the road, to kill Nick Martin. You made the lion's share of the money.'

'And when Martin died, we stopped,' Fox said.

'Only because you'd made enough money to float the company.'

'That's not true. We—'

'You then listened to the feedback. Everyone, except possibly you, was conflicted. You'd killed someone. Until then, it was only the trucking company's insurance claims and you were making a lot of money. Now, someone was dead.'

'Yes, but—'

'No *buts*, Mr Fox. Joseph Washington was scared to death. He felt terrible about the death, but my father, your business partner Andy Brion, he happened to mention to Joseph that they should come clean. My pop had a case of morality.'

'Dad?' Matty held his hands out. 'Tell me this didn't happen.'

'Your father,' Fox wiped his face, 'Andy, became a pussy. Yes. He was going to destroy what had been a very lucrative venture. Because he had a change of heart, he wanted to put all of us in prison. Washington came to me and suggested we needed to silence your father.'

Brion smiled. He was finally getting his answers.

'And your head honcho, the leader of your nefarious ring of outlaws, was now a cop. He had his ear to the ground and heard serious rumblings about my father and his interest in confessing.'

'Damn it, boy,' Fox clenched his fists. 'Joseph, Jack and I had long conversations about this. It didn't have to happen. If your father had just decided to keep his mouth shut it all would have blown over.'

'But you decided to kill Pop.'

'It was the three of us, OK? And it happened that André and Jack came together at a junction after a robbery and—'

Brion hit him again, across the nose with a vicious swing. Blood spurted from his face.

'You're going to kill my father?' Matty was now crying, obviously surprised with all the information.

'No.'

'What is this all about then?'

'Your father authorized the murder of my pop. There's only one way to get even for that,' Brion said. 'Your father has to pay. He took something I loved, I'm taking something he loves.' Aiming his pistol at Matty's head, he pulled the trigger.

FORTY-TWO

'So the old man just walked in,' Levy sipped his coffee. 'I'm guessing his kid owns the Corvette.'

'A high-level meeting,' Archer nodded.

'And who's that?' Levy pointed at the man walking up to the door.

They both watched the man with the sport coat enter the business.

'A worker? A client? It seems strange that on a curfew night Fox Glass would have a meeting.'

'Life goes on, Q. If there's business to be done, it's got to be done. Here we are involved in murder, yet our main investigation deals with the after-effects of death. We're working with people who are still alive. They still have business to attend to.'

'The guy who walked in with the sport coat. You think that's a client?'

'You know these people better than I do. If they're meeting at this hour, during this horrific time, it's a very important meeting. They could get caught up in the riot, still they're tending to business.'

They sat back, studying the lot in dwindling light. The noise from the riot-torn streets was louder. The odor of gasoline was strong.

'Josh, I'm not entirely comfortable with the guy who just walked into the building.'

'Not comfortable?'

'We're looking for Joseph Brion. He could look like anyone. It's not hard to disguise yourself.'

'Let's roll.'

Levy opened the car door, his weapon drawn.

Archer stepped from the car and they walked to the entrance.

Archer pushed the door open. There was no one in the lobby. Quietly they made their way through the entrance.

Muffled voices sounded from further back and they kept walking, pistols held at ready. The door to the meeting room was closed but they could make out some of the conversation.

'There's only one way to get even for that. Your father has to pay.'

The explosion was loud, and Archer flung open the door, gun ready to fire at anyone who was ready to fire back. The man in the sport coat spun around and dropped his pistol to the floor. Hands up he went down on his knees.

'Joseph Brion?'

'Son of André Brion,' he replied, grabbing the Smith and Wesson from where it lay. Aiming it at Archer's head, he put his index finger in the trigger guard.

Levy pulled the trigger on his Glock, the sound ricocheting around the room, and Brion collapsed, his bleeding body dead on the floor.

FORTY-THREE

'He lived. I read it in the paper.'

'Matty Fox was lucky,' Archer said. 'The bullet missed his brain by a fraction of an inch.'

'And you survived.' She reached across the table and touched his hand.

'Solange, thank you. I question how you come up with your ideas, but without them, without your insight—'

'*I* even question what input I have, Quentin. So please, don't apologize.'

'Are you ready to order?' The young lady stood there, pen and pad in hand.

'No, give us a little more time.'

They both reached for their glasses of wine, white and red.

'So, what you're saying is . . .'

'I'm never sure that my insights are correct. I pray every day, but there are times, many times, I don't understand it myself.'

'You gave me some powerful insight. I don't think we could have solved the case without you. You knew that Leroy was tied into the murder of Nick Martin. Without that connection, we'd still be out there looking.'

'I know how hard it is to believe, but he spoke to me.'

Archer shook his head.

'I'm not sure I want to go there.'

'It's a curse,' she smiled. 'I hear voices. It drove my ex-husband nuts.' She paused. 'It drives *me* nuts. Tell me more.'

'The idea was complicated. Matt Fox was struggling, the company wasn't doing well and he'd lost one of his biggest customers. Somehow, he figured out how to use a mirror to hijack trucks, but he didn't know anyone who would do the job. His circle of friends didn't include criminals.'

'So,' she said, 'one night it all fell into his lap.'

'As far as that group went, it was a win-win. They didn't do any time for the attempted heist and he gave them a very lucrative deal.

'Johnny Leroy had already applied to the department?'

'He was going to be a cop. It was already in the works, and it was a perfect fit. He followed up on the hijackings and was able to provide cover for the crimes. He misdirected, hid evidence and totally screwed up the investigation. He even got some award for the hard work he supposedly put in on the case.'

'But once Nick Martin was a fatality, they backed off the robberies?'

Archer nodded.

'I think they all decided that it was too risky. But then Joseph Brion's father, André, made some comments about coming clean. That triggered the rest of the group to make plans to kill him.'

'Did you really think this was the way our dinner conversation would go?' She gave him a grim smile.

'Yes. Because we came together over a murder several months ago, and I don't know what else we have in common.'

'Well, let's start here,' she said. 'Apparently we both like a good mystery.'

'We both enjoy wine.'

'We both live in the Quarter . . .'

Archer smiled, and put his left hand over her right hand. It was a comfortable moment, a chance to share feelings. And he had a lot of feelings to share.